THE MYSTERY OF THE MUD FLATS

'THE DETECTIVE STORY CLUB is a clearing house for the best detective and mystery stories chosen for you by a select committee of experts. Only the most ingenious crime stories will be published under the THE DETECTIVE STORY CLUB imprint. A special distinguishing stamp appears on the wrapper and title page of every THE DETECTIVE STORY CLUB book—the Man with the Gun. Always look for the Man with the Gun when buying a Crime book.'

Wm. Collins Sons & Co. Ltd., 1929

Now the Man with the Gun is back in this series of COLLINS CRIME CLUB reprints, and with him the chance to experience the classic books that influenced the Golden Age of crime fiction.

THE DETECTIVE STORY CLUB

E. C. BENTLEY • TRENT'S LAST CASE
E. C. BENTLEY • TRENT INTERVENES
E. C. BENTLEY & H. WARNER ALLEN • TRENT'S OWN CASE
ANTHONY BERKELEY • THE WYCHFORD POISONING CASE
ANTHONY BERKELEY • THE SILK STOCKING MURDERS
LYNN BROCK • NIGHTMARE
BERNARD CAPES • THE MYSTERY OF THE SKELETON KEY
AGATHA CHRISTIE • THE MURDER OF ROGER ACKROYD
AGATHA CHRISTIE • THE BIG FOUR
WILKIE COLLINS • THE MOONSTONE
HUGH CONWAY • CALLED BACK
HUGH CONWAY • DARK DAYS
EDMUND CRISPIN • THE CASE OF THE GILDED FLY
FREEMAN WILLS CROFTS • THE CASK
FREEMAN WILLS CROFTS • THE PONSON CASE
FREEMAN WILLS CROFTS • THE PIT-PROP SYNDICATE
FREEMAN WILLS CROFTS • THE GROOTE PARK MURDER
FRANCIS DURBRIDGE • BEWARE OF JOHNNY WASHINGTON
J. JEFFERSON FARJEON • THE HOUSE OPPOSITE
RUDOLPH FISHER • THE CONJURE-MAN DIES
FRANK FROËST • THE GRELL MYSTERY
FRANK FROËST & GEORGE DILNOT • THE CRIME CLUB
ÉMILE GABORIAU • THE BLACKMAILERS
ANNA K. GREEN • THE LEAVENWORTH CASE
DONALD HENDERSON • MR BOWLING BUYS A NEWSPAPER
VERNON LODER • THE MYSTERY AT STOWE
PHILIP MACDONALD • THE RASP
PHILIP MACDONALD • THE NOOSE
PHILIP MACDONALD • THE RYNOX MYSTERY
PHILIP MACDONALD • MURDER GONE MAD
PHILIP MACDONALD • THE MAZE
NGAIO MARSH • THE NURSING HOME MURDER
G. ROY McRAE • THE PASSING OF MR QUINN
R. A. V. MORRIS • THE LYTTLETON CASE
ARTHUR B. REEVE • THE ADVENTURESS
FRANK RICHARDSON • THE MAYFAIR MYSTERY
R. L. STEVENSON • DR JEKYLL AND MR HYDE
J. V. TURNER • BELOW THE CLOCK
EDGAR WALLACE • THE TERROR
ISRAEL ZANGWILL • THE PERFECT CRIME

FURTHER TITLES IN PREPARATION

THE MYSTERY OF THE MUD FLATS

(WO$_2$)

A STORY OF CRIME

BY

MAURICE DRAKE

WITH AN INTRODUCTION BY
NIGEL MOSS

COLLINS
CRIME
CLUB

COLLINS CRIME CLUB
An imprint of HarperCollins*Publishers*
1 London Bridge Street
London SE1 9GF
www.harpercollins.co.uk

This Detective Story Club edition 2018

1

First published in Great Britain as *WO2* by Methuen & Co. 1913
Published as *The Mystery of the Mud Flats* by The Detective Story Club Ltd
for W. Collins Sons & Co. Ltd 1929

Introduction © Nigel Moss 2018

A catalogue record for this book is available from the British Library

ISBN 978-0-00-816892-6

Typeset in Bulmer MT Std by
Palimpsest Book Production Ltd, Falkirk, Stirlingshire

Printed and bound in Great Britain by
CPI Group (UK) Ltd, Croydon CR0 4YY

INTRODUCTION

MAURICE DRAKE's more enduring legacy to date has been as a leading artist in glass painting and eminent authority on medieval stained glass, working in the early twentieth century. By contrast, his fictional writings and reputation as an author of seven popular novels, originally published between 1906 and 1924, have been largely neglected. This new release of the Collins Detective Story Club edition of *The Mystery of the Mud Flats* (1930), the first in 88 years, provides an opportunity to appraise Drake's most successful novel, alongside his other works; also, to reflect on his place within the Edwardian high adventure story genre, and to look more broadly at his influence on later authors of nautically themed mystery and espionage thrillers.

Born in 1875 in Newton Abbot, Devon, Frederick Morris Drake—better known by his pseudonym Maurice Drake—was educated at Teignmouth Grammar School. Along with his brother Wilfred, Maurice Drake represented the fourth generation of a famous glass painting family in Exeter, originally established by his great-uncle. He married Alice Wilson in 1897. The family home and glass painting studio were close to Exeter Cathedral, and he was an advisor to the Cathedral authorities on stained glass—a role to which his daughter succeeded him following his death. Maurice's best known art publications, which have become leading works in their field, are *A History of English Glass-painting* (1912) and *Saints and their Emblems* (1916), both co-authored with Wilfred. He was retained by leading museums and became a renowned lecturer and expert advisor on old stained glass, travelling widely in the UK, Continental Europe and USA.

During WW1, Maurice served both with the Infantry and

the RAF. In the early 1920s, he resumed his writing career, but in April 1923 died prematurely from pneumonia at the age of 48. It was the same year that saw the publication of his first novel since the Great War.

A popular British circulating magazine of 1913 described Drake as 'a big, brawny, moustached sunburned man . . . who looks what he is . . . an ardent amateur yachtsman. Everything in connection with the sea interests him, and it was this love for salt-water that led him, some seven years ago, to try his hand at a novel about life on the ocean wave.'

In *The Mystery of the Mud Flats* (also known as *WO2*), Drake's fourth novel, the sea and life aboard boats feature constantly. It proved to be his best-selling and best-received novel. Originally published by Methuen in 1913 under the curious title *WO2* (the chemical formula of the valuable substance at the heart of the plot), it was also released in the USA and Canada that year under the same title. Acclaim from reviewers and popular commercial success swiftly followed on both sides of the Atlantic; between 1913 and 1930 the book was published in 26 editions world-wide and in three languages. When Collins acquired the publication rights in 1930 for its Detective Story Club imprint, the title was changed to the more accessible (and thrilling) *The Mystery of the Mud Flats*, and subtitled 'A Story of Crime'. Interestingly, in 1913, the UK first edition of *WO2* was subtitled 'A Novel'; and the US first edition 'A Story of Romantic Adventure'. The later change of subtitle in 1930 reflects the rapid growth in popularity of crime stories during the intervening period. By then, the 'Golden Age' of mystery fiction was well under way.

Upon the book's original publication in 1913, the *New York Times* reflected on the market being flooded with tales of romance, adventure and melodrama, of which few could be classed as literature. While lamenting a lack of authors of the calibre of Dumas, Scott or Stevenson, it was nonetheless sufficiently impressed by *WO2* to comment that it represented 'a rift in the dark outlook for romance in a day of clinical novels and potboilers. The author . . . is on the right track, and his book is so far above the average hotchpotch of remarkable and incongruous events as to deserve special comment. *WO2* is a stirring tale of illicit sea-faring, full of open air thrill . . . a rattling good yarn, and stands well to the front among books of its kind.' *Scribners* magazine applauded the ingenious plot and originality in characterisation. *The Nation* reviewer concluded: 'It is not often that detective work, vagabond adventure and love-making are more pleasantly mingled'.

WO2 or *The Mystery of the Mud Flats* is a model of the Edwardian high adventure story—the tropes of thrills, heroism, mystery and romance are all present in good measure. It blends a mix of themes: a full-blooded, lively paced adventure story with an original and unusual plot and a varied and interesting group of characters; illicit smuggling; gripping and dangerous espionage activity; exciting action at sea, with plenty of sailing detail and sea-faring dialogue; wonderfully descriptive writing, especially of the Dutch Scheldt coastal locations, and evoking life at sea often in bleak conditions; a non-intrusive love interest involving a young woman with thoroughly modern ideas; and, written only a year before WW1, there is a clear foreboding of the growing menace of Germany as a military power. The story is narrated in the first person throughout, and the writing is direct, crisp and terse.

The narrator is James Carthew-West, a fiercely independent, educated young man from an upper middle-class background, whose reading interests include Marcus Aurelius, Balzac and Henry James. He has a consuming passion for the sea, and when we meet him is already an experienced and well-travelled seaman, the owner and skipper of a coasting ketch *Luck and Charity*, moored in Exmouth harbour. While resourceful and capable, Carthew-West is also prone to periods of idleness and impecuniosity. In the book's vivid opening passages he is found at a particularly low point:

destitute, hung-over, unwashed and unkempt, having slept out on a beach all night—'I woke on Exmouth beach that early summer morning much as I should think a doomed soul might wake, Resurrection Day'. But Carthew-West's ill-fortune is about to change for the better. His reverie is rudely disturbed by a young lady, Pamela Brand. A sparky personal chemistry between the two quickly develops. His initial views about Pamela being 'a sexless little guttersnipe' and 'viper tongued', and her corresponding disgust with his wasted life, gradually give way to a mutual love interest as the story progresses. Pamela is likewise a strongly independent character. She holds a BSc, and is an enthusiastic supporter of the suffragette movement, with forthright views on the role of women in society; very much a modern woman for her time.

Pamela introduces Carthew-West to her business partner, Leonard Ward, formerly an eminent Chemistry professor, now running Axel Trading Company which ships various goods between English ports and the Scheldt delta in the Dutch low countries. Ward is impressed with *Luck and Charity* as a shallow coasting vessel, ideally suited to navigate the waters of the Scheldt, and he charters the boat, along with Carthew-West and crew, on exceptionally generous financial terms. Axel's base is in the Scheldt at Terneuzen, located at the entrance to the Ghent ship canal, close to the mouth of the river. Drake's descriptions of the locale and setting are masterly—vivid and atmospheric, yet pared down and succinct (mud flats have rarely appeared so attractive!)

Prior to embarkation from Exmouth with the first shipment for Terneuzen, Drake introduces another central protagonist, Austin Voogdt. His initial appearance is comedic; one reviewer colourfully described him as resembling a debonair tramp. But this is no ordinary tramp. Of Dutch descent, Voogdt was previously an independent investigative journalist working for London newspapers, who swapped city life for the open road and exercise after being diagnosed with TB. Carthew-West takes to Voogdt, and hires him to work as a crew member on *Luck and Charity*. Upon reaching Terneuzen, they encounter Axel Trading's local representative, Willis Cheyne. He is a cousin of Pamela and fellow partner in the business; a secretive young man, with a volatile temper and unpleasant nature, prone to drink and gambling. Unsurprisingly, he later turns out to be dishonest and untrustworthy.

The charter operation runs smoothly and is financially rewarding for Carthew-West. But the trade is not all it seems. The cargoes delivered to Terneuzen are invariably loss-making, and the mud ballast brought back to England is apparently worthless. Yet Voogdt discovers that Ward and his partners have become extremely affluent of late. Increasingly perplexed, and with his investigative traits coming to the fore, Voogdt resolves to uncover the puzzle and find out what is really going on. At the same time, a German company begins setting up operations in Terneuzen, close to Axel Trading. Headed by its manager Van Noppen, its business is conducted secretively; initially thought to be fertiliser, then later explosives. But the Germans too exhibit a keen interest in the mud flats.

Voogdt displays talents and abilities more akin to a secret service agent than a journalist. Why does he initially disguise his true persona from Willis Cheyne and Van Noppen? How does he gain access to firearms at short notice, and what of his relationship with shadowy agents who look to him so admiringly as their leader in action? The allusion to British secret service connections is there, but ultimately Drake opts to keep Voogdt as an investigative journalist, motivated primarily by financial gain, rather than by national interest (although the latter is certainly served).

Stories dominated by sea adventures are at the heart of five out of Drake's seven novels. His knowledge and experience of sailing gives the books an authenticity which enhances their quality. The first, *The Salving of a Derelict* (1906), also known by its US title *The Coming Back of Lawrence Averil*, won a *Daily Mail* prize of £100 in 1906 for best story by a new writer (out of 600 manuscripts submitted). It sold well both in the UK and USA, and quickly established Drake as a popular adventure novelist. Lawrence Averil is the 'derelict' in the story's title, an Oxford-educated young man from a well-to-do family; inclined to the sea from childhood. He is fond of the essays of Ralph Waldo Emerson, and in particular 'Heroism' (apt, given the plot's development). Following the shock of his father's suicide after the discovery of financial embezzlement, Averil is offered a lifeline by one of his father's victims to work on a fishing trawler in the North Sea. Life at sea proves arduous and dangerous, as much from the hostility of other crew members as the bleak hardship of the natural elements. The challenges to Averil's character are formidable, and he is pushed to the limits. Ultimately, the 'derelict' proves himself, encouraged by the daughter of his boss, a modern, self-possessed London newspaper woman. There are clear parallels between the characters and personalities of Lawrence Averil and James Carthew-West (of *WO2*), as well as their respective female partners. Also, one of Averil's crew members subsequently appears in *WO2*, working for Carthew-West on *Luck and Charity*.

Salvage appears again in Drake's second sea novel *Wrack* (1910), but this time in its nautical form. A young naval officer, incapacitated from service early in his career, turns to salvage work at sea. The nature of salvage operations, with its risks and chances, is graphically described. The hero's efforts prove increasingly successful and highly rewarding; there is also a promising romance interest in the background. However, the story takes an unexpected dark twist following a fateful discovery, and subsequent emotional turmoil and tragedy overtake the previous happiness and good fortune of the protagonist.

In between these two sea adventures, Drake wrote *Lethbridge of the Moor* (1908). Set in Exmouth and Dartmoor, the story concerns the unfortunate and cruel consequences for the young hero, George Lethbridge, of an unpremeditated act, out of character, which causes injury to a gamekeeper during a foolhardy poaching expedition. Lethbridge is sentenced to five years' penal servitude. The remainder of the story focuses on the hardship of prison life and the misfortunes he suffers. The sensitive character of Lethbridge is sympathetically drawn. During his incarceration, Lethbridge displays admirable qualities of fortitude and stoicism, and commits acts of selfless virtue towards other inmates. A love interest also develops involving the wife of a fellow prisoner. The novel was praised by reviewers for its good and clear literary style, vivid description of Dartmoor scenery, and restrained yet forceful romance.

The popular success of *WO2* in 1913 led Drake to write a sequel. The follow-up novel was *The Ocean Sleuth* (1915), another sea adventure mystery and featuring the same main protagonists as in *WO2*. The sleuth is Austin Voogdt, now styled 'Sherlock of the Sea'. The newly married James Carthew-West and his wife Pamela also appear in the story, but only peripherally. Voogdt, the maritime detective, is the hero of the story. The plot is strong, exciting and fast-paced; but different in many ways from Drake's previous books. An absconding financier with £80,000 in notes is supposedly drowned at sea, after a foreign liner breaks up on rocks off the Lizard in Cornwall. Subsequently, many of the notes reappear as forgeries. At one point, there is an exchange of batches of real and counterfeit notes aboard a train in the Parsons tunnel at Dawlish. Spurred on by his love interest in a female suspect, Voogdt hunts down the real notes and solves the mystery. Both *WO2* and *The Ocean Sleuth* were sufficiently popular to be serialised in leading British adventure story magazines in their respective years of publication.

After military service in WW1, Drake returned to his writing career in the early 1920s. His penultimate novel *The Doom Window* (1923) was released in the same year as his death. An interesting and unusual story, concerned with the forgery of old glass specimens. The protagonist is with a firm of glass painters in Shrewsbury, and the plot centres on the famous 'Doom Window' of a local church. Like Drake, the hero is an expert in judging and making stained glass, and the book includes plenty of technical detail about its manufacture, as well as the ins and outs of the business. The blurb of the US first edition refers to the story being 'as colorful as the stained glass around which its plot turns'. The *Saturday Review* was particularly admiring of the scenes which describe the effect on the hero of his first visit to New York, where he visits as a consulting expert, and how he views all sorts of city life there through eyes fresh from an English cathedral town. We know Drake had himself made such a trip to New York to value a collection of old glass, and he will likely have drawn on his personal experiences when writing these descriptive passages.

Drake's final novel *Galleon Gold* (1924) was published posthumously in the year after his death. Fittingly a nautical story, this time set in the Hebridean Islands, it is an exciting and realistic sea adventure of mixed fortunes, complete with discreet romance element. The plot concerns the search for, and tracing of, lost galleons and gold. It particularly brings to mind George Birmingham's popular novel *Spanish Gold* (1908), which features treasure hunting off the west coast of Ireland.

While *WO2* lies squarely within the Edwardian high adventure tradition, it has a wider literary significance. There are parallels with the classic boating thriller *The Riddle of the Sands* (1903) by Erskine Childers, regarded as one of the finest early secret service stories of literary distinction (alongside *Kim* by Rudyard Kipling, published the year before). This well-drawn, exciting story of amateur espionage, involving two contrasting young male protagonists sailing in the Baltic and Frisian Islands who stumble across pre-invasion manoeuvres by the German navy, was prescient in calling attention to Germany as a potential threat to Britain, especially at a time (pre-*Entente Cordiale*) when France was perceived as the nation's principal enemy. *WO2*, with its allusions to Germany's international subterfuge and developing armaments programme, was published in the year leading up to WW1. It forms part of the small but influential body of fiction dubbed 'invasion literature', alongside *The Riddle of the Sands* and *The Invasion of 1910* by William Le Quex, published in 1906. All were stories with a purpose, written from patriotic leanings, and intended to raise public awareness of the threat of war with Germany and call for preparedness. Together, they provide an interesting insight into pre-WW1 British perceptions.

These novels were precursors to the adventure spy fiction of John Buchan's *The Thirty-Nine Steps* (1915), Conan Doyle's *His Last Bow* (1917) and E. Phillips Oppenheim's *The Great Impersonation* (1920)—all involving the rounding-up of German spy gangs at the outbreak of WW1. This influence carried over to WW2. A. G. MacDonell's *The Crew of the Anaconda* (1940) is in the same vein; it features the tracking down of German spies by the owner of a motor cruiser and his friends in the early days of WW2. It continues the literary association between small boats and international conspiracy threats, in the tradition of *The Riddle of the Sands* and *WO2*. One commentator has described *The Crew of the Anaconda* as a kind of WW2 equivalent to *The Thirty-Nine Steps*. Other espionage adventure thrillers with a nautical flavour from that period include Hammond Innes' *Wreckers Must Breathe* (1940), featuring the Cornish coastline, disused tin mines and a secret U-boat base; also John Ferguson's *Terror on the Island* (1942), which involves abstracting an invention from Germany prior to the outbreak of WW2.

R. Austin Freeman's *The Shadow of the Wolf* (1925) is a tale involving the forgery of banknotes and murder on board a yacht

off Wolf Rock in Cornwall. There is a significant boating influ-
ence in several thrillers by A. E. W. Mason, including *The
Dean's Elbow* (1930), and *The House in Lordship Lane* (1946)
featuring Inspector Hanaud. Mason was himself a secret agent
in WW1, as well as a keen yachtsman. One thinks also of various
sea mysteries of the 1930s, including those by Taffrail (Captain
Taprell Dorling—'the Marryat of the modern Navy') such as
Mid-Atlantic (1936), John Remenham's *Sea Gold* (1930), John
C. Woodiwiss's *Mouseback* (1939), Peter Drax's *High Seas
Murder* (1939) and Ernest McReay's *Murder at Eight Bells*
(1939). Later, a strong nautical theme can be seen in the novels
of Andrew Garve, for example *The Megstone Plot* (1956) and *A
Hero for Leanda* (1959); Edward Young's espionage thriller *The
Fifth Passenger* (1963); as well as several boating thrillers by
J. R. L. Anderson, including *Death in the North Sea* (1975) from
the series featuring Colonel Peter Blair, and *Redundancy Pay*
(1976), also known as *Death in the Channel*.

Maurice Drake's influence can also be seen in some of the
sea mysteries of famous Golden Age detection writer Freeman
Wills Crofts. The Golden Age commentator Curtis Evans has
noted that Crofts was a great admirer of Drake's sea adventure
stories, and interestingly maintains he borrowed the surname
of Maxwell Cheyne, the protagonist of *Inspector French and
the Cheyne Mystery* (1926), from Willis Cheyne in *WO2*. There
are similarities too between Joan Merrill, the heroine of Crofts'
story and Pamela Brand in *WO2*. Both stories feature Dartmouth
harbour in their plots. Crofts' earlier novel *The Pit-Prop
Syndicate* (1922) also displays the influence of *The Riddle of the
Sands* and *WO2*. It centres on investigations by amateur sleuths
into illicit smuggling activities, using boats ferrying pit props
which sail from the Bordeaux coast canals across to the Humber
Estuary.

Time now to rediscover and enjoy afresh the exciting adventures
of sea-farers James Carthew-West and Austin Voogdt, as they

tackle the strange mystery of the mud flats at Terneuzen, amid increasing dangers to themselves, and against a backdrop of the looming shadow of international conflict.

NIGEL MOSS
September 2017

CONTENTS

CONTENTS

CHAPTER I

CONCERNING A FOOL AND HIS MONEY

I WOKE on Exmouth beach that early summer morning much as I should think a doomed soul might wake, Resurrection Day. To the southward rosy, sunlit cliffs showed through faint haze like great opals—like the Gates of Pearl—and the bright business of getting-up was going on all around. Hard by the slimy piles of the wooden pier, in a corner tainted by rotting seaweed and dead shell-fish, I came slowly to consciousness, my eyes clogged and aching, a foul taste in my mouth, and in my mind lurking uneasiness as of a judgment to come. And lying out all night on dewy shingle had made me stiff in every joint, and sore as though I had been beaten all over with a stick.

The young day was one of heaven's own, all blue and gold. The two men whose crunching feet upon the shingle had roused me were aboard the dinghy that had been mine twelve hours before—my Royal Torbay burgee still fluttering gaily at her masthead. Her new owner was swabbing dew from off her seats, pointing out her merits to his companion the while. He spoke of me, a thumb jerked over one shoulder to show where I lay upon the beach. 'That there West'—the wind brought me that much; that, and a scornful laugh from the other. The whole bright day seemed laughing at me in derision, and I dropped my arms upon my face again and tried to get another hour of forgetfulness. I was at the bottom end of things. Poor comfort to reflect that I only had myself to blame.

I'd been on my uppers once before, at Kingston, in Jamaica, just after the earthquake; but I was fit then, with a clear conscience, and there was plenty to do. Now, with two years of idling and folly to my discredit, I only had the sore knowledge of chances thrown away. Besides, the past winter had tried me hard: poverty and loneliness and the sight of one's property slipping away day by day make a man ripe for any foolishness by way of a change. Only the day before I'd parted with the dinghy, almost my last asset, and now, on the morrow, the price didn't seem good enough. A rotten waterman's tub, scarcely seaworthy, in part exchange; a couple of pound's worth of loose silver in my pocket. And worst of all was the uncertainty as to what I should do next.

There had been no uncertainty at Kingston. There were more jobs there than men to do them, and I took the first that offered and did right well out of it. I had been with the Deutsche-West-Indie people till then, third mate on their *Oldenburg*, and we got into Kingston harbour the day after the town tumbled about the folk's ears. Trier, our skipper, did the right sort of thing—called at the Consulate and offered free passages out of the place to as many Germans as he could carry, and so on—and then, having done what he considered his duty, was all for the sea again. But I wouldn't go. Able-bodied whites were badly wanted ashore. Rescue parties were busy; there was a fearful mess to tidy up everywhere; there had been some bad cases of looting, and people were afraid the niggers would get out of hand.

My word, but that was work, that relief business! Awful, a lot of it—ghastly; but I don't know when I enjoyed myself so much in my life. There were still lots of people alive and buried in the ruins, and we had to get them out. At first I was in a mixed lot of whites and blacks and yellows; and they were a mixture, too! Our foreman was a full-blooded nigger carpenter, a fine chap, a devil to work, and as strong as a bull. We had two doctors, one of 'em off a Japanese man-o'-war in harbour and the other a visitor—a tourist. Their head assistant was another tourist, a woman, wife of a vicar in Lancashire when she was at home; but she'd been a hospital nurse, and she pitched in, like the rest of us. There were nine or ten American sailors, and three of them wouldn't speak to us English. There had been some fuss with our governor, who had declined the services of the American battleships' crews, I believe, and they were wild as hawks about it. Dozens of them had sneaked ashore to help, the officers winking at it. One of our three must have known something about permanent deserting unless he'd picked up his Cockney accent in the States. They were good men, those three, and the Cockney wasn't the worst of 'em. Then there was the son of the Mayor of Kingston and a yellow-bearded Finnish ship's cook and a Chinese laundryman. Those were all the notabilities. The rank and file were niggers, some of them women.

After a week there weren't any more of the living imprisoned, and we had to attend to the dead. Faugh! In the tropics. Awful! They broke our gang up and put the mayor's son and myself in charge of another lot digging out bodies and burning them. The mayor's son didn't work up to his collar, I considered. So we had words about it, and he went off with his nose in the air. To do the chap justice, I think now he only meant to go a hundred yards and come back again, but I hadn't time to think of that then, so I hove a half-brick at him and shouted to him to go to Hades. The brick got him in the back of the knee and brought him down in the road, and I sent a nigger to drag him into the shade and went on with the work. When I went to look for him he had cleared, and I never saw him again, but I fancy the incident had a good deal to do with my being left severely alone after things were tidy once more.

When the land breeze had blown the smoke of the last hideous burning away out to sea I was on my beam-ends, so I cabled the governor: 'Detained here for want of funds.' I might as well have saved my money, for I ought to have known what the reply would be. 'Capital experience. Pitch in and earn some, my son,' he cabled back.

A hard case, my old man. That's him all over. Nobody else in the world would have paid for those two unnecessary words at the end, just to show it wasn't because he was short of cash that he wouldn't help me.

The relief gangs had broken up and the sailors and most of the tourists departed—and there was I in a suit of rags, my hair about four inches long, and not a notion of what to do next. It was the long hair decided me, I think. I hunted up my nigger carpenter and got him to build me a little lean-to shack against the ruins of the Presbyterian church, promising to pay him when I could. Then I got a sheet of tin, painted a gaudy Chinese dragon on it with the words:

PROF. WATSON

TATTOOING ARTIST

and nailed it up over my door. I copied the dragon from the cover of a packet of Chinese crackers that was blowing about on a rubbish heap, and tattooing anybody can do, if they've got the sense to keep their needles clean.

As luck would have it, I hadn't long to wait for customers. In fact I was busy from the first day. When the shipping began to ply regularly again there were heaps of tourists to see the ruined town, and lots of them came to be tattooed as a souvenir of their visit. One chap gave me a photo of my shack, with me outside it at work on a sailor's arm. I begged the negative of him, had a few hundreds printed as postcards, and used to make a shilling apiece out of them. Things just boomed. I paid my carpenter and set him at work on a little frame house in a plot I hired, and when it was done I shifted my sign there and settled down to business in earnest. Then I got an assistant—a young Japanese from a sailing ship that had been wrecked on Culebra, in the Virgin Islands. He really was an artist, that chap, and his work put me out of conceit with my own botching. So after two years I sold him the house and business, lock, stock and barrel, and cleared out for home. As a souvenir he did a bit of his best work on my chest whilst I was waiting for my steamer. A lovely bit of tattooing it is: a masterpiece, an eagle holding a fish.

I landed in Plymouth with about six hundred pounds in my pocket, and knocked it down in two years. Lazy, lovely South Devon held me. I was fool enough to let the old man's cablegram rankle, and I never went near him—just sent him a card to say where I was, which he answered with another, and that's all the communication we held with one another. I loafed about from one place to another, idling, drinking more than was any use to me, and generally wasting my time. I'd earned six hundred pounds as easily as falling off a log, and thought it would be easy enough to earn another lot when that was gone.

There's a class of man common on the south coast of England, and especially in Devonshire, who is no manner of use to himself or anybody else. The natives call them remittance men, and that exactly describes them. They're idlers, mostly sons of busy professional men or manufacturers in London, the Midlands or the north. They idle more or less gracefully; they go fishing and sail small boats, or get drunk and sleep in the sun. They're very little use to anybody, as I've said already, and I wouldn't mention them if I hadn't lived with them—been one of them, if you like. They were my only associates for two years, and they and sleepy South Devon brought me down to sleeping out on Exmouth beach.

It was just after Christmas when I landed at Plymouth, and by the spring I'd got tired of messing about and fuddling in a garrison town and thought I'd like a bit of sailing for the summer. Of course every waster I'd picked up with knew of the very boat that would suit me, and I should think I inspected half the rotten tubs in Devon and Cornwall before I found the packet I wanted.

I only heard of her by accident. A boat-builder at Yealmpton had built her as an experiment to the order of his brother-in-law, who was a fisherman in the Brixham fleet. The brother-in-law—a man with more notions in his head than money in his pocket—had died bankrupt before his boat was rigged, and the

Yealmpton man had her left on his hands, and half the south Devon coast was laughing at him, for it appeared she was useless to anybody, being the wrong build for a trawler and too small for a coasting boat.

I went over and saw her one Saturday afternoon and fell in love with her on the spot. Her hold, too small for freights, was amply big enough for me, and besides it left more cabin room at each end of her. She was a beauty, to my thinking; a good, beamy boat, not too deep in draught, and built like a house. The builder, normally an honest man, in building for his sister's husband had put real good stuff into the boat. The day I was there two other fellows had come down from Brixham to see her and were jeering at her, to cheapen her, I suppose. The builder was raving her praises, and I got into his good graces at once by speaking the truth, saying that she was a well-built craft, honest material and honest work in her.

That was the way to tackle the man, for he'd put his heart into her timbers. The other two sheered off and I bought her, hull and masts only, as she stood, for a hundred and ten pounds, and she was dirt cheap at the price. For another hundred he rigged her, fisherman fashion, rough hard gear throughout to stand any weather, divided her hold with cheap matchboard bulkheads into a saloon with two cabins, and decked over her hatch with four skylights. And I got to sea with her, well-pleased, before the middle of June.

Brett had named her the *Luck and Charity*, of all outlandish names, but I didn't bother to change it. Sure enough she brought me luck in the end—the best of luck—and at first she was a charity to the fraternity of wasters, and no mistake.

With her hold turned into cabins she was a very roomy packet. Though she was only forty-five feet or so between the perpendiculars, she was fifteen in the beam, every inch. There was a little skipper's cabin aft, about twelve feet by nine, with just head-room enough to stand upright, two bunks and a flap table; the big square hatch we decked over was about eight feet

by thirteen, and there was a roomy forepeak—almost fit to be
called a forecastle—with two bunks on each side. Altogether
we could shake down ten men without crowding, though I've
often slept fifteen aboard, the extra members of the family
sleeping on the cabin seats or on the floor.

It was an idle time, those two years, but past question I
enjoyed it. The wasters were delighted, of course, and I was
the dearest old chappie in the west of England whilst funds
lasted. It worked out about level, though; they had cheap quarters and I had a cheap crew, so everybody was pleased. We put
to sea or stayed on moorings just as the weather served or the
whim took us, so mostly we had fair-weather cruising. Ashore,
there was plenty of company. There's a freemasonry of sorts
amongst remittance men: they snarl behind each other's backs
pretty much, but can unite upon occasion. I happened to be
the occasion this time, and there was plenty of visiting, and
card-playing, and fuddling, and remarkably mixed company
whenever we went ashore to revel.

The first winter I tied her up in Teignmouth harbour and
lived ashore, and when the spring came started off again. Not
being built for a yacht the *Luck and Charity* wanted a lot of
ballast, but she wasn't too deep for getting in and out of those
little west of England harbours, and by the end of the second
summer I knew the coast from Swanage to Land's End like the
back of my hand. And very useful knowledge it has proved to
be since then.

It didn't seem so useful, though, when I came to tie up for
the second winter. I chose Exmouth Bight for anchorage this
time. You can't play the fool without spending money and I
was cleaned out down to the last fiver. Exmouth is a free
harbour—no dues unless you go into dock—and so Exmouth
looked the place for me. The winter before I'd had plenty of
invitations ashore, but this time the wasters had got wind of
my circumstances and invitations were off. On the whole it
seemed a cheerful prospect.

I kept my one paid hand hard at it, lowering topmasts and stripping gear, and, when the lot was snugged down for the winter, paid him off and told him to clear out and go home. He was a stolid shockhead from Topsham, called Hezekiah Pym. The wasters used to laugh at him, and certainly he was the quaintest sample of a yachtsman I ever met. But he might have been born on the water, so handy was he afloat, and he had served my turn so well that I felt sorry to part with him. I had to pawn my watch to make up the money I owed him, and even then it was a near thing. It was a real good watch that my father had given me when I was twenty-one; but the pawnbroker wouldn't advance me more than the value of the gold case because, he said, the crest and motto engraved on it spoilt its sale value. The result was that when I'd made up 'Kiah's money I hadn't half-a-sovereign to my name.

When I paid him he looked first at the money and then inquiringly at me.

'That's a fortnight's brass extra because you haven't had notice,' I told him.

'Aw,' said he, and put the money in his pocket. Then, as an afterthought: 'What be yu gweyn t' du fer th' weenter, sir?' he asked.

'Stop aboard and catch flukes.'

'Aw,' said he again meditatively, and went ashore, leaving me to moralise on rats and sinking ships. But I did him an injustice for once.

Next morning he was aboard again before I was out, and brought me my breakfast in bed.

'What brings you back?' I asked.

'Come back t' catch flukes 'long o' you,' he said.

'Look here,' I said, 'I'm broke, 'Kiah, and I can't afford to keep you. So you just slip off to Topsham again, and get another job.'

'What for?' said the fool.

'Because I'm broke.'

'I thought you would be, mighty soon,' he said slowly. 'Yu been kippin' all they lot tu long.'

Not once had I ever caught him in the slightest act of incivility all the time I'd had the boat, yet that was how he regarded my guests—'Yas, sir'; 'No, sir'; 'Surely, sir.' Never a word out of place; but that blinking, stolid lump had all the wasters sized up, all the time. Like their own bogs, South Devon men are. They smile and look tranquil, but you never know what's under the surface. There's good rocky ground in them to stand on, though, sometimes, if you've the knack of finding it.

After I'd had my breakfast I went forward and told him again I hadn't a job or pay for him and he must go. He only said 'Aw' protestingly; and he didn't go, and hasn't gone to this day. He never alluded to the matter again except one day in mid-winter when we'd had a good haul of flukes and could spare some to send ashore to sell. Then he looked up from the loaded dinghy alongside, blowing on his half-frozen fingers.

'Nort doin' up to Topsham now,' said he. 'I'm better off yere'n what I should be 'ome.'

The winter came in wet and cold, and I nearly went melancholy mad with the sheer monotony of it. With each rising tide we swung our nose towards the harbour mouth and watched the water cover the mud-flats. At flood, we laid up or down or cross-channel before the wind and cursed the swinging round because it tangled our fishing lines. At ebb, our bows pointed up river and the mud-flats became uncovered again. We could only fish at dead water, flood or ebb, and between times we went to sleep or watched the scenery—dirty water or dirty mud, according to the state of the tide.

On the whole I can't say I was pleased with that winter, and indeed it would take a man with queer tastes to admire wet mud-banks with the thermometer at freezing point, and wind and rain enough to keep you in the cabin for days on end.

Man cannot live on flukes alone, and to get bread and matches and paraffin—to say nothing of an occasional orgy on butcher's meat—I began to sell the boat's fittings. First the side-lights went, the spare anchor, the compass—things I thought I could replace cheaply or do without; but by early spring we were pretty well stripped—the fittings and bedding, from the cabins, the saloon table, crockery, spare rigging, any blessed thing that was detachable and had a market value. The saloon and cabins had relapsed to their original condition as hold, the matchboard partitions having been chopped up and burnt in the after-cabin stove, to save buying coal. The hold was a picture with its broken bulkheads jutting from the sides and the floor littered with driftwood and rubbish—anything we could pick up ashore that we thought would come in handy. A marine store dealer's shop was a fool to it. To save keeping two stoves going 'Kiah came aft and shared my cabin. He never sulked or lost his temper or grumbled once all the winter, and though he never had a word to say for himself, he was company for me of a sort.

Lying on Exmouth beach the day after the dinghy had gone, not the least sore thought I had was that I'd spent money to which he had as much right as myself. I groaned aloud as I tried to get to sleep again, and as the sun rose and warmed my aching bones I fell into a uneasy doze that brought some short forgetfulness.

CHAPTER II

CONCERNING A STROKE OF GOOD
LUCK AND AN ACT OF CHARITY

WITH the sun warming me, I must have slept for over an hour; but, lying face downwards as I was, even my dreams weren't pleasant. I thought I had fallen overboard from the *Luck and Charity*, and rising half drowned under her stern called to 'Kiah for a rope. He was steering, but, instead of throwing me the mainsheet, he reached over a long arm, caught me by the side and pushed me under again. Drowning, I gulped salt water, and woke with a jerk, to find a girl standing over me prodding me in the side with her toe. Stupid with sleep, I rolled over and sat up, blinking to stare at her.

The sun, just over her head, dazzled my eyes so that I couldn't clearly see her face; but from her get-up I judged her to be the usual type of summer visitor to the town. A big straw hat, a light blouse and dark skirt, and a bathing towel in one hand; but with the towel she held her shoes and stockings, and I saw that the foot that she had stirred me with was bare.

I asked her what she wanted, sulkily enough.

'We want to go across the river.' She pointed to the yellow sand-hills on the Warren side.

'Well?' I said.

'There doesn't seem to be a ferryman here. Don't you want to earn a sixpence?' Her tone was not conciliatory.

I looked down the beach. A man and woman stood by the waterside, but the boatmen had gone—to breakfast, I supposed. For a moment I was minded to tell her she must wait till they came back, but the thought of 'Kiah came into my mind. I owed it to him to make up what I could for the money I'd spent overnight.

'I don't expect my boat's smart enough for you,' I said, scrambling to my feet.

'I didn't expect anything lavish,' she snapped; and at her tone I looked down over my clothes and passed a hand over my head and face. I didn't look prosperous. One boot was broken at the toe, and my serge coat and trousers were stained with every shade of filth, from dry mud to tar, by the winter's 'longshoring. I wore one of 'Kiah's jerseys, *Luck and Charity* in dirty white letters across the breast. Bare headed, my hair was full of sand, and there was a fortnight's growth on my cheeks. My razor, an elaborate safety fakement, had been sold early in the winter to get 'Kiah an oilskin jacket, and though I considered I had a right to shave with his, it was a right not often exercised. He'd inherited the thing from a grandfather who'd been in the army, and I didn't share his high opinion of it. But in bright sunlight, with this girl staring at me, I wished I'd done so more recently.

The boat was in a state to match its owner. It couldn't have had a coat of paint for two years, and to make matters worse the beach children had been playing in it and left it half full of pebbles, seaweed and sand. With the girl looking on, I started to clean out some of the rubbish, and the man and woman strolled along the water's edge to join us. Feeling ashamed of myself and my shabby craft, I kept my head down and went on with my work till the man spoke.

'An old boat?' he said, civilly enough.

For an answer I mumbled some sort of assent.

'Is she tight?' he asked.

'I don't know,' I said. 'I only bought her yesterday. She'll take us that far without sinking, I suppose.'

He said no more and we pushed off. The filthy tub leaked like a basket, of course, and the water was level with the bottom boards before we reached the Warren. I saw what was going to happen when we started, and rowed my hardest to get across before their feet were wet, but facing them I had time to look them over and see what sort of people my first customers were. The other woman was a beauty—a real beauty, of the big, placid type. She said very little on the way across, just trailing one hand in the cool water now and again, and listening to the talk of the others. The man struck me favourably. He was tall and gaunt, with a bit of a stoop in the shoulders. His clean-shaven face was sallow and he wore spectacles, which gave him the air of a student of sorts. His big square mouth was immovable as the slot in a post office, save for an occasional movement at the corners that seemed to hint at a laugh suppressed. A man you took to at sight: straight as a line, you could see he was.

The girl who had waked me was of a different class from the other two. Now that I could see her more plainly I saw that she had a likeable little face enough, but you couldn't call her a beauty anyhow. Big eyes and short upper lip were her best features; her nose was a snub, and she was well freckled, and wore her hair in a club sort of short pigtail. Her dress was shabbier than the other woman's, and I took her for a paid companion, or rather a poor relation, which would account for their tolerating her impudence. She was full of life, chattering nonsense the whole way across.

I've learnt since that that young woman's manners do occasionally cause embarrassment in well-bred circles. Blood will out: her grandmother was a mill hand, and the grand-daughter's thrown back to the original type. She's told me since that 'Guttersnipe' was one of her school nicknames, and like most school names it's deadly appropriate. She's got the busy wits and the quick tongue of the gutter, combined with the haste in action and the discerning eye for essentials that lifted her forefathers out of it.

The Warren beach was steep, and when they got out of the boat they had to scramble up a high slope of sand. The girls reached the level beach at the top and were out of sight at once;

the man lingered to pay me. He hadn't anything less than a shilling, and I couldn't change it.

'Take the shilling and call it square,' he said, blinking at me through his spectacles.

'The fare's twopence a head. I don't take charity,' I said rudely.

'No need to be rude, my man,' said he. 'Either you can trust me or you can take the shilling and bring me the change later. Here's my card. I'm staying at the Royal.'

'I don't know when I shall be ashore again,' I told him. 'When are you going back to Exmouth?'

'In about an hour, I expect. The ladies are going to bathe.'

'Then I'll wait till you come back and put you across again,' I said. 'That'll make up the shilling's worth.'

He nodded and scrambled up the beach after his womenfolk. No sooner was he out of sight than the younger girl's head appeared against the sky and came slipping and sliding down over the steep bank of sand again. When she reached me she was breathing fast as though with running.

'How old are you?' she jerked out.

'Twenty-eight.'

'You were drunk last night, weren't you?'

'I was.'

'You fool!' she said.

Words can't tell the scorn in her voice. It brought me up all standing, as though she'd slapped me in the face. Literally I couldn't answer her; before I'd thought of a word she'd scrambled up over the slope again and was gone, leaving me staring after her like a baby.

When I got my wits about me I don't know when I was in such a rage. The cheek of the little slut!

One thing I would do. I'd show her I was independent, at all events. Somebody else could row them back and spend my sixpence. I got into the boat again and pushed off to where the *Luck and Charity* lay at anchor.

It's queer the way one's resolutions change with one's moods. 'Kiah was getting breakfast, but I kept mine waiting whilst I had a shave with his awful razor. After a wash I felt better and got overside and had a swim. Scrambling aboard the small boat her looks disgusted me, and I tidied her up as best I could, next thing, and put a couple of cushions from the cabin into her.

Doing this I heard a clock at Exmouth strike nine, and remembered it was eight o'clock when I had left Exmouth beach. I don't pretend to explain it, but almost before I knew where I was I was rowing back to the Warren beach to await my fares.

I'd been thinking hard about the ckeeky girl, you may be sure, and a good breakfast and a wash had revived my self-conceit. Her slanging indicated that she took some interest in me, I thought, and I made up my mind I'd rout out my last decent suit of clothes and go ashore in the evening and try and pick her up on the promenade. Her behaviour had confirmed me in my notion that she was some sort of dependent, and I thought I could furbish up sufficient togs to impress her with the fact that I was a yacht owner. I'd take the starch out of her, I reckoned. No denying she'd waked me to an interest in her.

They kept me waiting half-an-hour longer. Whilst I was waiting I remembered the card the man had given me and searched my pockets till I found it. 'Mr Leonard Ward' was the name, and the address 'Mason College, Birmingham.'

When they came down the beach the little girl gave me one look up and down, and then sat in the boat with her back to me all the way across, ignoring my existence. The man Ward gave me my shilling and offered to pay me for waiting, which I declined, and the three of them were strolling up the beach together when I was seized with a diabolical impulse.

'Here,' I called after them; and as they turned round, 'You—the little girl. Miss—Pamily, is it? I want you.'

Her face went crimson, but she walked back to me.

'My name is Brand,' she said, very stately.

'Pamela Brand?' I asked.

'Pamela Emily Brand. And what do you want of me, pray?'

'I want to ask you something—two things. Why did you go for me just now like you did?'

'Because I hate waste,' she said. 'What's the other thing?'

'Will you meet me this evening?'

It was her turn to be struck speechless now; she couldn't get any redder than she was already. She looked over her shoulder to see if the man Ward was within call, and then, her face quick and alive with resentment, leaned over and with her open hand fetched my face a smack you could hear fifty yards down the beach. She's a lady, I tell you! And before I'd recovered, she was marching off with her nose in the air—just boiling with rage, I knew; and I laughed aloud, for all my stinging cheek. I'd drawn her. I'd teach her manners—the gutter-bred little prig.

Rowing back to the *Luck and Charity* I resolved more than ever to go ashore and seek her out that very evening. Now that she was piqued, I knew she would welcome any advance on my part as giving her an opportunity for revenge. So the first thing I did after scrambling aboard was to look out my best suit of clothes and give them a brush up. Then I turned in to get an hour or two of decent sleep.

Judging from the way the ship's head was laying, and from the sunlight streaming through the doorway on to the floor, I guessed it must be about half-past two, and three-quarters flood, when I was waked by a boat bumping alongside and by someone climbing on our deck. 'Kiah was about, I knew, and reckoning he could attend to any visitor, I turned over and was trying to doze off again when he swung himself down the companion stair, barefoot.

'Gen'leman to see you, sir,' he said.

'What name?' I called after him.

A mumbled inquiry, and the voice of my morning customer in answer.

'Tell him Mr Ward wants to see him. He had my card this morning.'

So Miss Brand had called in male assistance. Somehow I hadn't thought that of her; but I hadn't any particular objection to a row, so pulled my boots on and went on deck, stretching myself. He was sitting on the bulwarks, looking aloft, a hired boat and man hitched alongside.

'Good afternoon,' he said civilly.

'Afternoon,' I answered. 'Want me?'

'Yes. I—I—want—' He hesitated. 'I understand you want to hire this boat on a charter?'

'I wanted to sell her and clear out to sea,' I told him. 'Failing that I wouldn't mind a charter, certainly. But she's not fit for a yacht. Her cabin fittings are stripped, and there's nothing under this hatch roof but smashed bulkheads and driftwood.'

'I don't want a yacht. It's for the coasting trade. How many tons could you get into her, and what water would she draw, loaded?'

'Not more than about sixty tons, I should think. And I don't know about draught. Something under nine feet, for certain. She'd never pay. You'd want three men, and how's the freight on sixty tons to pay their wages?'

'The draught is the point,' he said. 'They're shallow waters I want her for. We can't use a bigger boat very well. In fact, it's just this small class of vessel I'm down here to look out for. She's staunch, isn't she?'

'Sound as a bell,' I assured him. 'Come below and have a look at her, and then you can tell me just what you do want.'

We went all over her, and he seemed an intelligent man, from his comments. Being evidently shore-bred. he couldn't see how badly she'd been stripped, of course, but the few questions and remarks he did make were all to the point. After going through the hold and forepeak we went aft into my cabin and sat down.

'She'll suit my purpose,' he said, and looked across the table at me inquiringly.

'Where do you want her to go to?' I asked.

'To and from the Scheldt,' he said. 'I am a director of a small company trading at Terneuzen, in the Isle of Axel. We have a couple of boats on charter now, but we're busy and can do with another, for a year at least. You would take our goods from English ports here on the south coast, returning in ballast. What ballast did you say this boat wanted?'

'Summer, fifteen tons or so; winter, twenty-five, I daresay.'

'You can allow for more than that,' he said. 'We're excavating beside our wharf there and are glad to get the mud taken away. So you needn't blow over for want of ballast. And now as to terms.'

We discussed terms easily enough. Thinking such a small company as he described would be sure to haggle. I asked twice what I was prepared to take, and he accepted on the nail. After that, I was almost ashamed to point out that I should have to ask for an advance.

'The boat isn't fit for sea as she is,' I explained. 'I've sold all my spare stores, and shall have to pay for labour as well as fit her out. If you're in a hurry, that is. I daresay my man and myself could get her rigged in a month or five weeks.'

'That won't do,' he said. 'I want you to get under way just as soon as you can. We'll advance you fifty pounds. Will that be enough?'

I nodded. 'That'll be ample. As to security? I'll give you a mortgage on the boat herself.'

He seemed to approve of the suggestion. 'That's business,' he said. 'I'll get the mortgage prepared at once, and you can have the cheque when you please. You'll want to take on another man or two, won't you?' He got up and went on deck, me feeling almost dazed with my good luck.

He shook hands as he was going over the side. 'By the way, I shall want your name and address.'

'My name's West—James West.' It didn't seem quite the occasion to drag in the Carthew hyphen part of the business. 'As to address, I haven't one ashore. You'd better describe me as master and owner of the ketch *Luck and Charity*, registered at Plymouth.'

'That'll be good enough,' said he, and went down into his boat and was rowed away, leaving me fit to jump with delight.

'What du he want?' 'Kiah asked.

'Sir,' I shouted at him. 'Say "sir," you uncivil Topsham dab.'

'Yu 'eaved flukes at me for callin' 'ee "sir" yes'day,' he protested.

'That was because you were my partner then. Now you're my crew, my first orficer, my navigating loo-tenant, my paid wage-slave. We've got a job, 'Kiah. Your wages are doubled as from last October. You'll have a lump of arrears to draw tomorrow. Go and wash your face, and then go ashore and spend the money I got for the dinghy last night. In meat, d'ye hear? A duck, and green peas, and a cold apple tart at Crump's, and cream to eat with it. Us'll feed like Topsham men when the salmon comes up river, 'Kiah. Us have got a job, 'Kiah—a twelvemonth charter-party at good money—and us draws fifty quid tomorrow. D'ye understand, you plantigrade?'

'Caw!' said 'Kiah cheerfully, and went forward to wash himself before going ashore.

When I woke next morning it struck me I'd been in rather a hurry to take the man Ward at his word; but the confidence wasn't misplaced, for he came aboard at eleven with the cheque in his pocket and the mortgage deed ready for signing. That was soon done, and he handed me the money and my first instructions. I was to get the topmast up; replace the missing stores and victual the boat; hire an extra hand and proceed to Teignmouth, there to load clay for Terneuzen. My consignee was a Mr Willis Cheyne, the company's representative on the spot, and I must look to him for further instructions.

The rigging once started we worked double tides. I took on two men instead of one, and drove them for all I was worth, intending to take whichever proved the better of them to sea with me. They turned out to be a pair of crawling slugs, and I sacked them the third day and looked for another couple to take their place. But the tourist season was beginning, all the best men on the beach were busy, and the report spread by my two failures discouraged the others. In the end 'Kiah went to Topsham one evening and returned with a cousin of his, a Luxon—everybody in Topsham is called either Pym or Luxon—and we three finished the job in a week from the day the other two were sacked. Ward was aboard nearly every day, and once he brought his womenfolk with him. I was aloft, too busy to do the polite, so I shouted to him to make use of the cabin and went on reeving the peak halliards. The Pamily girl scowled up at me till she must have nearly got a crick in her neck, but I gave her a friendly wave of the hand and after that saw no more of her than the top of her big straw hat. Foreshortened, she looked like a mushroom wandering about the deck.

Luxon was just such a silent shockhead as 'Kiah himself. I never learnt his other name; 'Kiah always called him 'Banny,' which was obviously impossible. The job done, he drew his money arid went ashore without a word to me of his future intentions, but 'Kiah explained he wouldn't come to sea with us. "'E reckons 'e'd ruther stay 'ome,' was all I could get out of, him.

The evening before we left Exmouth I was in the dock entrance, filling our water-breakers from the hose where the ferry steamers water, when a voice hailed me from the top of the steps and asked if I was the ferry.

'What ferry?' I asked, without looking up.

'Across the river. To—Dawlish, is it? I want to keep along the coast road.'

'You'll find the Warren ferryboat on the outer beach. There's a steam ferry leaves here for Starcross in half-an-hour or thereabouts.'

'What good's a sixpenny steam ferry to me? I'm on the road;' and the owner of the voice came down and sat upon the steps just above me.

He was on the road and no mistake about it. I never saw such a long, lean, broken-down tramp in my life. His coat and shirt were worn through at the elbows, showing his thin, bare arms. The holes in his ragged tweed trousers showed he had on another pair of blue serge underneath, both pairs frayed to fringes at the heels. He wore no hat, and his boots were past even a tramp's repairing. As he sat, he took one off, looked at it whimsically with his head on one side, and threw it into the dock, and then served the other in the same way.

'It's a pity to separate 'em,' he said cheerfully. 'True, they never were a pair, but they've done a good few miles in my company.'

'You're a chirpy bird,' I said.

'Of course I am,' said he. 'Why not? Six months ago I wasn't given as many weeks to live, and yet here I am, fit and well, thanks to God's fresh air and a sane life. I've neither house nor farm nor fine raiment to bother me, nor woman, child nor slave dependent on me. I've even half-a-lung less to carry than you have, by the healthy look of you. My hat once on, my house is roofed.' He put his hand to his head. 'I forgot. It blew over the cliff a few miles back. All's for the best in this best of worlds. That's another worry the less.'

'You've got two pairs of trousers,' I suggested.

'True, O seer. A concession to public tastes. They are selected so that the holes in the inner pair do not correspond with those in the outer, and thus decency is observed. And now what about this ferrying business?'

I had got my water-breakers aboard the boat and was stowing them between the thwarts. 'Jump in,' I said. 'I'll put you across.'

'I may as well warn you that I haven't a sou to my name,' he said. 'You'll have to work for love. I'll take an oar and work my passage, if you like.'

It wasn't the first time he'd been in a boat, evidently, for he came aboard neatly, without stumbling or awkwardness, took the oar I proffered him, and handled it very fairly.

Half-way across I asked him what he was doing at Dawlish.

'Nothing, I expect. I've given up asking for jobs. It's much easier to ask for grub. Almost anybody'll give you that in this dear land of mine—poor folk especially—but work isn't so easy to get. Besides, I'm an unhandy fool at the best. I never learnt any trade worth knowing.'

'Have you a trade?'

'Bless you, yes. I'm a pressman—or was, before my lungs began to go. The doctors ordered me fresh air and exercise in a mild climate and I'm getting them tramping the South of England. Then I was fat and flabby and unhealthy and morose; now I'm the lightest-hearted wastrel on earth, and I've stopped spitting blood these last two months.'

'What are you going to do when the winter comes?'

'Don't know. Same thing as before, I suppose, unless I can ship south in some packet or other.'

I pricked up my ears. 'Ship south, eh? Are you a sailor man?'

'I used to report the big regattas for *The Yachting Gazette*,' he said. 'I had to know one end of the boat from the other to do that.'

'Feel like supper aboard my boat?' I pointed to where lay the *Luck and Charity*, just visible in the gathering dusk.

'Nothing I should like better,' he said airily, so we went aboard and I set before him cold fried sausages and baked mackerel.

The man was ravenous—almost starving—and he ate like a shark, I watching him across the table. In the lamplight one could see him better, and upon examination he wasn't such a bad looking tramp. He had a short black beard and moustache, his hair was close-clipped, and, for a wonder, he was clean, save for the dust of the roads upon his tattered clothing. Lean as a lath, his cheekbones stuck out and his eyes were sunk in their sockets, yet he looked like what he had claimed to be, fit and well and sunburnt to a healthy brown.

After he wiped the dishes clean he got up.

'Shall I wash up after myself?' he asked.

'No hurry. Sit down and chat. D'you smoke?'

'When I get the chance. Thanks.' He produced cigarette papers from some corner of his rags and rolled and lit a cigarette of my tobacco. Inhaling a few breaths luxuriously, he began to look about him. 'Books—books,' said he, and got up again to run his nose along my little shelf. '*Practice of Navigation, Ainsley's Nautical Almanac, South of England Cruises.* Hullo! *Pecheur d'Islande.* D'you read Loti?'

'With a dictionary handy.'

'Good man. *Pecheur d'Islande* takes a bit of beating, don't it? Henry James's *American,* too.'

'I'm trying to break myself in to him. *The American's* readable.'

'Readable! You savage. Half-a-mo', though. Balzac. Marcus Aurelius. What sort of ship d'you call this?'

'The *Luck and Charity,* coasting ketch.'

'The Luck's mine, the Charity yours. Extend it to a night's shakedown, will you? A heap of old sails in any lee corner'll do me well. I'm dog tired—and I give you my word I'm not verminous.'

'You're welcome,' I told him. 'Turn in when you like. I've got to be about early tomorrow morning—we're going round to Teignmouth to load.'

As luck would have it, the Teignmouth tug brought up a vessel next morning, and as she was going back alone I bargained for a cheap tow round. In the hurry I forgot my guest, and when he came on deck we were passing the harbour mouth.

'Shanghai'd me, have you?' he said.

'I forgot you. We're only going as far as Teignmouth this trip. That won't take you off your road, will it?'

'Any road's my road,' he said philosophically. 'Can I be of any use?'

'Can you cook?'

'Near enough, I expect,' said he, and set 'Kiah free by frying the breakfast, which he did very well.

I was messing about the deck afterwards, tidying up a little, and took a pull on the topsail halliards, which were new stuff and were loosening in the sun. The other end of the rope was insecurely hitched, and my down haul pulled it off the pin and just out of reach. It began slowly to slide aloft over the sheave and was quickening pace when the tramp went up the shrouds like a lamplighter and caught it at the crosstrees.

'You've done some sailoring,' I said, when he came down, the free end in his teeth.

'Yachting,' he said shortly. 'Just enough to know my own uselessness.'

'Good talk,' I said. 'Care to ship with me aboard this packet. We want a man.'

'What's the trade?'

'South Coast to the Scheldt, I understand.'

'Sounds good enough,' he said. 'But I'm supposed to be an invalid of sorts. I may not be up to the mark, but I'll try it for a bit, if you'll have me, on one condition. I'm to chuck it any day I please without any nonsense about giving notice on either side.'

'All right. We'll see how it works. If you can't stick it, you can't; if you can you'll be company for me. What's your name, by the way?'

'Voogdt.'

'What a name! Dutch?'

'My grandfather was. It's a good enough name for me.'

'No offence,' said I, for he sounded testy. 'Only we seem to have a rum collection of names here. Mine's Carthew-West, the boat's the *Luck and Charity*, the first mate is Hezekiah Pym, and now we've shipped a crew called Voogdt.'

'Austin Voogdt, if you want the lot of it,' he said, in perfect good temper once more. And so we came to Teignmouth with our full ship's company.

CHAPTER III

CONCERNING A COMPANY OF
MERCHANT ADVENTURERS

WE took forty tons of clay from Teignmouth, and with fair weather all the way up Channel reached Terneuzen on the fourth day. We made a lighthearted crew, all three: for me, I was to continue the cruising, that had amused me for the past two years, and be paid well for it, to boot; Voogdt, for all his baresark philosophy, was well enough pleased to have a roof over his head, warm clothing and regular meals; and as for 'Kiah, give him three meals a day and tell him what to do next, and he asked nothing more.

Voogdt got on wonderfully well with 'Kiah. A bundle of nerves, he used to almost dance with irritation at his deliberate speech and gait, slanging him in many-syllabled terms of abuse, which 'Kiah, strangely enough, seemed rather to enjoy.

'Move. Get a move on you, you slab-sided megatherium,' he would say; or, 'Gangway! Make way for your betters, you hibernating troglodyte'; and 'Kiah would grin as he shambled about his work, peaceful and undisturbed. ''E's a funny blook, id'n' 'er?' he said to me once, almost admiringly, as he was doing his trick at the wheel. 'Uses longer words'n what yu du. French, I reckon.' I fancy he thought Voogdt complimented him by assuming him proficient in that foreign tongue.

Personally, I got on very well with the man, too. He was mad, if ever a man was; but he was a gentleman and a good sort as well. His attitude towards life was recklessly joyous. 'I lost half-a-lung in a month,' he told me once. 'Any shift of wind may finish me—a drop or rise of temperature in the wrong direction, or a degree more or less of humidity or dryness. Nobody really knows much about tubercle—how it may flourish or die in any given individual. I'm like a child wandering in a whirling engine-room in the dark. A false step or a lurch, and—whisk I'm gone. What's the use of taking care?'

He couldn't do the heaviest work, but, apart from that, was as good as any other man—better than most, because he was willing. In fact, he steered better than 'Kiah, who, having held a tiller before he could read, steered rather by instinct than conscious effort. 'Kiah would lean over the wheel as though half asleep, swaying to the motion of the vessel, and although he steered as well as the average fisherman, carelessness born of familiarity often let him half-a-point or so off his true course. He steered as much by the feel of the sails as by compass, and so rarely needed to exert himself. Steering well enough for all practical purposes, he didn't try to do better. Not so Voogdt. His eyes never left the bows except for an occasional quick glance at the card, and he put his uttermost muscle and will-power into his work. It exhausted him, of course. I've seen him mop the perspiration from his face when he was relieved; but he steered to a hair-breadth nicety all the time.

I was thankful to have found him, and when I found out what manner of man he was, I offered him the spare bunk in my cabin, thinking he would be more in place there than sharing the forecastle, good chap though 'Kiah was. Voogdt said as much at once.

"Kiah's an awfully decent sort. Think it'd hurt his feelings if I shifted?'

'Ask him,' I suggested, and Voogdt did so. I fancy he told him my bookshelf was the principal attraction aft. 'Kiah displayed no wounded feelings whatever and Voogdt's thought for him only rendered him the more welcome in my quarters; so it was a very merry and bright ship's company that entered the Scheldt the fourth morning after leaving Devonshire.

The Deutsche-West-Inde boats used to call at Antwerp, so I'd been in and out of the river often enough before. Terneuzen lies on the south bank, at the entrance to the Ghent ship canal, about a couple of miles from the mouth of the river, and as tide was making we managed to get there without a pilot. It seemed to me a queer place for an English company to open shop, yet there were the sheds, plain enough to see with 'Isle of Axel Trading Company' painted upon them as large as life. They were built on the big embankment that keeps the tide off the fields, a good mile from the town and lock-gates, flat Dutch pastures and tillage all around them, and I never saw a place that looked less like business in all my life. Four small sheds of wood and corrugated iron sufficed for office and warehouses, and a chimney smoking behind the office hinted at some sort of dwelling under the same roof. The wharf was a mere skeleton of wooden piles sticking out into the water, with a six-foot planked way along the top leading to the sheds. According to the chart, the whole lot, houses and wharf, would be half-a-mile from the river at low water, and separated from the stream by dreary mud-flats. It was just high tide when we got there, and so were able to float alongside the wharf, a red-faced youngish man with short curly hair shouting directions from the shore. We rode so high that we could look over the embankment right down on the cows feeding in the green pastures behind it. The place was as peaceful as a dairy farm, no houses nearer than the town, and I wondered more than ever what trade any company could do in such a deserted spot. As soon as we were made fast the curly-haired man came aboard, very busy about nothing.

'My name's Cheyne. I'm the manager. Capt'n West? With clay from Teignmouth?'

'Forty tons,' I said.

'Good. May as well get your hatch cover off, Capt'n. Then come ashore'n have a drink. We'll get it out of her tomorrow, 'n then ballast you to rights, 'n off to sea again, eh? Too long in port's bad f'r th' morals, eh?'

'Shouldn't think there was much chance of going on the

bend here,' I said. 'Unless you go bird-nesting or chasing cows.'

'Y' can go on the bend anywhere, cocky,' he said, and hiccupped, and I noticed he'd managed it all right. 'Terneuzen's a hot little shop, lemme tell you. 'T least I've livened 'em up a bit. Sleepy hole it was before they had me t' liven 'em up. We'll go into town this evening an' shake a leg, what?'

I took my papers to his office—the untidiest hole I was ever in—sat among the litter for half-an-hour, had a drink and a chat, and then went aboard again.

Voogdt was stowing the foresail when I got back and looked at me inquiringly.

'That cove full?' he asked.

'Full as an egg. Useful sort of manager, eh?'

'Useful sort of business generally, I should say,' he replied. 'What the dickens are they going to do with this clay here? Feed cows on it? Is your money all right, skipper?'

'I haven't earned my advance of fifty yet. When I have, I'll ask for another.'

'I should, if I were you,' said he, and then the matter dropped.

However, there were more signs of activity next morning. We rigged a rubbish wheel at the gaff-end, and with the help of four hired Dutch labourers started to get the clay ashore. Even Cheyne put on an old suit of clothes and bore a hand, but I never saw such slack methods as his in my life. The man worked like a navvy, I grant, but I should have thought he'd have been better employed in tallying the tubs of clay. As it was, he'd pull and haul with the rest of us, very noisy and hearty, and I admit he hustled those slow-bellied Dutchmen better than I could, knowing the language as he did. Then, when we'd got out a half-dozen or dozen tubs, he'd pick up his tally-book again.

'How many's that?' he'd cry.

'I make it a hundred and twenty-three.'

'Hundred and twenty-three goes,' he'd say, and tick them off without checking my figures, and then back to the tackles he'd go again. I put him down as unmethodical but a man-driver;

and the driving was wanted no denying that, for those four Dutchmen might have been picked for their stupidity. In fact, two of them were no better than sheer imbeciles.

When we came to the bottom of the forty tons Cheyne began to get fussy. He was as careful to have the last pound or two of clay out of her as he'd been careless about the two-hundredweight tubs. He even had the tubs and buckets scraped and the sides of the hold cleaned down as though he wanted to make up for his slackness in the tallying. It was high water again by the time we had done and he said we could knock off till half-ebb.

'Your chaps had better turn in for a spell,' he told me. 'We work at low water after this. I'm going up town now to get some grub. Care to join me, Capt'n? Yes? Come along, then.'

On the way he explained how he wanted us to ballast. 'That mud you're lying on is always silting up and we ballast with that to keep the channel open to the wharf. See?'

'How are we to get it aboard?'

'By brute force and bally ignorance, my son; same's we got the clay out with. We can't afford a dredger yet. All you have to do is to lower the tubs on the side away from the wharf, send two or three men overside with shovels, and the rest pullihaul, and there you are. How much d'ye want to steady that packet of yours?'

'Twelve tons'll be ample, this weather.'

'Take twenty—take twenty,' said he. 'You never know when it may come on to blow off this coast. Besides, we want the stuff taken away, and it's a charity to give those Dutch lumps another day's work. Bright lot, ain't they?'

As we walked along the top of the embankment I couldn't help wondering where he was taking me, for not a sign of any town or village could, I see. On our left was the river, shallow water over mud-flats, broken here and there by a red or white iron beacon pole marking the channel to the entrance to the canal; on our right flat pastures divided by long lines of poplars, receding in perspective to the flat horizon. Dominating them, the great ship canal ran inland, its high banks planted with avenues of lime-trees, and, save for a block of buildings at its entrance, behind which rose a little church spire, not a house was to be seen.

Once we crossed the lock-gates the town, such as it was, became visible lying low in the farther angle formed by the embankment of the canal and river frontage. It proved to be the usual 'longshore Dutch village, half nautical, half pastoral: two or three tiny streets of one or two storeyed houses, red tiled, gay with green and white paint, and clean as rows of new pins. They clustered round the foot of the grey church tower, church and cottages alike dwarfed to toys by the great locks of the canal. The block of buildings I had seen proved to be a modern hotel, pleasantly placed for summer trade with wooden benches outside it under the lime-trees, a pilot-house, built of little Dutch bricks and looking for all the world like a doll's house, and a tobacco shop, clean as a dairy, much patronised by the sailors passing through the locks. I never saw a quainter, prettier little place—a sleepy little farming village, with the canal alongside to smoke your pipe by, and watch the passing ships. The girls are pretty there too: big-eyed, pale and dark, which is not what one expects to find in Holland. The head-dress of the district is a wide-winged thing of white linen like a Beguine nun's, and instead of the usual golden cups to hide their ears, the women wear thin fluttering plates of gold on either side of their forehead, which flip about and tinkle like golden butterflies. Under the summer evening light, I took to the place at once.

Contrary to all Cheyne's talk of bad business and economy, he wasn't mean about his personal expenditure. He stood me a thundering good dinner in the hotel, and a first-rate bottle of hock with it, and as many cigars as I could smoke. But somehow I couldn't take to the man. He let on to be a square, hearty chap enough with no nonsense about him, but his manner was too uncertain for me. One minute he was over-effusive, slap-on-the-back, hail-fellow-well-met, and the next was standoffish, as though he'd remembered he was one of my employers and wanted to remind me of it too. He wasn't as good a man as Ward, but he didn't think so, and made no secret of his opinion.

'Oh, Leonard's all right,' he said once, when I was telling him how I'd been chartered. 'He's all right enough, but he's a squaretoes. I wonder he gave you a job, if you had on a brass hat when he first met you.' Another time he said he was a fossil. 'He's too slow to come in out of a shower, is ol' Len. Good job for him I'm here. He'd be robbed right and left else.'

He was ready enough to talk about himself. He'd been a sailor, too, it seemed. 'With Warbeck's, of Sunderland,' he said, with an air, as though he expected a lowly coasting skipper like me to grovel at the very name of his tinpot firm. 'I was third officer on their *Gloucester*.'

'A fine boat that,' I said, and let him gas about her for a while.

Later on I tried to sound him about the two girls, but all I could get out of him was that the Pamily one was his cousin, and the other—a Miss Lavington—was her cousin on the other side.'

His business talk varied between over-confidence and sudden reticence or evasions of the point under discussion. He gave me the notion, somehow, that he was rather incapable, but was trying hard to impress one with his wits and ability. If he'd been altogether reserved, I should have liked him better. It was none of my business, the way he conducted the company's affairs; but his half-chummy, half-patronising way made me tired, and I was glad to get back and start ballasting the *Luck and Charity*.

The wet mud was stiff, awful stuff to shovel and worse to stand on. We put some planks on it to give foothold, but we were slipping about all the time, and in half an hour all hands were slime from head to foot. Voogdt chucked it. 'I can't shovel this stuff,' he said. 'It's man's work, and I'm only half-a-man. Am I sacked, skipper?'

'Not you,' I said. 'Get aboard and find something to do on deck. This job 'ud kill a horse.'

Cheyne came down soon after in dirty clothes with a shovel, and asked what 'that chap' was doing aboard. He grumbled a little when I told him Voogdt couldn't do heavy work. 'This is an all-hands job. If I can take a shovel, he ought to.'

'He can't,' I said, 'and that's all there is about it,' and Cheyne said no more.

I'm bound to say he worked like a good one himself: by my reckoning we got a hundred and twenty tubs aboard in three hours. That made a good twelve tons and when the tide drove us off the mud I told him we were ready for sea.

'No hurry,' said he. 'I haven't got your sailing orders yet. Turn your chaps in for a spell, and we'll get a few more tubs aboard next ebb.'

Next ebb wasn't till midnight, and I told him so.

'Can't your tender babes work after dark?' he sneered.

'They'll work when I tell 'em,' I said rather hotly, for his tone annoyed me.

'Then tell 'em now,' he said. 'Tell 'em it's pay and a quarter for night work, if you like. I've got plenty of lanterns in the shed.'

Who could make anything of such ways? Employing fools because they were cheap, and paying able seamen pay and a quarter to help them! Extra pay for night work at putting more ballast in a boat than she needed, because he wanted mud cleared away! A dredger would have cleared the lot in a couple of days. I thought of Voogdt's warning, and decided I might as well see if I could get another advance. I'd spent thirty pounds in fitting out and victualling, and clothes and things for the three of us, but that left me nearly twenty in hand, and of the money spent certainly ten or twelve pounds had been unauthorised expenditure on our personal needs. On the other hand, the freight worked out at about thirty pounds, so that really I still owed the company the twenty I had left. However, when I asked for an advance, Cheyne made no bones about granting it. 'How much?' was all he said.

I hung in the wind a minute, uncertain what to ask. 'I spent thirty fitting out,' I said, 'and the freight's thirty. Would another twenty be too much?'

'Say thirty, to be on the safe side,' said he. 'The Oost-Nederland Bank in Terneuzen'll cash my cheque for you,' and he drew me a cheque on the spot. This after his harping on economy and grumbling about Voogdt being idle! I concluded finally that he was an unbusinesslike fool.

As I was leaving the office he called after me. 'We're paying two bob ballast allowance,' said he.

'Two bob?' I was ashamed to confess my ignorance of what he meant by ballast allowance.

'Two bob a ton. So it's worth your while to ballast pretty deep. Two quid in your pockets if you take away twenty tons, and only four and twenty bob if you go as you are. So you'll see it pays you to wait a tide.'

'It would pay me to fill her full, then,' I said, surprised.

'A sure thing it would. But of course that's nonsense. Twenty tons is ample, as you say. Take twenty-five if you've got time; but you must get away next tide. I'm expecting the *Olive Leaf* tomorrow from Grangemouth, and there's no room at the wharf for the two of you.'

When I got aboard after cashing the cheque Voogdt was standing by the hatch looking at the heaps of slimy muck in the hold. I jingled the canvas bag in his face.

'Did you touch him?' he asked.

'For thirty. So we're still a quid or two ahead of 'em.'

'What d'ye make of the man?' he asked, jerking his head towards the office.

'A bumptious, silly fool. That's what I make of him.'

'What was the man Ward like? Another fool?'

'Not he,' I said. 'Unbusinesslike he may be, but a fool he is not, if I'm any judge. I hope this chap isn't going to let him down.'

'So he isn't going to let you down, that don't matter much,' Voogdt grunted. 'When are we going to get hatches on?'

'Next tide. There's some more ballast to come aboard first.'

'What on earth d'you want more ballast for?'

'I don't want it,' I said. 'At least the boat doesn't. But there's two bob a ton allowance on all we take away it seems.'

'That's a rum notion, paying on ballast, isn't it?'

'I don't know,' I said. 'I've only been in steam since I served my apprenticeship. Come to think of it, I've never carried ballast before. Even when I was serving my apprenticeship in sail we always had freights both ways. I suppose ballast allowance is a custom in this coasting trade.'

'A rum custom,' said Voogdt. 'Tempting skippers to strain their vessels with useless stuff. And seems to me I've heard of paying for ballast before now.'

'Well, that's possible,' I said. 'P'raps the ship that left just before had a good ballast allowance and swept the quay clean. Besides, they want this stuff cleared away.'

'Ah! That explains it,' said he. 'Why didn't you say so before? How d'ye expect to make a sailorman of me if you don't instruct me as we go along?'

We worked that night by the light of hand-lanterns, but all hands were tired out, and though I promised 'Kiah and Voogdt to share the new allowance equally, we couldn't get more than about ten tons aboard. Cheyne said that would do. 'It'll have to. The *Olive Leaf* 'll be here next thing. You can charge for twenty-three tons, Capt'n. That do you? Here's your papers. You're for Dartmouth, to load deals. Now get your hatch cover on, and slip it with the morning tide.'

It came on to blow a little when we got outside. Nothing to hurt; a northerly breeze, too, which was all in our favour, but we had a bit of bucketing in the Straits of Dover. The *Luck and Charity* I knew I could rely on; with her extra ballast she was as stiff as a church, and I felt a bit more amiable towards Cheyne when I saw how well she behaved. We got wet jackets, of course, but nothing worse. 'Kiah I'd tried before and could trust, too, but Voogdt and the running-gear were new, and I watched them both. The man shaped as well as the hemp and manilla: both were inclined to give a bit under the strain at first, but a brace now and then to the tackle and a helping hand and a joke with the man did wonders. Both, were working sweetly before we reached the Race of Portland, and Voogdt took us through it, only laughing whenever some nasty cross-sea slopped aboard and slatted down over him. It was pretty to see him, the veins standing out like twisted wire on his wet, lean hands as he strained to steady the kicking wheel, and to think how scared he'd looked when he came on deck two days before and found me driving through it with the lee rail under water and the hatch cover awash. Working like a Trojan, laughing at the smashing of our bows and the cataracts the Race was sending over him, he didn't look much like an indoor man with his death warrant signed, sealed and delivered by the doctors.

'Gad! This is fine!' he cried, when I went to give him a hand. 'No, let me go, skipper. I can take her through it myself. I like it.'

He was able to bear a hand in Dartmouth now, when it came to loading the deals. In fact I think he handled more of them than did the quay-lumpers, who were half asleep, like all Devonshire men. Good food and a regular life were telling on him; he was putting on flesh, and the sea air was beginning to colour his sallow sunburnt cheeks a bit.

We got our ballast out on the quay, and the deals aboard in four days, but then had to wait a day or two, the wind having shifted round to the east. Voogdt spent his time idling about the old town, and 'Kiah had a half-day's holiday and went to Topsham. I was sitting on deck smoking and thinking about the spree I'd had at last Dartmouth regatta when somebody hailed from close alongside.

'*Luck and Charity* ahoy!'

'Ahoy!' I answered, and jumped up to see who it was. I don't think I was ever more staggered in my life, for there in a waterman's boat just under our stern was the Pamily girl!

I threw a rope ladder overside and she scrambled aboard, and I stood staring at her, with my mouth open, I expect.

'Good afternoon,' she said shortly. 'You're loaded, I see.'

'Y-yes,' I stammered. 'We got away from the wharf yesterday afternoon.'

'I'll see your papers,' she said, most businesslike, and turned to the man in the boat. 'You'll wait for me, please,' and she led the way to the cabin.

Dumb with surprise, I got the papers out and laid them on the table before her. She went through them all, her brows knitted, for all the world like a young housewife trying to check the butcher's bill. I couldn't believe she knew anything about the business, but she made no remarks, only folding each paper as she read it and handing back the lot when she'd done.

'Thank you,' she said. 'You brought ballast, didn't you? How much?' Twenty-three tons, Mr Cheyne made it,' I told her.

'Where is it?'

'On the ballast quay.'

'Thank you. That's all I want.' She got up, and looked me up and down. 'You're looking very well,' she said.

'I'm very fit, thanks. Regular employment and—and all that sort of thing, you know.'

She nodded and went on deck, and I followed her. Just as she was going down into her boat I asked her if I could offer her a cup of tea.

For one minute I thought there was going to be more face-smacking, but she suddenly turned dangerously pleasant.

'I should love it,' she gushed. 'But I mustn't stay long, Captain West. Miss Lavington's waiting for me ashore.'

'It won't take any time,' I assured her. 'I've got one of those oil blast-lamps that boil a kettle in about five minutes.'

She let me get tea and we drank it on deck, and all the time I felt like one sitting on a powder magazine. Her manner was atrociously correct—demure and sweetie-sweetie, prunes and prisms all the time; and she was making eyes at me most affectedly with every word. But I thought I could read behind that; I guessed she was trying to lure me out into the open and destroy me, and I wasn't taking any. I was a coasting skipper; she the friend and, in a sense, the representative of my employers. So the more she gushed the politer I got, and when she rowed away I swear she was biting her lip. That sort of sexless little guttersnipe just loves a row, and she didn't bring it off that time.

Voogdt hailed me from the quay soon after, and I went to fetch him in the dinghy. He had learnt that the deals we had shipped were from the Baltic and fell to discussing the matter with me.

'More paying trade for our employers,' he said. 'Shipping deals from the Baltic to Terneuzen via Dartmouth. You note the direct and economical route, skipper?'

'Oh, hang the company!' I said. 'If they're going scat, they're going scat. Meanwhile we're being paid to learn the coasting trade.'

'It'll take a bit of learning, I can see,' said Voogdt dryly. 'I hope it won't be too much for my poor brain.' And not another word could I get out of him. 'Kiah came back that night, silent as ever, and next day the wind went south with the sun and we got under way for Terneuzen again.

CHAPTER IV

CONCERNING A CARGO OF POTATOES

Voogdt worried me with questions about the cargo all the way up Channel, and for the life of me I couldn't find an answer for him that even satisfied myself. Here were we being paid on the tonnage of the boat—sixty tons burthen—and only carrying thirty. Last voyage it had been forty, so that in two voyages we were drawing money for fifty tons of cargo which we had never shipped. For the sake of argument I put it that their customer might only have ordered forty tons of clay, and as to the deals, they were ugly stowage for a boat as small as the *Luck and Charity*. Anyhow, I didn't see why we should worry so long as our charter money was paid.

His words had stirred my curiosity a little by this time, and when we reached Terneuzen my first care was to see whether any of our clay was left over from the last voyage. It was all gone, however, and I nudged Voogdt, drawing his attention to the fact. In its place was a large heap of broken stone. He looked at it, rubbing his bearded chin in meditation.

'What's that stuff for?' he asked.

'How should I know?' I said impatiently. 'To feed cows on, I suppose.'

'Looks like road metal to me,' he said musingly, and sure enough when Cheyne came aboard he told me that was what it was.

'It came as ballast,' he condescended to explain. 'We can use it very well. Some of it'll stiffen the mud behind the wharf and the rest mend the cart-track between here and the town.'

I told Voogdt this and he nodded. 'So the *Olive Leaf* brought ballast, did she? I wonder what she took away?'

By the evening I was able to tell him that too. Cheyne asked me to dinner, as before, and casually mentioned her at the table as having gone farther up river.

'To Antwerp?' I asked.

'Yes. She took up some of your clay. It was sold to Ghent, but the buyers sold again to an Antwerp pottery.'

I didn't question him farther, but chuckled rather as I thought what a mare's nest Voogdt would find in that announcement. Cheyne saw my smile and without more reason fired up in a moment.

'What the—do you see to grin at in that?' he demanded. 'Don't you believe me?'

'Of course I do,' I asid, surprised. 'I wasn't laughing at anything you said.'

For a moment he looked threatening, then calmed down and passed the bottle along.

In the intervals of getting out the deals, I told Voogdt where the clay had gone, but he displayed no surprise.

Ballasting was done the same way as before, except that Voogdt was able to help part of the time, and we sailed with a full twenty-five tons of mud instead of a bare twenty-three. As before, Cheyne was in a hurry to get rid of us at the last.

'Off with you,' he said cheerily. 'On hatches and clear out and make room for your betters.'

'The *Olive Leaf* again?' I asked.

'The *Kismet*. She passed the *Hasborough* last night with a fair wind. Guess she's outside the river now, waiting tide.'

'What's she bringing?' I asked.

'What business is that of yours?' He put on his standoffish manner in an instant. 'You're not paid to ask questions, but to obey orders. Just remember your place, Capt'n, and I'll remember mine.'

I raged inwardly for having laid myself open to the snub. The brute had been genial as a blood-relation till then. But it was no good quarrelling with one's livelihood, so we got away without another word. Voogdt took the wheel when we got into the main stream.

'What's the *Hasborough*?' he asked.

'A lightship off Norfolk.'

'Then if the *Kismet* passed her yesterday, she's been north, that's obvious. And if she's been north, it's a hundred to one she's carrying coal. And if she's carrying coal, which is saleable anywhere, she'll be loaded deep.'

'Sherlock Holmes,' I said, and went below.

When I came on deck half-an-hour later we were passing Flushing, and out at sea a small coaster about our own size was lying at anchor. She was comparatively light, riding high in the water.

'There's the *Kismet*, Sherlock,' I jeered. 'And if she's got more than thirty tons aboard, I'm a Dutchman.'

'Then either 'tisn't the *Kismet* or she isn't carrying coal,' he said quietly. Half-an-hour later I had the laugh of him again, for we passed near enough for a glass to show her name in dirty white letters under her bows.

'What d'ye make of that?' I handed him my glasses and took the wheel.

He had a long stare and then turned and looked at me queerly.

'*Kismet* it is, right enough. Down helm a wee, skipper, and get a bit closer.'

'What for?' I said; but I did as he asked.

'Now hail 'em,' he said, when we'd got close enough. He was itching with excitement and curiosity.

'Ahoy!' I shouted. '*Kismet*, ahoy!'

'Ahoy!' came down the wind.

'Ask 'em where they're bound,' Voogdt prompted.

'Where—are—you—bound?'

'Goole to Terneuzen with coals,' came the answer.

'There you are,' I said. 'Now you know. Like most of you private detectives, you're half right and half wrong. She is the *Kismet*, and you said she wasn't. She's come from the north and she's got coals, just as you said. And she's got half a cargo and not a full one, which is flat contrary to your notions. Now what d'ye make of it?'

'I make rank unbusinesslike ways of it,' he replied. 'And on the face of it, that's all one can say. I'm beat I admit.'

'Well, what odds?' I said. 'We've got our money, and that's enough. If the thing's being mucked I'm sorry for Ward, but he's big enough to manage his own affairs. I'll mind mine, you mind yours, and everybody'll be pleased.

'Poking my nose into things has been my business for some years,' Voogdt snapped at me. 'You can't drop the habits of a lifetime in ten minutes, you dunderhead,' and after that stuck to his wheel, grumbling about dolts and thickwits under his breath.

We were bound for Poole this time, and no sooner had we got our ballast on the quay than Ward made his appearance. Voogdt stared at him hard, and late in the evening came aboard full of information about him.

'He's a chemist. He's got a professor's job at Mason College, Birmingham.'

'He's a sound man—a worker. He's had the gold medal of the Royal Society of Arts, is a Felton prizeman and heaps more besides. What on earth can he be doing dabbling in a little trading concern like this? A man with his record could get to the top, if he liked, and yet here he is tinkering at this business with a cub like Willis Cheyne for a manager. He isn't a fool, yet he behaves like one.'

'Oh, hang!' I said. 'You worry me with your twaddle. Let's do our work, and draw our pay and live in peace. Go to bed. We start loading potatoes tomorrow at six a.m.'

'Potatoes!' he said wearily. 'They're shipping potatoes to an agricultural country now. Next time we shall carry windmills in sections, or canal water. They're short of both in Holland, and naturally can pay big freights on 'em. Good-night, o massive-brained ruminant. Good-night.'

I thought potatoes were a funny cargo myself, but I wouldn't encourage him in his silly ways and so swore I considered it natural they should be imported. 'There's Ghent handy,' I said, as we were squabbling about it on the way up Channel. 'Ghent and all the other Belgian industrial centres close by. A big population wants food, don't it?—and industries want deals and clay and coal.'

'In half cargoes!' he jerked out; but I had him there, having been thinking about the *Kismet* myself.

'That's because of the tide,' I said. 'How could they get deep-laden boats, even of our light draught over those mud-banks at neap tides?'

That shut him up and so ended the discussion for the time being and we got in, discharged our potatoes and ballasted as before. Some of the *Kismet's* coal still lay by the warehouse, but not more than ten tons at the outside. The rest was gone. Even Voogdt grudgingly admitted there was nothing unusual to comment upon.

But the evening before we sailed we had a shock. Our bags of potatoes were lying neatly stacked by the wharf, twenty-five tons of ballast were aboard, and the hatches were on, ready for sailing. Having an hour or two to wait for the tide I suggested to Voogdt that we should stroll along the bank to Terneuzen and have a drink before we went. When we got to the canal entrance we had to wait, the lock-gates being open. Right beside us was a German coasting schooner, and I thought I'd air my German a bit and impress Voogdt.

'Wo gehen sie?' I said to a boy on deck.

'Emden. Mit Erdapfeln.'

He used the slang word 'Erdapfeln' instead of the more correct 'Kartoffeln' and I turned to Voogdt to translate without thinking of the sense of the words. But he needed no translator, it was evident.

'Potatoes,' he said under his breath, like one dazed. 'Potatoes! Hear that?' He leaned over and spoke to the boy himself.

'*Woher sint sie gekommen?*'

'*Sas van Gent.*'

The thing had soaked into my thick head by this time and we stared at each other in silent amazement. I was being paid a sovereign a ton to bring potatoes three hundred miles to Terneuzen; whilst Sas van Gent, only ten miles up the canal, was exporting them in bulk to Emden. No explanations could spare that. We forgot the drink we'd come out for, and turned to walk back to the *Luck and Charity* with our heads in a whirl.

Half-way back I stopped in my stride. 'I read a yarn once,' I said, 'about a man who saw a Government announcement in the papers that the Woods and Forests had oak-trees to sell, and another from the Admiralty to say that they wanted oak timber. So he stepped in and sold England her own property and retired on it.'

Voogdt patted me on the shoulder softly, speaking with exaggerated gentleness, as though to a sick child.

'Don't fash yourself, my son,' he said. 'This thing is beyond your great brain. 'Tisn't a fool Government this time. It's the rules of trade, and demand and supply, and a dozen other things, all being turned upside-down. It's water flowing up a hill, James, that's what it is. It's rank raving lunacy, apparently run at a profit, and that's impossible. Impossible, I tell you.'

Walking slowly and thinking hard, Cheyne overtook us as we neared the wharf, and asked us into the office for a drink. To my surprise Voogdt, answering him, put on a raw Cockney drawl, and spoke as though he were an illiterate coasting hand.

We sailed for Torquay this time, but conversation languished on the voyage. The more I thought of that German-bound boat the crazier the whole thing seemed, and, think as I would, I couldn't see a light anywhere, Once or twice I made some sort of suggestion, more in protest against the clashing facts than anything else, but each time Voogdt shut me up sharp.

'Oh! go and boil your head,' he said rudely. 'I've been over and under and all round it; and all I can say is that it's against nature. But you mark my words, Mr James Carthew Hyphen West, if any more funny things like that happen, I shall go slap off my rocker.'

Another cargo of potatoes awaited us at Torquay, and Voogdt nearly danced on the deck when I told him so.

'I hate being beat. That's what I'm suffering from,' he said, half laughing at himself. 'After all, the explanation's clear enough. Ward or somebody in the company has money, and Cheyne's induced 'em to put it in this fool venture. When it's gone the company will shut shop and Cheyne'll go to sea again, having had a royal holiday ashore. That's all. It can't be anything else Let's get the spuds aboard I hate doing it I hate waste. But after all we may as well have some unknown fool's money as anybody else. Here's my last word about it, skipper; always see you're paid in advance and lay by against a rainy day.'

There was no difficulty about that. Cheyne was always ready to make an advance whenever I asked him, even when sometimes the money was for my own purposes. We sprung our topmast a month later, and though, strictly speaking, I ought to have paid for repairs myself, Cheyne authorised me to get a new spar at his expense. 'Get a good stick and don't waste time about it.' That was always his cry. 'Hurry. Hurry. Make quick voyages.'

'And he's losing money on every voyage, sure,' Voogdt said once almost despairingly.

After the second potato trip he wrote to a friend of his in London, asking for particulars of our employers, only to find the so-called company was not registered as a company at all. He showed me the letter.

'There you are,' said he. 'That settles it. They must have got hold of a capitalist mug, and they're bleeding him. Only—' He stopped.

'Only what?'

'Well, I should have thought a fellow like Cheyne would have opened his sham store in a more amusing place. The Riviera, say. And there's Ward. Cheyne may be a rogue and a fool, but Ward's neither, if I'm any judge of a man. What's he doing in that galley?'

It didn't worry me that I couldn't answer his questions—if I can't understand a thing, I just disregard it and get on with the work; but to him unsatisfied curiosity was like a prickle in his flesh.

However, as time wore on he seemed to be easier in his mind, and after a few trips we'd got the hang of the trade and were just making voyage after voyage without remark. Each voyage was much like the last. We nearly always had light cargoes, and took away as much ballast as we could get in two tides. We always traded in the English Channel, and nearly always to different ports. In fact the only port we called at twice was Dartmouth, and on our second visit, three months after the first, we lay at Kingswear, on the other side of the river. In those three months we'd made about ten journeys: to Looe, Penzance, Falmouth, Fowey, Teignmouth, Plymouth, Newhaven, Southampton and Kingsbridge. By that time we were so accustomed to the round that even Voogdt accepted each new order without remark.

My bank account was growing and as I'd given Voogdt and 'Kiah bonuses from time to time, we were a flourishing concern. Whatever folly the company represented we had no reason to complain.

Early in September we were ordered to Guernsey, but just outside the Scheldt it came on to blow real nasty from the south-west. It looked like an equinoctial gale, and we stood across to the North Foreland intending to drop anchor there till it blew itself out. It lasted two days, and whilst we were lying at anchor we saw the *Kismet* coming down river towards us, reefed down but with a bit of topsail hoisted. Just as she passed Birchington, about a mile from us, she got a sudden buster of a squall off the shore, and before you could say 'knife' her topmast was over her side. She luffed up towards the shore, all she could, and dropped anchor to clear away the raffle and mess. At Voogdt's suggestion we rowed over in our dinghy to proffer assistance. The wind was gusty and strong, but the water smooth, and we soon reached her and climbed aboard.

The skipper, elderly, and a typical coasting master, stood in the waist placidly directing his three hands as they hacked and cut away the wreckage. He was dressed coaster-fashion, in blue coat, guernsey and trousers, gaudy red carpet slippers and a bowler hat, once black, but now green with age. He nodded to us as we went to bear a hand, and when things were getting tidy invited us into his cabin and offered us a drink.

I told him we were from the *Luck and Charity*, and that turned our talk on our only mutual acquaintances—our employers. The old man seemed well pleased with them, and apparently knew a good deal more about them than we did.

'Mr Cheyne—a fine young fellow 'e is. A true sailor, I call i'm. Miss Brand's 'is cousin—she's a most amoosin' young person; and there's Miss Lavington. She's a real lady, that.'

'Have Miss Brand and Miss Lavington got anything to do with the company, then?' I asked in surprise.

'Sure-ly. It's mostly Miss Lavington's money in it. Mr Ward, 'e's a partner, too. Them four.'

I caught Voogdt's eye. 'Only those four?' I asked.

'I don't know of any other.'

'Have you been with them long?'

'Jus' over a year. I signed charter for another year only las' month. Good people, they are. Mr Ward spoke mos' complimentary about the last year's working, an' gave me a fifty-pound bonus an' a shilling a ton rise.'

'What are you getting now, then, Capt'n?'

'Nine-an-six a ton burthen between the Tyne an' Terneuzen.'

'Don't you go farther north than the Tyne?'

'No. The *Olive Leaf*, she trades from the Scotch ports. They're thinking of putting on another boat for the Irish Sea. If they can't get one to suit them, Mr Ward says they'll build.'

Voogdt asked a question, forgetting that etiquette demanded he should hold his tongue in the presence of his betters, and the old skipper shut him up at once. After that we both felt rather uncomfortable and took our leave as early as we could.

Next day the wind eased a bit and shifted into the north-west, so we set sail for Guernsey. The last we saw of the *Kismet* as we rounded the Foreland her people were getting their new topmast aloft.

CHAPTER V

IN THE MATTER OF A DESERTING SEAMAN

As a general rule one of the most talkative of men, Voogdt none the less had his silent days, days when he grudged even mono-syllables, only grunting assent or dissent in answer to direct questions. Sometimes such a mood would last him half-a-week; once it was over he talked like a mill, as though to make up for lost time. He was a good talker, and his silences were the less agreeable for the contrast.

Throughout the summer I had never known him so silent as during this trip to Guernsey. The gale had left a long sea behind it that did nothing to enhance our comfort aboard, and a sulky shipmate only added to my annoyance. By the time we reached St Peters Port I could have kicked him with the greatest goodwill in the world.

He cheered up a bit when we got in harbour, and I began to be sorry for him—with a little touch of contempt, perhaps—thinking that it was the roughish weather he had been suffering from. He worked well, as he always did now, getting out the ballast, but in the evening staggered me by announcing that he was leaving the *Luck and Charity*.

'What on earth for?' I asked, fairly taken aback.

'That was our agreement, James, if you remember. I was to leave you where and when I pleased. Well, I please now and here.'

'But why? Have I done anything?'

'What haven't you done? You picked me up out at elbows and starving, and you've put fresh life into me. That's what you've done. And I'm going to repay you by deserting just as the winter's coming on. I feel a sweep, old man, but I must go.'

'Is it the winter you're afraid of?' I asked.

48

'Call it that. I can't give you a better reason or I would. Don't make any more difficulties about it. I feel ashamed to leave you like this, but I tell you I *must* go. That's all.'

'What are you going to do? Have you enough money to get on with?'

'No; I haven't. That's another thing I had qualms in tackling you about. Will you lend me forty or fifty quid? I can't give you any security beyond my bare promise to repay.'

That was a surprise. Of course his pay hadn't been large—only thirty bob a week—but, as I was doing well, I had considered it my place to make things easier for the other two. On weekly boats the men are expected to find themselves out of their weekly thirty shillings, but Voogdt had messed with me, and both he and 'Kiah had drawn good bonuses on each voyage. 'Kiah I knew had banked nearly twenty pounds, and I told Voogdt so.

'You ought to have done as well,' I said.

'I've done better, if you want to know,' he answered. 'Thanks to you I've banked over twenty, but I want fifty more for a special purpose. Now don't bother me with more questions, there's a good chap, but just let me have the money and be gone.'

I grumbled a little, but drew a draft for fifty on the company's agents, and Voogdt buttoned it up in his pocket.

'That's one more good turn I owe you,' he said. 'If I live through the winter you shall have a hundred per cent. on that loan. If I don't you've lost your money and must grin and bear it. Goodbye, old chap. Keep all my loose traps and use what you want. I shall be with you again in the spring.'

We shook hands and he went on deck. I heard him shout to 'Kiah and say he was off on a holiday, and then his footsteps went over our plank gangway and he was gone. I had shipped him on a quayside without warning, and found him a good man throughout, and now I lost him in the same way on another quayside, and missed him more than I can say.

We took road metal from Guernsey. It really amounted to a trip out and back in ballast, but Voogdt wasn't there to jeer, and I felt too low-spirited at his loss to think much about it. I shipped an islander in his place, a man by the name of Rance, a pilot who had lost his certificate. He was a smart sailor, but a quarrelsome little brute when in liquor, and as he drank heavily in port—which was, I suspect, the reason for his losing his ticket—we were no longer the happy family we had been.

The first night he came aboard he had a violent row with 'Kiah, and his trident snapping and squabbling drew me forward to see what was the matter. Looking down through the companion, I could see them both by the light of the hanging lamp. 'Kiah was in bed trying to sleep, his blankets drawn above his ears, and the new hand, a rather bow-legged little beast with an enormous moustache, stood in the middle of the fo'castle rating him in French and English and Guernsey patois mixed.

'Cochon!' he yelled. 'English pig!' But still 'Kiah lay inert. 'You English pig! You dir-r-ty Topsham dab!'

Why the name of his birthplace should have roused 'Kiah I can't tell, but it did. He put one bare leg over the side of his bunk and blinked at the gesticulating figure before him.

'You say that again,' he demanded.

'Dir-r-ty Topsham dab. I will say eet twenty times. Dir-r-ty Topsham—'

'Kiah moved as slowly as a bear, but in his sluggish way he was immensely strong. He caught Rance by the feet and the man was on the floor on his back in an instant. Then, in a short shirt and nothing else he started to climb the ladder, dragging his adversary after him by his ankles. When he had got him on deck, open-mouthed and staring, I thought it was time to intervene.

'What are you going to do with him, 'Kiah?' I asked.

''Eave 'm auverboard,' he said stolidly.

'You mustn't do that, man.'

''E caaled me a dirty Topsham dab,' said 'Kiah placidly.

'Well, he doesn't know any better,' I told him. 'Now you've got him on deck, kick him down into the fo'castle again, and tell him we don't allow quarrelling on this boat.'

'Kiah did as he was told, and Rance, stupefied with sheer funk, behaved comparatively well henceforth.

The winter trade in the Channel was no joke, and threading the shoals off the flat Dutch coast was worse. But we were well clothed and fed and earning good money, and remembering the last winter neither 'Kiah nor myself felt inclined for grumbling. Cheyne showed himself desirous of our comfort: our cargoes were lighter; a couple of additional men were hired at Terneuzen to help get extra ballast aboard, and we helped ourselves at will to as much coal as we wanted from the company's stores.

Nothing happened. It was just one dreary, cold, wet voyage after another, with an occasional spell of idleness, waiting for the wind to shift or lull in our service. I even began to welcome the idea of reaching Terneuzen and having a decent meal and a talk with Cheyne at the end of each voyage.

'That's a new man,' he said, when he first saw Rance. 'Where's that long, lean Cockney of yours gone?'

'I don't know,' I said. 'When he joined he said he might ship south for the winter.'

'I don't like changing men,' Cheyne said, which rather surprised me, for I hadn't given him credit for that much decency. 'What's this chap like?'

'I don't care for him. He's a sailorman, though.'

'Oh, is he?' said Cheyne, and later had him ashore and gave him a drink or two.

After that Rance always spoke of him with great respect: 'A tr-r-ue gentleman, Mr Cheyne.' A good job somebody thought so; but, as I say, I was glad of the man's company myself at that time.

We made pretty much the same round of voyages as we had been making through the summer: in and out of bleak, cold little ports, now deserted, that had been gay with summer visitors when we had seen them last.

One visitor seemed loth to leave the south coast, though, and that was Ward. I hadn't seen either of the two girls since Miss

Pamily boarded us at Dartmouth but Ward came aboard two or three times. Even in the winter he paid us a visit or two, and the more I saw of the man the better I liked him. It seemed a pity he should take so much interest in such an obviously rotten affair as this company; but it was none of my business to say so.

One day early in the new year as we were entering Terneuzen we found a big galliot, of Dutch build, but flying German colours, lying at anchor about a mile down the river-bank from our head-quarters. It seemed a queer place for such a boat to anchor, and when we got ashore I asked Cheyne what she was doing there.

'You'd better board her and ask,' he said rudely. 'I've enough to do minding my own business.'

Next day there was no reason to ask. The people aboard were broaching her cargo, apparently of deals, and floating them ashore. Cheyne got out a pair of very fine glasses he had and spent most of the morning watching them, and in the afternoon he went for a stroll in their direction.

'Do you know any German?' he asked me next morning.

'A few words.'

'Then knock off for an hour and see if you can find out what those chaps are about down there. Looks to me as if they're bringing some sort of portable house ashore, but I can't under-stand German, and can't make head or tail of what they say.'

I went down, dirty as I was, and fell in talk with the skipper of the galliot, a German Frieslander from Delfzyl. His cargo was building material, but he didn't know what it was to be used for, so after a chat I went back to the A.T.C. offices, not much wiser than I went.

'What is it?' Cheyne asked. He tried to make the question sound casual, but he was obviously ill at ease.

'Building material,' I replied. 'Deals and corrugated roofing principally. There are a lot of sheets of heavier iron plating, like boiler-iron.'

'Yes—yes. I saw that myself. But what's it for?'

'The skipper didn't know,' I said.

'Or you couldn't understand his talk?' Cheyne sneered. 'I thought you said you understood German. I wouldn't have wasted your time like that if I'd known you didn't.'

'I can talk it better than you,' I said, inclined to lose my temper, like a fool.

'That don't say much. I told you I couldn't speak the language at all. Now, come on; get that stuff out of her and don't stand jawing here.'

Our next trip took us to Penzance, and we were away ten days. I've good cause to remember it, for it was very near being my last trip for the Axel Trading Company. When we got back to the Scheldt the galliot had gone, but another vessel was moored in her place, and ashore the deals and iron were materialising into one small shed and two larger ones.

Cheyne was fidgeting about like a cat on hot bricks, and when I asked him what the sheds were for, he fairly snarled at me, all pretence to civility gone.

'Go and find out. Do, there's a good chap. If you really can find out I'll give you a fiver. I will, straight.'

I earned the fiver easily enough, for there was no difficulty this time in finding out what the sheds were for. A young dapper German in charge explained in pretty good English that they were the new premises of the Delfzyl Handeln Gesellschaft, and would be opened for general trading purposes at the end of the following week.

Cheyne almost foamed at the mouth when I told him. He wasn't particular about his language at any time, but I never heard him blaspheme as he did then.

'Well, what else can you expect?' I said, when he'd done. 'If you're running a show like this you must expect competition. Good job for you they're a mile farther from the town than you are. That's one good thing in your favour. They'll get fewer callers than you do, for certain.'

He turned on me, furious.

'What the—do you know about it? In our favour? . . . Why,

you born flaming fool, you don't think our business is done over a—shop counter, do you?'

'I don't know how your business is done, and I don't care.'

'Don't look as if you did, idling ashore here when you might be at your work. Get aboard, d'ye hear?'

'Look here, Cheyne,' I said. 'You say two words more and I'll see if I can't manage to lay you out. You offer me a fiver to get you information, and when I come back with it you behave like the gutter-bred swine you are.'

I naturally expected the sack, after that, and I determined if I got it I'd kick him round his own wharf as a farewell, just to square up for past favours. However, instead of sacking me, he was a shade more civil than before, so I'd no reason to regret talking straight for once. But he never paid me the fiver, after all. In the excitement of the moment I forgot it, and when I remembered his promise we were at sea again and it was too late to bother about it.

For all his civility he was still uneasy in his mind about the new company. No one could help seeing that, and again I began to reconstruct my notions about him. I wondered whether he'd invested any money in the concern himself, but somehow couldn't think him fool enough for that.

He was, though. That afternoon, when he came aboard, he apologised for his language of the morning, and then admitted he was a shareholder.

'I lost my temper, Capt'n. I'm sorry. You must overlook it. Fact is, this new concern worries me. All my savings are in this venture, and naturally I was a bit upset to learn these other people were on our track.'

I said I'd find out all I could, and next afternoon came back with a pretty considerable budget for him. He took me into the office, shut the door, produced a bottle of whisky and told me to fire away; and I told him all I could.

'The two big sheds are fifteen paces long by about seven

wide—say forty feet by twenty. That's as near as I could guess without its being noticed that I was pacing them out on purpose. They're about eight feet high to eaves and thirteen to ridge. The small one's half that size, say twenty by twelve. The man in charge is a clerk from the company's head office in Delfzyl—a Frieslander. Van Noppen, he's called.'

'A smart chap?'

'He seems so.'

'Any machinery there?'

'Didn't see any. Why?'

'What's become of that boiler plating the galliot landed, then?'

'I asked him that myself. He said it had been loaded again for Ghent.'

'He's a liar, then. I should have seen— But go on. What's in the sheds? What's that ship brought down there now?'

'Some patent fertiliser or other—in bags. I couldn't see into the sheds. The doors were closed, but the sills were clean and there's no litter about, so I expect they're empty yet.'

Cheyne nodded approvingly. 'Skipper, you've got eyes in your head. Where's this chap Van Noppen living?'

'In one of the big sheds, I think. At least there's a stove pipe at the end of one of 'em. The windows are high up under the eaves, and the little shed's got no windows at all.'

'Anybody there besides the manager?'

'Half-a-dozen lumpers getting bags ashore and piling them on the bank.'

'Lumpers? You mean hands off the vessel?'

'No, I don't. They weren't sailors—not smart enough. Just clay-smeared shore lumpers, like your lot here.'

'Where did they come from then?'

'Terneuzen, I suppose.'

'I should have seen them pass here if they did. What did that galliot sail with?'

'Ballast, I suppose. I didn't ask. They couldn't get anything else from here, could they?'

'Are they—are they digging out a wharf—like ours?'

'They've made a start. The barrows and planks are lying about.'

'What do they want barrows and planks for?' he asked sharply.

'They're wheeling the stuff across the bank and dumping it down the slope inside.'

'Inside?'

'Yes, inside—inland. Away from the river. I suppose they've dumped fifty or sixty tons down over the grass on the inside of the bank. It's sliding out over the field behind the sheds.'

'Now—what—the—devil—is—that—for?' said Cheyne, in a whisper to himself, pausing between every word. Upset? He couldn't have looked more scared if he'd seen a ghost. I stared at him hard and he did his best to resume the conversation. But I'd done talking. No need of all Voogdt's warnings to rush back into my mind; no need for me to warn myself that there was something fishy doing. Plain, honest business—even unprofitable business—don't scare a man like that.

He cleared his throat and reached for the bottle. 'What do you reckon that is for?'

'What is what for?'

'Why are they throwing the mud on the inside of the embankment?'

'Where else can they put it?' I asked.

'Well—we ship ours as ballast, as you know.'

'Perhaps they've got more paying cargoes than ballast.'

'Yes—yes. P'raps so. Very likely,' said he, plainly unconvinced, and so I left him, wondering what on earth was up, and wishing more than ever that Voogdt hadn't left me as he did.

What ever it was that worried Cheyne it didn't interfere with business. He was up bright and early next morning, driving away as usual at the ballasting. The wind was strong, nor'-westerly, but he expected one of the other boats next tide, he said, and so sent us off to drop down with the ebb. 'Anchor off Flushing, if you can't get out,' were his parting instructions.

We had to anchor, the wind being almost dead ahead and a

lumpy sea outside, and next morning I was waked by the hooter of the Harwich daily boat. It struck me they'd be getting a dusting, so I went on deck to see her come in.

Sure enough they were getting it. The following run of sea made steering difficult, I suppose, for she was yawing about rather badly, and taking it green over her stern every now and then. Naturally there weren't many passengers on deck—I pictured them all mighty sick in their berths, and pitied the stewards—but two people, a man and a girl, were standing a little way apart in the bows. For the moment the man reminded me of Voogdt, but as the steamer neared us he walked to the other side of the deck and I lost sight of him. The girl, wrapped to the chin and wearing a fur cap or toque, waved a hand cheerily as she passed. I waved back, as one does wave to a stranger's greeting from a passing boat or train, and then went below to the warm stove, thinking she must be a hardy sort of girl to be on deck in such bitter weather.

The wind lulled in the day, and then shifted to the northward, so that we were able to get under way next morning, but we were past the West Hinder before her face came back to me as something quite familiar. Even then it took an hour of brain-racking before it came to me with a shock that she was Pamily Brand.

CHAPTER VI

OF A PRODIGAL'S RETURN

OF course I made sure she must be going to Terneuzen, and did my best to make a quicker voyage in consequence. She'd annoyed me from the very start of our acquaintance; flicked me on the raw of my vanity, as it were, and I wanted a chance to get level with her. But besides that there was something interesting about the girl that occupied my thoughts, and, anyhow, to see her at Terneuzen promised some sort of change from the usual sitting and drinking with Cheyne.

There was very little else to interest one in the life, as things were. The winter coasting trade was a cruel business, and if it hadn't been that I was saving money fast I think I should have tried to break charter and lay by in some harbour till the spring.

But I was doing very well, and hideously uncomfortable though the cruising was, I still flinched at the memory of the winter before. No more idling on an empty stomach for me, if I could help it So I stuck to it, and 'Kiah backed me up in his stolid way, and we both took it out of Rance whenever he seemed inclined to get slack.

We were for Lymington this voyage, and even 'Kiah seemed ready for a grumble at the way I drove the pair of them. I forget now what we brought back; some fool cargo or another, for certain. Since Cheyne's outbreak I'd made up my mind that the ostensible trade of the company was only a cloak for some other more profitable business—probably fancy smuggling of some sort, like saccharine, perhaps. I didn't know, and I didn't care. Besides, that girl's face stuck in my mind—a little roundish oval with dark hair and fur all round. It struck me she'd look rather well, seen close at hand, in that get-up. Her big eyes and short lip seemed the right features for a merry sort of winter picture.

It was nearly dark and raining heavens hard when we got off the Isle of Axel, and the office seemed deserted, but I got the dinghy overside and went ashore to report myself. The place was all locked up, so off I went to Terneuzen in search of Cheyne. As I expected he was at the hotel by the locks: 'Dining with his friends upstairs,' the landlady said.

'What friends?'

'The English friends. The tall man and the two young vroowen.'

'Ask him if he'll see me,' I said, and the landlady departed, and presently called down over the stairs to say I was to come up. I'd had a shave the night before and a pretty good washing with rain and salt water all day, and as for my guernsey and rough serge, they were clean enough, as such clothes go, so up I went.

It gives you a queer feeling, intimate yet strange, to see a girl indoors and without her hat for the first time. They had a private room, only lighted by a fire on the hearth and candles on the table at which they sat. Miss Brand, facing the door, had the shaded candlelight on her face and big eyes as she held her head on one side to peer across the dim room. The man—Ward, as I had guessed—got up and shook hands, and the girls nodded pleasantly and gave me a good-evening. Cheyne sat back lounging in his chair, his legs stuck straight out under the table.

'Perhaps Captain West would like something to eat?' Miss Lavington suggested.

'I should. I haven't had anything to eat since breakfast,' I confessed.

They cried out at that, and shifted their chairs so that I could sit between Miss Lavington and Ward. The Pamily girl stared at me unwinkingly as soon as I came into the light from the candles on the table.

'What does Captain West drink as a rule?' she asked.

'Whisky, generally, isn't it, West? But he doesn't drink much, do you?'

For once I felt friendly towards the bounder.

'What do you call much?' the girl asked carelessly.

'I don't think I've ever seen him drink more than two glasses at a sitting, and weak ones at that.' He said it as though he intended to sneer at my unmanly habit. If he'd only known I felt like patting him on the back I expect he'd have changed his tune.

The girl said nothing, but went on staring at me curiously, with her head on one side like an inquisitive bird.

'After a pause: 'You're wet,' she said.

'Only a drop of rain.'

She pushed back her chair, put her napkin on the table and walked round to me and felt my coat.

'He's soaking,' she announced.

Ward looked on with a smile on his post-office mouth, and Miss Lavington's eyebrows lifted wearily, yet amused, too, I thought. As for Cheyne, he grunted some sort of protest. I think he said I could go downstairs and get a change. But the girl didn't take the least notice of any of them.

'Get up and go over by the fire,' she ordered. 'Take your plate with you. Take off your coat. Here.' She put it on the back of a chair before the blaze, and then stood over me with a stiff glass of whisky and water. 'Drink that,' she ordered.

No good resisting. There really wasn't much sense in sending me to the fire, for I was wet rather than cold, having walked fast. But she had a whirlwind way of her own it was useless to try and resist. Besides, thinking of her as the poor relation, I judged she didn't get many chances of bossing people about. So I drank the spirits, and very strong and good they were, and then sat obediently before the fire, steaming as I ate, with the rain from my hair running down inside the collar of my guernsey.

In a minute she noticed that too and brought me her table-napkin to wipe my head and face on.

'Rather have a towel?' she asked.

'This'll do, thanks'; and I rubbed my hair dry and went on eating till the plate was empty. She refilled it, waiting on me, going to and from the table, the others handing her whatever she wanted; and whilst I ate she stood and held my glass.

The Pamily girl took my plate as I rose.

'You'll have another glass of spirits before you go?'

'No, thanks.'

'Yes; you must. And then go aboard and get into dry clothes as quickly as you can.' She filled another glass at the table and gave it to me as I stood before the fire.

'I can't tell what it was made me break out as I did—the warmth and food after a day's hunger and cold had as much to do with it as anything, perhaps; or maybe it was drinking strong spirits after some days of abstinence. Whatever the cause, it suddenly dawned upon me what awfully decent people they were. Anybody else would have sent their employee downstairs to get dry and presentable before they talked to him, as Cheyne had wanted to do; but Ward and Miss Lavington had only aided their little spitfire of a companion to make me comfortable where I was. It came over me with a shock that I was really making my living by helping to rob them, and on the impulse spoke out the truth for once.

'Look here,' I said. 'I—I think you ought to know how things stand. He'll never tell you,' and I nodded towards Cheyne. 'This business here is all sham, you know. Your money's being dribbled away gradually in these rotten voyages. The charter I made with you, Mr Ward; I as good as swindled you. I never thought you'd pay me the sum I asked. Why, it's twice the current rate of freights. And the cargoes aren't what they ought to be—I could carry twice as much as I do. Here, this last voyage: I go to Lymington in ballast—two shillings a ton allowance on it—and come back with thirty tons of unsaleable rubbish. What goods can you expect to get at a village in the New Forest? And I've taken out ballast before now, and been paid freights back here on road metal—for mending a path nobody uses. You'll never make money that way. You're paying us to waste your capital for you. You—Miss Lavington and Mr Ward, I mean—you're being robbed daily. It's only common honesty to tell you so.'

For a few moments not one of them answered or moved. They might have been wax figures rather than men and women. Then Ward lit a cigar—and did it jerkily, I thought, just as a wax figure would move—blew out the match carefully and put it on his plate.

'What makes you think that?' he said very quietly.

'A hundred things. The rate you're paying me—light cargoes—the waste and want of economy everywhere. I've brought potatoes here—a quid a ton freight, from Dorset—and found Sas van Gent exporting them to Germany when I arrived. That's business isn't it?'

Ward looked at Cheyne, who nodded and then turned to me. 'That'll do,' he said. I naturally expected he would rage, but he spoke quietly enough. 'You've proved yourself a zealous servant, and now you can get aboard. We'll sack you in due form tomorrow.'

'As you like. My charter lasts till June, but I'm ready to break it if Mr Ward wishes. I've seen you rob him long enough'; and I shuffled on my wet, warm coat and ran back to the boat as fast as I could. I didn't want to be laid up with a chill just as I must look out for a new job.

But it was to be a night of surprises. I got into my cabin and lit the lamp, and just as it was flaming up somebody coughed softly in Voogdt's old bunk. I pretended not to hear, changed into a dry shirt and trousers, and then pulled back the curtain suddenly.

'Come out of it, whoever you are,' I said.

The huddled figure under the blankets stuck up a pale, startled face, half laughing, and it was Voogdt himself.

'Good Lord! Austin!' I cried. 'How did you come aboard?'

'Hush,' he said in a whisper. 'Don't shout so you bullock! Swam aboard—me the consumptive invalid. Man, I'm nigh dead with the cold. Where on earth have you been till now? On the bend?'

'After a fashion. I've just got myself the sack.'

'Tell us all about that later on. For the present light the stove and get me something hot—quick.' He got behind the curtains again his teeth chattering audibly.

I guessed Rance might have some spirits, so went forward and woke him. As I expected, he had managed to get a bottle of Schiedam aboard by some mysterious drunkard's means, and I took it aft, lit the stove, and made Voogdt a rank brew, disguising the taste with a double allowance of sugar. He drank it greedily, demanded more, and got under the blankets again. After three glasses he declared that I'd saved his life.

'Can you talk now?' I asked.

'Yes. But you first. Tell us all about getting the sack.'

I told him the whole story without interruption, but when I'd done he announced that his tale could wait.

'First thing to be done is to hide me. Ward'll be aboard in the morning and neither he nor Cheyne must know I'm here, whatever happens. Next thing is for you to apologise to Ward, and offer to stand to the charter. He'll accept, I fancy; but if he's nasty, insist as your right on working it out to the end of the twelve months. Understand that. At whatever cost you've got to stick to the firm like—like a bug to a blanket. But I must be hidden till you touch at your next port. Then I rejoin.'

'Well, that's good hearing, anyhow. Where've you been all this time? South, for your health?'

'No, north. And I haven't been there for my health either, since you use the most apposite form of words. All the same, I've precious little to show for my journeying. And that's enough for now. Warmth—blessed warmth! I was nearly frozen stiff when you came, James. And now for sleep. Let me know where I'm to hide when I wake.'

He turned his face to the wall and was snoring before I got to bed, though I turned in immediately.

He was up before me, too. When I woke in the dim light of the winter morning his bunk was empty. I whipped out of mine quickly, and just missed breaking a leg, for he'd pulled up a trap-door in the floor which gave into a three-cornered hole we called the after-peak. In the summer we used to store milk and bottled beer there for coolness, but it was only about two feet high, and I shouldn't have thought he could have got into it. However, there he was, lying on his back, and pushing the rubbish it contained back into the less accessible corners.

'What are you doing?' I asked.

He didn't hear me, so I stirred him with my foot until he squirmed his face under the hole, and then asked again.

'Making a nest,' he said, and grinned. 'There's nowhere else I can go without being seen.'

'But you can't stay down there till we fetch another port.'

'I don't intend to try. I'm going to live in the cabin here and dodge below when anybody comes aboard.'

He put a spare mattress and blankets down the hole and soon had a chance of trying its capabilities, for, as he had prophesied, Ward came aboard the moment we touched the wharf.

I tackled him at once. 'I want to apologise for my behaviour last night, Mr Ward.'

He took it very quietly. 'Very good,' he said. 'We accept your apology. Miss Lavington and myself were not disposed to make any bother about it. You're a bit over-zealous, perhaps; and—you will please consider this as an order from your employers—we wish you to avoid further friction with Mr Cheyne. We are perfectly satisfied with his management, and have no complaints to make about the way in which the business is conducted. I may say we are perfectly satisfied with your work as well.'

'As long as you're pleased—' I began lamely.

'We are pleased, I assure you. The—er—the conditions of our markets are not a thing you can be expected to understand. Very likely you thought you were opening our eyes to short-comings last night, but I can assure you that all the company's transactions pass under my own eye. Light cargoes, for instance: there's this shallow river as a standing excuse for them. And there are other points you're not able to consider—the size of our customers' orders, and so on. I quite understand that it must seem queer to you, this small class of trade of ours done at the very door of a great market like Antwerp, but you know the old saying that where big businesses can live, small ones can do with the crumbs they let fall.'

'I never heard the saying.'

'Perhaps not. But it's true. We—we are even doing fairly well, since you seem anxious for our interests. Er—in fact I had proposed to pay you a fifty-pound bonus at the end of the charter, if you were disposed to renew it. Are you prepared to go on with us?'

'I'm prepared, fast enough. But how about Ch—Mr Cheyne?'

'Mr Cheyne will make no objection. We'll regard that as settled, then. One thing more: whatever you may think of our unbusinesslike methods, don't talk about them to anybody. To anybody, mind. Already some information about us must have leaked out, and now we've competition at our very door—this German firm. So hold your tongue. That's all.'

Before he went he stood a moment by the hatchway where I was helping Rance at the hand-winch.

'Excuse me,' he said, 'but you—you're an educated man, aren't you?'

I told him where I'd been at school, and he went ashore. In the afternoon a boy came down from the hotel with a note for me.

'DEAR CAPTAIN WEST,—Would you care to join us at dinner tonight. Yours faithfully,

'ANNE LAVINGTON.'

I went below to write an answer and found Voogdt with his body under the floor, and his head up through the trap-door, reading.

'What's on?' he asked.

'Look out,' I said. 'There's somebody coming.'

It was a lie, but I meant going, and couldn't stop to argue with him about it then. He popped out of sight like a hermit crab into its shell, pulling-to the trap-door over him, and I sat on it on a camp-stool and wrote my acceptance, laughing to myself.

I was glad I went, for the evening proved thoroughly enjoyable. For one thing it was a godsend to sit at table with decent women once more, and for another Cheyne was savagely annoyed at my being there, though he did his best to conceal it. Miss Lavington made a very good hostess in her sleepy, kindly way; her slow, lazy smile set you at your ease and banished stiffness from the very start. She was certainly a very lovely woman, and Ward was evidently very sweet on her in his reserved way, so that I judged they would be partners before long in a closer concern than the Axel Trading Company if he had his way.

As for Miss Pamela Brand, all I can say about her is that she puzzled me. I misunderstood the sort of girl she was at our first meeting, and I don't profess to understand her to this day any more than I can understand why spring weather should drench you with cold rain one minute and set you steaming in hot sunshine the next. I've read poets who compare a girl to April weather, showers and sunshine: you couldn't find a seasonable comparison for this one without dragging in every month of the year from sultry August to December ice.

Most of the talk was about business. Meeting as we did, comparative strangers with one common interest, there weren't many subjects we could all touch on. After making an exhibition of myself the night before, I couldn't well ask many direct questions; but the Pamily girl wasn't bound in the same way, and she made me talk about my work no end, till I even got the notion that the candlelights shining in her big eyes took the shape of question marks. What ports had I called at since she came aboard at Dartmouth? How did I like the winter trade? What sort of men did we employ?

I told her of Voogdt and how I picked him up at Exmouth, and she seemed very interested. Then Cheyne cut in:

'That black-bearded Cockney you had aboard? He was no class, was he?'

'A better man than you,' I nearly said; but remembering how Voogdt had played the low Cockney before him, and his present mysterious ways, thought better of it.

'He was a better-class man than he looked. He'd been on a newspaper before he went on tramp.'

The other three looked not at me but at Cheyne for enlightenment. He made a little shake of his head, as though he were denying something.

'No class,' he said. 'No doubt he managed to impose on the good nature of our friend here, but you can take it from me that if he was on a newspaper it was on some low job—driving a wagon, maybe. I had him ashore and stood him a drink and had a chat with him.'

I confess I felt offended at the cad contradicting me like that to my face. They were all so intent on what he said, and so obviously disregarding me, that just for a moment I felt out of it. However, before I could say anything or show my resentment, the exclusive atmosphere had passed, and Pamela Brand was talking to me of something else as agreeably as you please, and the others were backing her up in making me feel I was one of a family party rather than the stranger I'd felt a minute before.

Towards the end of the evening the talk shifted round from coasting to deep-sea cruising; and of course the Brand girl must know all about where I'd been. When I told her, Cheyne wanted to know what boats I'd been in.

'The D.W.I.,' I said.

'What D.W.I.?'

'I only know one company of the name—the Deutsche-West-Indie Company.'

'Oh! a German line. That's a swell company though. What were you? Quartermaster?'

'I was third officer on their *Oldenburgh* when I chucked the job at Kingston,' I said.

That took Master Cheyne back a bit. I wondered whether he remembered about his blowing-off about having been in Warbeck's. Ward and Miss Lavington looked at him with surprise—and again with that queer air of accusation. From their faces one would think he'd been remiss in something. But I hadn't time to take much notice, for the interrogation lights were waking in the Brand girl's eyes again, and she started another catechism. Where and why had I chucked the *Oldenburg?*

Of course that meant telling her all the yarn about Kingston and the earthquake, and when I'd done it was time to go. They were all very nice, shook hands all round, and Miss Lavington hoped I'd join them again when next in port if they were there, and so on, and so on; but even so there was something in their manner I couldn't fathom, and I came away with the notion that I'd left Cheyne behind me to undergo a heckling about something he'd left undone.

It might have been a strange echo of my own thoughts that came from behind the curtains of Voogdt's bunk when I got down into the cabin.

'Well, have they pumped you dry?' were his first words.

CHAPTER VII

CONCERNING A PENALTY FOR CURIOSITY

VOOGDT asked me the same question once or twice next day, but for once I had an answer ready for him. Each time 'Somebody coming, Austin' sent him down below like a trap-door spider, and though I had him that way over and over again, and though he knew I was fooling him and cursed me for it, yet he never hesitated an instant, but, even whilst he doubted me; dived into his hole again and again. It was very evident he was extra anxious to keep out of sight.

I resented his repeated question all the more because I felt there was some great reason for it. Worrying wouldn't mend it, though, and so as usual I put the whole thing out of my mind and drove the work as hard as I could, in order to get Voogdt away from Terneuzen unobserved. Cheyne was down the day after the dinner-party, working as hard as ever, and a bit more civil to me—in consequence of the D.W.I. revelation, I suppose— and we took in a good thirty-two or three tons of ballast and got away to sea again early next morning without seeing any more of Ward and the womenfolk. When we got clear of the shore Voogdt was able to come up from his hole in the cabin. If 'Kiah or Rance came aft he could hide in his bunk, and with the skylight shut down the noises of the wind and water outside would keep our voices from the helmsman, provided we spoke low.

'What a time you've been,' Voogdt said, when he'd dragged up his mattress and blankets and replaced the trap-door. 'I thought for certain you'd get away last night.'

'We got in a bit of extra ballast.'

'How much this trip?'

'Thirty-three tons, I expect.'

His face showed unbounded astonishment, eyes and mouth open.

'Why—why—? What on earth d'ye want that lot for? We used to reckon twenty a heavy load.'

'We don't want it. That is to say, it's not necessary, of course. But, as you know, they want it cleared away.'

'How much cargo last voyage?'

'Thirty-five tons.'

'And now you're taking away thirty-three of ballast. It's mad—sheer lunacy. And it pays.'

'They say so, at all events.'

'They tell the truth, then, for once. I know it pays—have spent my last summer's savings and most of your loan just to find out that much.'

'Where've you been?' I asked.

'In Birmingham and the surrounding district, poking my nose into other folks' affairs. And bar that one fact, that Ward and Miss Lavington are making money, I haven't got a penn'orth of information worth the having. How are they making it, Jem? That's what beats me. Not at this trade. We know that, don't we?'

'They say it pays.'

'How can it? I've been into the thing like an auditor. I've gone over every trip we did last summer; priced the cargoes, found out current freights, read up old market reports, and generally put the business through a sieve. And every voyage shows a loss—every single voyage. What d'ye make of that?'

'You must have got hold of the wrong prices. They say it pays.'

'Oh, dry up,' he cut in. 'You make me tired, you poll-parrot. I tell you I've been into the thing to the uttermost farthing. I've assumed them buying and selling in the best markets. I've allowed for the fact that they've no competition.'

'But they have.' It was my turn to interrupt this time.

'What competition have they got?' Voogdt asked scornfully

'This German firm. Didn't you see their sheds about a mile below us?'

'How could I see anything when I left Terneuzen by night, and haven't put my nose outside this hole since? What sort of crowd are they? Tell me all about them.'

I told him all I knew, and when I'd done he beat his forehead on the cabin table and groaned.

'That finishes it,' he said. 'I'm gone in—dead—done for. There's something in it, now, for certain, and I've spent hard money looking for it and can't find out what it is. Never call me a pressman again. Call me a—you're a sailor, aren't you, you lump?—call me a sailor, for the future.'

'I'll call you a sailor when I've done with you,' I said. 'You've something more to learn first, though. You haven't tried this winter cruising, deserter.'

'And I'm not so sure I will, either,' he said thoughtfully. 'Where are you for this time? Newhaven? I've good mind to borrow more money from you there, and jump the ship again.'

'Don't do that,' I said. 'I'm sick of this lonesome cruising, and it's even a sort of pleasure to see your ugly mug again. Stay on. We'll keep Rance to help do the heavy work.'

His eyes twinkled. 'That's all right,' he said. 'But I may have to go, Jem, all the same. I must get to the bottom of this business, or I shall die of complicated interrogation marks in my innards. This German firm settles it. They must be getting something out of the trade somehow; but for the life of me I cannot see how it's done. Get that into your head.'

'How do you know they're making money then?' I asked.

'Two years ago Ward had a job at Mason College worth three hundred a year. He lived in diggings and lived small. Miss Lavington was a bit better off, but not much. She and Miss Brand were both students at the same college. Her income—Miss L's, I mean—was derived from two steamers her father left her. The Brand girl had some small property as well, I believe, and they lived together, also in digs. Little Brand was then under age, and your lovely Lavington was one of her trustees.'

'Miss Brand was a student, was she? What was her line?'

'She was a student. Now she's a B.Sc.'

'That little guttersnipe a Bachelor of Science?'

'Where was I? Oh, about the money. Well, Ward's thrown up his paid professorship, and now holds a sort of honorary visiting appointment, and Miss Lavington's sold her steamers.'

'That doesn't sound like making money.'

'That's the funny part of it. On the face of it that's what any casual observer would say. But they're just dripping with money, Jem. I've got behind the scenes, which used to be my business, and there I learn that Ward and his girl are investing money—big money—in dozens of concerns. To give you only one instance, they took up ten thousand quid of that Japanese municipal loan only last November. And the allotments in that loan were twenty-five per cent. of the applications. Those two between 'em had applied for forty thousand quid's worth of scrip! It's unbelievable, isn't it?'

'What other business concerns have they?'

'Not a thing—except as shareholders. And every investment they hold has been taken up since the opening of these tin sheds at Terneuzen. You take my tip, there's something devilish fishy in it. Big smuggling think? We should surely have spotted that, shouldn't we? And now this German firm are on their track. It beats me! It beats me!' And he slammed his hand down on the table with a bang.

'Don't make such a row. D'you want Rance to come down to see what's the matter? Tell me more. Are they living in a big way?'

'No. In diggings, just the same; but they seem to make holiday all the time, as you see. Ward does his correspondence from the Birmingham office of the company, a shabby hole near Snow Hill, giving on the railway goods shed at the back. There seems to be very little business done there; but I didn't bother about the place much. Only one queer thing about it; and that's the clerk in charge.'

'What about him?'

'Well, he used to be a solicitor, and was reckoned one of the smartest men in the city, until he came a purler—gambling on 'Change. That put his light out. He was struck off the rolls and hung about at a loose end for months. Then Ward took him on, and he sits in that office all day, doing nothing, apparently. I tried to make his acquaintance, and, building on his past record, was a sporty, devil-may-care, boon companion. But it was the wrong prescription. He was as close as an oyster and cut me dead a dozen times before he could shake me off. The Birmingham office itself isn't any size, and I thought the profits, if they really came from this trading, would be more easily detected at the Terneuzen end of the business. In fact I still think the Snow Hill office is only a blind.'

'Are the other two boats making the money?'

He shook his head. 'I had one look at the *Olive Leaf* and, as far as I could make out, she's on the same lay as we are.'

'How did you find out where she was?'

'That was an accident, I admit. Fact is, I—er'—he stammered and got rather red over it—'I may as well own up that I was shadowing Ward. He was constantly leaving Birmingham, and I thought I'd find out where he went. A nice long chase he let me in for, too—all the way to Bo'ness, on the Firth of Forth, a bitter Scotch port, all granite and coal dust. And the first call he paid was aboard the *Olive Leaf*.'

'What was she doing there?'

'Fetching coal to Terneuzen. The same old tale, half cargoes at high freights. At least I suppose they're high, for the boat's well found, and the men seem content enough with her. I couldn't find out what the freights actually were, for the skipper's a dour Scotsman, with a fine notion of minding his own business.'

'And Ward? What did he do aboard?'

'That's more than I can say. I wasn't in the cabin with him and the skipper. But I hung about till the boat cleared the port, and then came back to Brum. She had nothing aboard but coals, though, I'll swear—unless the lumps were hollow and filled with saccharine or opium or such dutiable goods of value. Besides, that's nonsense. If there's smuggling going on, it must be into England, not out of it. No, it beats me. Here's the situation in a nutshell: they lose money on every voyage, and put away money all the time. How's it done? Tell me that.'

'I don't explain it at all, and I don't want to. I'm like your Scotch skipper—have a fine notion of minding my own business. We're doing well, they're doing well, and everything in the garden's lovely. Why bother about it?'

'Because I was made that way, I suppose. I can't rest in the face of puzzles like this. And I will get to the bottom of it before I'm done—I will, mark you, or I shall bust. And now, sailor, hand me down *Ramuntcho* from that shelf and then go on deck and 'tend to your business. I'm a passenger for once, and don't you forget it.'

I hung in the doorway a minute. 'Is the Brand girl making money, too?' I asked.

'Dunno. I daresay—it looks like a family party. But the lovely Lavington's the Catch of the Season. When next I go to Terneuzen I shall clip my beard and go ashore and make goo-goo eyes at her. Now go away. Loti's better company than you are.'

We made a short voyage of it, and the first night in port, 'Kiah and Rance being ashore, Voogdt went on deck, and on their return greeted 'Kiah and announced his return to duty.

'Kiah grinned all over his face.

'Glad t' see 'ee agen, Mr Vute,' he said. ''E—that there Rance—'e id'n no comp'ny fer a man.'

'You'll find me comp'ny enough,' Voogdt announced. 'I've a-learnt a braave lot o' new naames t' caal 'ee by 'Kiah. As for 'e'—he jerked his head Devonshire fashion towards the forecastle where Rance was retiring—'us'll talk to 'e proper, in's own lingo.'

He had a passage of arms with the islander before twenty-four hours had elapsed, much to 'Kiah's gratification. I wasn't present officially, but some of the echoes of the strife reached the cabin and 'Kiah afterwards retailed to me as much of it as he could understand.

'I d'no what they was a-sayin' of,' he said. 'Frenchy talk, 'twas. But Mr Vute, 'e went for Rance, proper. Rance, 'e 'adn' nothin' t' say tu un, after five minutes of it.'

'So you've been upsetting the peace of the ship,' I said at tea-time.

'That little beast. He's a pig—sneering at 'Kiah and his ways. 'Kiah's worth twenty of him.'

'Was that it?' I asked. 'What did you say?'

'Oh, just told him what I thought of him, and gave him a breezy sketch of his family and forbears. We shan't have any more trouble with him in the future, I fancy.'

However, when we got back to Terneuzen we found ourselves let in for a mild row. The man had made no complaint to me of Voogdt's behaviour, but the day after we landed Cheyne came down to the *Luck and Charity* and said Rance had told him he would leave the ship.

'Let him,' I said. 'I don't want him.'

'We don't like sacking men,' Cheyne explained. 'Besides, this Cockney hand of yours seems unreliable. He jumps the ship and rejoins at his own sweet will, whilst Rance is steady and sticks to his job.'

'I can't allow any dictation as to the management of my crew,' I said.

'No dictation at all, my dear chap. Only, you see we want to have a name for fair dealing with our men, and both Mr Ward and Miss Lavington dislike change. I don't even want you to sack your Cockney, but Rance says he'll leave unless he has an apology from him, and—well, I don't want Rance to leave.'

'I don't want four men to work this boat,' I said. 'I admit Rance had been with me through the worst of the winter and

I've no wish to sack him, but if he wants to go, let him go, and welcome.'

'I'd rather he didn't go, I tell you,' Cheyne repeated. 'Of course you can run the boat with three hands. I know that. But four can make things easier, and—and we're prepared to make you an allowance towards the pay of a fourth hand, if you'll keep him on.'

'All right,' I said, trying not to look surprised. 'If you wish it I'll tell Voogdt to apologise.'

'Thanks. I shall be much obliged,' said Cheyne, and departed.

Voogdt heard what I had to say in silence. 'Rum game, isn't it?' he remarked when I'd done. 'But of course I'll apologise—I don't take my dignity seriously like that little animal. Call him down now and I'll get it over. And see here, Jem; when I've grovelled, do the friendly and produce a drink. I'd like to know what hold the little swab has over Cheyne.'

He apologised in due form—a genial, pleasant apology that any decent man would have accepted at once. Rance, like the ill-bred little beast he was, looked down over his nose and was stiff as starch, and Voogdt went all over it again, smiling. His repetition and my whisky made the peace in the end, and they left the cabin like brothers. In the afternoon I heard Austin arranging to stand the little brute a dinner at Terneuzen in the evening.

He got back at midnight in a vile temper.

'My head,' he complained. 'Like a kettle. And I've got the hiccups. That vermin insisted on my drinking level pegs with him, and I'm half screwed. "To bed, to bed, quo' sleepy-head." . . . And all to no purpose. I've spent good money feeding a pig, and I shall have a ghastly head in the morning—and I don't believe he's got any hold over Cheyne after all. I'm sure he hasn't. And yet Cheyne requests me to apologise to him and salve his wounded feelings, and offers to pay part of his wages if he's kept on. All of a piece, Jem—all mazed, crazed, dazed. All of it. Sleep, blessed sleep. "Hush me, O sorrow."'

All next day he was like a bear with a sore head, but I didn't trouble much about him, because the two girls came down to the wharf and paid me a visit, and I was put about to make them reasonably comfortable. Being cold on deck, they had tea in the cabin, which, with the stove alight and the skylight open, was bearable, if draughty. Both of them were as nice as could be, and their chatter and furs and scents made the bare cabin seem a very pleasant place for once. Ballasting had started, but it was flood tide and the men were ashore, Voogdt having gone for a stroll and 'Kiah and Rance to Terneuzen marketing, so everything was quiet.

It was a still, cold winter's afternoon without a breath of air, and as we sat at tea the only sound audible outside was the lip-lip of the tide against our wooden walls. Then we heard music—a big liner going up-river to Antwerp, a string band playing in her saloon. Whilst we were listening three or four gunshots sounded in rapid succession somewhere down the river and the girls wanted to know what they were.

'Somebody shooting duck or seagulls,' I suggested.

'If it's duck, I've nothing to say. If it's seagulls, it's a shame. They're no good, dead,' said Miss Brand, in her downright way.

'You don't object to shooting duck?'

'No sense in carrying sentiment too far. Man must eat. Besides, I like duck and green peas myself, though it's too early yet for them.' She laughed a little, and the talk went on in other channels.

It might have been half-an-hour later when somebody jumped aboard and came across the deck. I didn't recognise the step, but it came down the companionway and proved to belong to Voogdt.

'Beg pardon, Cap'n,' he said, in his Cockney accent. 'Didn't know you wasn't alone,' and disappeared at once. Ward came aboard soon after, and as it was getting dusk the girls shook hands, said thank you very prettily and went off with him. I went forward to see if Voogdt was in the forecastle and found him sitting on one of the empty bunks, looking pale.

'Are they gone?' he asked. 'Yes? Good. I'll come aft.' He limped as he walked.

'What's the matter?' I asked.

'I've been shot, Jem. In the leg.'

'Shot? How? An accident?'

'Useful sort of accident,' he said grimly. 'Here, lend a shoulder and help me down the stairs. I've had a fright, I can tell you.'

'How did it happen?'

'I went down to those German sheds this afternoon,' he said. 'Thought I'd like a look round and see what was doing. I walked down through the fields inside the embankment, and when I turned the corner of the sheds one of the doors was open. Inside was machinery—a big press, amongst other things—and in one corner two-three men were making and laying concrete, I thought they didn't seem over-pleased to see me; but I did the low-down 'foremast hand and asked if I could get a job there. The man in charge—was that the one you saw? Young and clean-shaven? Fair? . . . That's the chap, then—said he couldn't give me a job, and I was rather put to it for an excuse to hang about. However, I did, most barefacedly, and asked this man what the machinery was for. "Agricultural machinery," he said. I suppose he took me for a sailor, and thought I shouldn't know.

'Like a fool, I said—in German, too—"What use is a heavy-weight press to a farmer?" And he told me it was for packing hay. I just had sense enough to see I'd made an abject ass of myself, so I didn't comment on the concrete—which I'll swear was being laid as a bed for the thing—but said, "Oh, yes," as if convinced and started to walk home. That was about an hour ago.'

'Well?' I said.

'Well! Listen, and tell me if it's well. I'd got about a couple of hundred yards along the bank, and was walking along with my head on my chest, puzzling over that press, when suddenly I thought I heard somebody smack a whip behind me. At the same time a bee flew by, with a rather shrill buzz. Thinking hard as I was, I took no notice. Then the whip smacked again and another bee flew by, and all at once I tumbled to what was going on and jumped over the embankment down among some cows at pasture. Oh! the sweet smell of cows, Jem! The dear beasts!'

'I don't understand you,' I said.

'My son, the third bee touched ground by my foot, hit up a splash of gravel and sang off over the river with a note I haven't heard since Pieter's Drift; and the fourth bored a hole through the calf of my leg as I jumped. If it had touched bone I shouldn't be here now.'

'Good Lord!' I said, startled. 'D'you mean—?'

'I mean they were out to kill,' he said. 'Man, think of the barefaced devilry of it. Daylight, our sheds here within a mile, and out in stream, a C.P.R. liner going up to Antwerp with a band playing. I could hear the tune distinctly. It's a serious business that makes men risk their necks like that by light of day, alongside one of the biggest highways of Europe. If they'd broken my leg and brought me down, I should have been buried in Scheldt mud tonight, and no questions answered. As it was, the cows saved me. Even as I jumped I thought that out. A dead man's easily moved, and who's going to ask after one missing 'foremast Jack more or less? But a dead cow's another matter. If they'd shoot a man for asking a single question they wouldn't do anything that would bring indignant farmers asking hundreds more round their agricultural sheds.'

'How did you get home?'

'Drove the herd this way, keeping carefully in the middle of them—not so easy a business as it sounds, either, especially with a hole in your calf, and the cold fear of death on you. My word, but I was a frightened man, I can tell you. And now—now—now—we come back to the old question, rendered much more anxiously. What is it all about?'

'But you don't think this has anything to do with the company, do you?'

'I'm positive it has. How, I don't know. But when you get two abnormal things both happening at one spot, you can't help connecting them. I'm too badly scared even now to think the thing out properly, but I'll swear that the same cause underlies both Ward's investments and the hole in my leg. And now this is where you come in, at last, you who refuse to meddle. Ward's investments aren't your affair, you say. Are flying bullets your affair?—the attempted murder of a member of your crew? Besides, who's to say you yourself won't be the next? You're in just the same employ as I am; you've been messing round those sheds making inquiries, just as I have. I tell you, Jem West, it may become your business—your vitally important business—before you expect it.'

I ran my hand up through my hair, puzzled as a man could be. I didn't know what to say, the whole thing sounded so impossible. For a minute I was half inclined to think Voogdt had illusions or had been drinking, but one look at his serious face dispelled that idea, and, moreover, there was the blood-stained bandage round his leg—incontrovertible evidence.

'Was more than one man firing?' I asked.

'I didn't look back to count,' said he dryly. 'But if there was only one he had a magazine rifle, for the firing was too quick for anything else. It's wicked, isn't it? Now I'm recovering from funk I'm getting in a rage about it. The cold-blooded wickedness of the swabs!'

'It is a bit hot,' I admitted. 'What are you going to do? Tell the police?'

'You bet I will. If there's law in Holland I'll go for 'em. And yet—' He stopped.

'Yet what?'

'I don't know. I'm thinking. Go and wash off any blood that may have dropped on deck—I'd keep under cover as much as possible if I were you. Meanwhile, say nothing to any single soul about it. This matter requires deliberation.'

I searched the deck with a lantern and a bucket of water,

and found and washed away a few stains. There were some on the companion stairs as well, which showed he must have been bleeding fast, for he hadn't been on them more than a very few seconds. More than ever I was puzzled, and rather scared too, and inclined to get angry as one does when frightened. I was all for laying an information with the Turneuzen police at once, and I couldn't see any reason for Voogdt's delay.

'Kiah and Rance came aboard as soon as I'd washed the deck clean, and the ebb clearing the banks, we had three hours to work before I could talk to Voogdt again in private. He came on deck, concealing his limp, and did his work at the hand-winch without remark. When the rising tide sent us aboard, I went down after him into the cabin.

He hummed and hawed a little over his tale, but eventually got it out that for his part he'd rather not have the police called in.

'I'm shy of asking it,' he said, 'because I'm asking you to risk your life, and that's the plain truth. But see here, now. If you fetch them to meddle here matters won't end with jailing the men who tried to shoot me. There's something big behind this—big and dishonest. Before you know where you are our people'll be in the dock with their German competitors, and Cheyne and Ward, and perhaps the two girls, may all smell the inside of a Dutch prison. Would that please you?'

'No, it wouldn't. Not but what it'd do Cheyne good, maybe.'

'Exactly. Well that's the only real reason I can give for keeping the police out of it. On the other hand we may be risking more lives than our own if we don't inform. That's the deuce of it—we're working in the dark. And that's what really is influencing me, Jem. I won't be beat by these people. They're all in it—from the little Brand girl to the son of a gun who fired at me this afternoon—and I'm out of it, and I hate the feeling. Here I've made myself conversant with this trade at both ends: I've shovelled their mud and audited their accounts, and I'm still gaping at the business like a fool, unable to see where the profits come in. D'you think I want to call in a fat-headed Dutch policeman to tell me what I ought to have found out for myself long ago?'

'Speaking for myself, I'm more afraid than curious.'

'On my honour, I don't believe I am,' he said. 'Oh, I'm afraid all right—I was in a stinking funk this afternoon. But curiosity's eating me alive. What is it? What is it in this trade that allows Ward to bank money in thousands and incites a German trader to risk hanging? I'm in it up to my eyes. I've got the Axel Company's grime on my hands and their pay in my pockets, and their competitors' trade-mark on my leg, and here, in the middle of it all, I can't see how it's done. And I will!' He almost shouted it. 'I will! I'll get to the bottom of this business if I've got to run through storms of cursed bullets. No police, Jem. Hang the police! I'll find out what the game is if I spend half my life at it. And then, my noble captain, we'll go into it ourselves—you and I. That'll hurt the thieves worse than anything else, I'll swear.'

CHAPTER VIII

FURTHER RESULTS OF CURIOSITY

WE had no sleep that night, either of us: Voogdt because of his excitement and the pain in his leg, and I because he kept me awake arguing the matter to and fro until the morning ebb, when we turned out, got the last of the ballast aboard and put the hatch covers on. At first I was inclined to treat the whole affair as an accident; but Voogdt convinced me, as he had a way of doing and by daylight I had come round to his opinion that it was a deliberate attempt to get him out of the way. Not that I was persuaded so much by his words; it was his evident anger and fright that weighed with me, for I knew it took a good deal to scare him in earnest.

I was so thoroughly convinced by the morning that when two figures came marching down the bank from the German sheds I proposed to Voogdt to be ready to resist an armed attack.

'Pooh!' he said. 'What nonsense! They've come to explain the matter away. You say nothing. Leave it to me.'

When they reached the wharf they hailed us and asked if they might come aboard. The taller man, whom I recognised as the manager, Van Noppen, had a little gun in his hand, and with him was a hobbledehoy youth with a broad, cheerful face, dressed in the clay-smeared clothes of a lumper.

When they got on our deck Van Noppen led off with abject apologies in English.

'Dis young fool here'—he indicated the boy at his side—'he has yoost bought a new rifle, an' yesterday afternoon he must start shootin' at a paper target, de fool. He never looked to see vhere his shots vass gone vhen dey hat gone t'rough de target.

83

One off your men vass on de bank an' I see him yoomp away off it. I hope he vass not hurt.'

I looked over my shoulder as though beckoning Voogdt, and he came to my assistance.

"E was, though,' he said truculently. "E was shot in the leg. Look 'ere.' He pulled up his trouser-leg and displayed the bandage. 'Nice thing, thet is. Shootin' blind an' large. 'E might 'a corpsed me. A bloomin' nice thing, I call it.'

'He is very sorry,' Van Noppen said, but Voogdt was not to be appeased.

'Sorry! Thet's a lot o' good, ain't it? Thet'll mend my leg, won't it? S'pose I gets blood poisonin,' an' as to lay by an' loses my job.' He turned to the boy and abused him in such execrable German as 'foremast hands pick up in the ports, and then turned to Van Noppen again. 'I'll 'ave the law on yer both.'

Van Noppen shrugged his shoulders. 'The law? Oh yes. But how vill that do you good? If any leedle compensation—'

Voogdt cut in.

'Compensation. Oh yus, I don't think. 'Ow can 'e pay compensation?'

'I haf no doubt our company vill make him an advance on his wages,' Van Noppen suggested.

'Then I want a 'undred quid. One 'undred pounds. Savvy?'

'But that is reedeeculous,' Van Noppen said placidly. 'A pound, yes—or two. But a hundert for a leedle accident is foolish talk.'

I stood back and let them squabble over the sum, Voogdt playing the half-angry, half-frightened 'foremast hand to perfection, and Van Noppen quietly persuasive. If Voogdt's strident accents hadn't been a constant reminder that he was playing a part I should have been less interested. As it was, he had so convinced me that I seemed to be looking on at a play. The German clerk, well clad and businesslike, with the silent, sheepish lumper at his side, only filled me with suspicion, and their argument, all about money compensation, seemed a thin veneer of civilisation over some hidden abyss of savagery. I almost expected Van Noppen to bring the rifle to his shoulder and shoot one of us on the spot, and half unconsciously put one hand towards the weapon. He handed it to me at once and went on talking to Voogdt, whilst I examined the weapon with curiosity. It was a little Belgian rook-rifle, such a cheap toy as is made for export at about half-a-soverign. I opened the breech, looked through the barrel and was idly sighting it out across the water when Van Noppen appealed to me.

'I ask you, Captain. I offer feefty pounds to your man. Ees it enough?'

'I should take it, if I were you,' I said to Voogdt. 'You'll very likely get nothing if you go to law, you know.'

'Aw right, sir,' he said. 'If you sye it's aw right, I'll take it. 'And it over,' he said to Van Noppen.

The money in notes was immediately forthcoming, and I saw that the bundle the German returned to his pocket was far larger than the sheaf he handed to Voogdt. Their business being concluded, Van Noppen held out a hand for his rifle, but Voogdt made a gesture to restrain me from returning it.

'Thet bloke ain't fit t' be trusted wiv a gun,' he said. 'I'll 'ave thet too—'e can chuck it in to make up the bargain. It'll come in' andy f'r shootin' gulls.'

Van Noppen hesitated a moment, but finally handed over the rifle with a box of ammunition which the hobbledehoy produced from his pocket, and the pair went ashore just as the *Luck and Charity* floated. Voogdt watched them start on their homeward journey and then handed the notes to me. 'The fifty I owe you,' he said. 'The hundred per cent. interest will follow later, I fancy,' and before I could say a word, he had gone forward and was rousing out the other two to help cast off from the wharf.

Once outside the breeze fell light, and we drifted aimlessly. Off the Weilingen, Voogdt amused himeslf by bringing up the rifle and shooting at the razorbills on the water round us.

'Don't do that, you bird-killing Cockney,' I said.

He wheeled round.

'Who's killing birds, you fool? I haven't touched a bird, and don't mean to. I'm trying the range of this kid's toy. I must have been over two hundred yards from the man who potted at me, and this fool thing won't carry half that distance.' He paused, looking thoughtfully out across the water. 'What a game it is,' he said slowly. 'Fifty pounds out of a labourer's pocket to salve the leg of a coasting hand! It all points the same way. Cheyne talks of losses, whilst Ward is banking big money. Both they and the German crowd lie like steam, and both are very anxious to avoid inquiry into their business. Cheyne doesn't like sacking men. Why? Because it means employing new ones. And the Germans try and shoot a man for asking a simple question, and then come and tell lies and pay up hard money to square it. Why, again? To keep strangers—the police—out of the way of their wharf. What other points have they in common, Jem?'

'Well, they both open tin sheds and do the same class of general trading business in the same district,' I said.

'That's true.' He seemed to ponder on my rather obvious suggestion. 'That's true. But why the secrecy, and the shooting? And where do the profits come in?'

'Beats me,' I said briefly, looking over the side at the birds. As I watched a tiny catspaw broke the glassy surface of the water like anyone breathing on a window-pane. 'And here comes a fair breeze, so we shall have something better to do than sit here and cackle and vex our brains. Ease that sheet a bit, Austin, and then get a cup of tea.'

After the first few puffs it blew steady, and by the time tea was over I had half-a-mind to take in the topsail. However, we were only for Southampton, and I thought that by carrying it we should save a tide, and very fortunate it was for us I did, for we had a bad scare before we rounded the Nab lightship next evening.

Three or four pilot cutters were cruising about off Dungeness, and with them was one small steamboat, slowly doing the same aimless round. She had the appearance of an old tug, being very shabby and narrower in the beam than the great modern ocean towing boats. I pointed her out to Voogdt and drew his attention to her shape.

'She'd be faster than the modern broad-breasted tug?' he suggested.

'Faster, yes. But a modern tug 'ud pull this one backwards whilst she went full steam ahead.'

'That's be funny to see,' he said. 'Suggestion for a *fête maritime*—tug-o'-war between two tugs. What's she doing here, think?'

'Brought down a crowd of Channel pilots to wait for upward-bound vessels, I expect.'

That was about six o'clock. Past Dungeness we laid our course for the Owers light, and I went below to catch a short nap, leaving Voogdt in charge. At a quarter-past eight I was waked by his usual signal—three bumps with his heel on the deck above my head—and went up the stair, yawning.

'What's the row?' I asked.

'Something's gone wrong astern of us,' he said. 'I saw the lights of a steamer there ten minutes ago, and now she's disappeared.'

I got behind the wheel and peered out through the darkness—dark as the inside of a bag, it was—but not a sign of any steamer's lights could I see. The breeze had freshened, and we were slipping along at a good rate, and the sea just lively enough to give a pleasant rise and fall here aft. Shoreward a blur of light on the sky showed where Brighton lay, but the town itself was below the horizon and not another light was visible.

'Are you sure you saw her?' I asked.

'Positive. Overhauling us, she was. I could see all three of her lights not ten minutes ago.'

I stared again, but could make out nothing, and turned on Voogdt, rather annoyed.

'What d'ye want me to do?' I asked.

'That's for you to decide. I called you on deck for instructions. I tell you I saw her as plainly— My God, she's on us! Shout! Shout!'

She was right on top of us, no lights showing, and ploughing through it like a liner. My heart went into my mouth, and we shouted at the top of our voices, hoarse with alarm, dragging at the wheel like maniacs. For one moment despair succeeded despair, for Voogdt lost his head and was shoving the wheel hard-a-port, to luff, whereas I saw our only chance was to wear ship. He being at the wheel had the start of me, and the *Luck and Charity's* bows had commenced to swing shorewards before I could tear the wheel from his hands and jam it over hard-a-starboard with all my force. We were just in time: the steamer went by us at a good ten knots, actually grazing our stern as she passed.

'Kiah and Rance were on deck shivering in their shirts by this time, and Voogdt cut short my abuse for his stupidity.

'Never mind that now. We aren't out of the wood yet. Tell 'Kiah and Rance to pull on some clothes quick and come on deck again, top speed.'

'What d'ye mean?' I asked.

'That was deliberate, man,' he said, excitedly. 'Didn't you see their look-out? He was crouching in the bows. I saw his figure against that patch of light in the sky. They were trying to run us down; and they may be back any minute, and here we are with all our lights to guide 'em.'

He flung his coat over the binnacle and ran forward, extinguished the side-lights, and was back in less than half-a-minute. 'We must get the dinghy overside.'

'What for?'

'To save my skin, since you don't seem to care about your own. Here's Rance. Take the wheel, Rance. Your look-out,

'Kiah, and keep your eyes open. There's a foreigner with his lights doused trying to run us down. Watch out, 'Kiah, for God's sake. You watch too, Rance. She may come round and have another try at us astern. Come on, West, bear a hand.'

'You're mad,' I said.

'Very likely. Move, all the same.'

I made some other foolish protest, but he wasted no words in answer, only disappearing into our cabin. When he came out he had a bundle of blue lights and rockets in one hand and the little rifle in the other. The bundle he threw into the dinghy, then brought the rifle to his hip, pointing straight at me.

'Mad am I,' he said excitedly. 'Call it so, to save time. I tell you straight, I'm mad enough to shoot even you, Jem, if you don't help all you can. You'll be dead, anyhow, if that boat comes back. Come, help me with the dinghy. That's better. Overside with her. Half-a-minute—a match. Now, over she goes.'

The dinghy floated away behind us, a mixed heap of rockets and coloured fires sputtering and blazing on her bottom boards.

'Now shout,' said Voogdt. 'Shout like fury—at the top of your voice. Rance—'Kiah: shout, men! Come back to the wheel, Jem. We may want to be extra nippy there in a minute or two. Now shout again.'

We shouted together, again, and yet again—poor attempts to wake the appalling emptiness of the night. The wind caught our voices from our very mouths and whirled the cries ineffectually away to leeward. Astern the dinghy blazed fainter and fainter as we left her farther behind, and then suddenly went out. Her last flare showed distinctly the bows of the darkened steamer that cut her down, and I admit I felt as sick as a man could feel.

'There goes our last chance,' said Voogdt despairingly. 'Stop shouting. It'll only help them to find us and when they do, the game's up.' He picked up the little rifle again. 'I'll give that look-out a flea in his ear, though . . . What's that?'

Away to the southward a rocket leaped, pricking into the night like a red-hot needle.

'Thank God!' he said fervently. 'Somebody's seen the flare. 'Send it's a King's ship. Get another blue light to show when we see 'em close, Jem.'

It was a King's ship—four King's ships, in fact—torpedo boats at night exercises. They came up hand over fist, and Voogdt answered their inquiries through our megaphone.

'Just been run into by a steamer goin' down Channel . . . Leakin' streams . . . One o' you stand by us so far as the Nab, will 'ee? . . . We'm in a sinkin' condition . . . No, us don't want t' leave 'er.'

The might of England, speaking through another megaphone, was reassuring, if scornful.

'What do you expect if you go barging about all night without lights?' queried a clear voice with acerbity. 'You slovenly fishermen are the curse of the Channel.

Voogdt whipped his coat off the binnacle, and set about relighting the side-lamps. Since we were sinking, the voice went on, a torpedo boat would stand by us, and did, taking no notice whatever of our shouted thanks when we parted company at the Nab light-vessel.

'A nice cheery trade, this,' Voogdt grumbled, as we bowled along past Spithead. 'When they can't shoot you ashore they try and run you down at sea. I saw that look-out man against the sky as clearly as I see you now. And I'll tell you another thing: that indecision of ours at the wheel saved us. When that chap saw our bows swing shorewards, theirs swung after us. If you'd wore ship as you wanted to without a hitch they'd have followed us in that direction and cut us in two, sure as fate. Next time the *Luck and Charity* goes to sea she goes armed. I'll see to that. I tell you that was a carefully schemed plot to wipe us out. Why were they waiting for us at Dungeness else?'

'What d'ye mean?' I asked.

'Why, you blind mole, that steamer was the one you drew

my attention to as being an old tug. Pilots be hanged! She was chosen for her old-fashioned build. "What narrow beam you've got, grandmamma." "The better to chase you with, my dear." But what a noble service is the King's Navee, Jem, eh? I've never fully appreciated it before.'

CHAPTER IX

OF CURIOSITY REWARDED

VOOGDT kept his promise about going armed when next he went to sea, and when he spread his purchases out upon the cabin table the place looked like an artillery museum. There was a condemned Mauser rifle, its barrel drilled out smooth to convert it into a cheap shotgun; a Martini; two clumsy great navy revolvers; and a little Browning repeater with a clip of cartridges in its handle and a long-heeled barrel that suggested some snarling beast with its ears back as it lay across the top of the fist that held it. As for ammunition, I should think the heap of packages on the table would have filled a bucket. I laughed at the array.

'What on earth are you going to do with those things?' I asked.

'Bust somebody if we get any more funny business,' he said grimly. 'Fifteen pounds that lot's cost me, and I don't spend money like that for nothing. Happen the next boat that tries to run us down may get her paint chipped.

'Don't kill yourself or any of the rest of us, that's all,' I said, and left him stowing away his weapons out of sight.

The cargo awaiting us was of pig-iron this time. There were only twenty-five tons of the stuff, but neither Voogdt nor myself were moved to offer any remarks about it, only setting mechanically about the usual business of emptying and refilling the hold, our minds still full of our recent experiences. Knowing no one ashore, neither of us said anything about the matter to any outsiders, and if Rance and 'Kiah talked they were probably disbelieved, sailors' tales not going for much in seaport towns. At all events, no reporters called on us for information, and by the time the monotonous business of loading was over I felt rather inclined to be ashamed of the warlike preparations concealed below.

The breeze still held, and leaving Southampton on the morning tide we reached Dungeness about two in the afternoon. The steamboat was still there, steaming round and round at half-speed in a five or six mile circle, three big pilot-cutters cruising up and down to keep her company.

'We'll give them an exhibition,' Voogdt said to me. 'Can you shoot, Rance?'

Rance pronounced himself something wonderful as a marksman, and Voogdt fetched up a couple of empty bottles and all the contents of the armoury. The weapons were handed out, the bottles thrown overboard, and we woke the sandy flats of Dungeness with a noble banging. I think one bottle got away, and the other must have cost several shillings' worth of ammunition before it was sunk, but the noise and splashing of the bullets were impressive. The people on the steamer took no notice whatever of us and we saw no more of her; but whether she feared our artillery, or whether there were too many craft about for her to have another try at us, or whether perhaps Voogdt was mistaken in her altogether, it was impossible to say. Whatever the cause, she left us alone, and we made a quick and uneventful voyage, arriving back at Terneuzen inside of four days.

The first thing we noticed was that the German settlement was in a state of great activity. No less than three barges lay at their half-built wharf, one of them spritsailed after the Medway pattern, and the other two clumsy Scheldt pontoons, only fit for towing. Thirty or forty labourers ashore were building a second embankment inside the first, and another cargo of deals and corrugated iron was being unloaded from the river barges. When we reached our own wharf Cheyne was waiting for us, cheerful as a cricket.

'Busy times down yonder,' I remarked.

'They're going in for explosives,' he said. 'That's the factory coming ashore in pieces. They're going to put up the sheds between the two embankments.'

He was very full of their business, and on the best of terms with himself and all the world. 'Decent chap that Van Noppen— their manager. Generally has grub with me evenings;' and he went on to describe the German company and their trade as though he were a partner.

'They're doing a *bona-fide* business, then?' I said, surprised.

'Yes, of course,' he answered casually, and then paused. I could have bitten my tongue off as I saw him gradually realising what my words implied. 'Of course they're doing a *bona-fide* business,' he said slowly. 'What the—do you mean by saying that?'

'I didn't mean anything,' I said lamely.

'Then what d'ye say it for? D'you mean to imply that we're not doing a *bona-fide* business as well—you? Haven't you been told off once already about that?'

I tried to wriggle out of it by assuring him I believed the Axel Trading Company to be the soundest of concerns, but nothing would pacify him. He was scared, or had lost his temper, or both, and like a fool went on bully-ragging me when he had better have held his tongue. At last my temper wore thin, too, and I blurted out the truth.

'Since you want to know, I reckon you're doing very fishy business,' I said angrily. 'I didn't mean to let it slip, and I don't mean to mention it outside. I owe some sort of duty to my employers, even whilst you're one of 'em. So you can reckon on my holding my tongue so long as I'm drawing your pay—and that'll be just as long as you keep civil, I tell you straight. I know these voyages don't pay, and I know you're making money. I know Ward invested ten thousand pounds in a Japanese loan recently. In fact, I know a lot more than you think, and the best thing you can do is shut your head and thank heaven I can keep mine shut as well.'

He tried to answer, but literally he couldn't speak. It was

strange to watch him lick his lips and twitch about the mouth trying to get the words out. He just mumbled something inaudible that might or might not have been an apology, and then turned on his heel and went back to his office without a word.

'What d'ye make of that?' I asked Voogdt.

'Isn't he in a funk? "Fishy business" is right, anyhow. I never saw a man look so sick. As to the Germans'—he shrugged his shoulders—'either legitimate business is their line, or they're cleverer rogues than our lot. The explosive manufacture wheeze is a great idea—accounts for choice of position and everything else, besides keeping inquisitive strangers away.'

I had to go to the office within the hour and Voogdt insisted on accompanying me. 'It's no time to play with a bear, just after you've been stirring him up with a pole,' he said, so we walked up the wharf together, and he waited outside the office whilst I went in.

Cheyne, writing letters, looked up as I entered, and I stated my business briefly and cleared out. All through the interview neither of us said a word more than the business required; and Cheyne's manner might be described rather as cowed than merely civil. All the starch was gone out of him; you could scarcely recognise in him the cheerful, easy manager who had greeted us an hour or two before.

'He'll go on the loose,' I said to Voogdt on our way back.

'Not till he's come and had another talk with you,' he said. 'You've frightened him too much. Is Ward here still?'

'I forgot to ask.'

'Then run back and ask now. I'll wait.'

I stuck my head in round the door. 'Mr Ward still here?' I said.

'He went back three days ago.'

'I, guessed that,' Voogdt said, when I told him. 'Cheyne's writing him now, reporting your conversation and asking for instructions.'

'You know a lot, don't you?' I said, inclined to be sceptical.

'Ward's the controlling brain of this show. If he was in

Terneuzen Cheyne would have been up there by this time. I'll bet anything you like a code wire meaning "Be on your guard," or "Suspicions aroused," precedes the letter.'

We had reached the ship and were going aboard over the sloping plank gangway, which, having been used as a platform for ballasting, was caked with mud. A little rain the night before had made it very slippery to walk on, and it was necessary to tread delicately.

'You're good at guessing,' I said, picking my steps with care.

'Up to a certain point,' said he, putting a foot on the plank behind me. 'But every time I get past these elementary questions I stumble—' There was a scuffle and a bump, and I turned round to find him sitting on the planks. The fall had startled him. His mouth was open and he stared in a strange, set way.

'Hurt?' I asked.

'Hurt? No. I stumbled over something, I was going to say. And I did—I stumbled over something . . . Good Lord! Good Lord, I say.'

'Well, get up, if you aren't hurt.'

His face made me nervous, he looked so queer. I thought perhaps he'd injured his back.

'Are you sure you aren't hurt?'

'No, I tell you. Of course I'm not hurt. Shut up. You worry me.'

'Get up, then.'

'No hurry.' He slid his hands over the planks on which he sat and then looked at his muddied palms like a man stunned, or waking from a sleep. I felt sure he must be seriously injured, and got back on the gangway to help him to his feet.

'Here, let me help you up.'

'I'm all right,' he said. 'All right. All right. All right. Sound in wind and limb. Can't you understand English?' He jumped up and ran lightly aboard. 'Does that look like serious damage?'

'You looked funny.'

'You'll look funny when I've done with you. My sainted aunt! Jem West, I've tumbled.'

'I saw you.'

'You blithering precisian. Don't you know what a *double entente* means? I stumble, I said, and I stumbled. I've tumbled, I say. In my tumble I tumbled.' His eyes were dancing, his speech was jerky with excitement, half hysterical. 'You simple-minded, one-idead old thickhead. Let's see how much I can tell you without your comprehension. Did you see me tumble?'

'Not actually. You were behind me.'

'Well, I did, didn't I? You know I've tumbled?'

'Of course I do.'

'You saw me actually sitting on it, didn't you?'

'On that plank. Yes.'

'On that muddy plank. That's what I mean by it. It. See?'

'Look here,' I said, 'you've jolted your spine, or something, and it's made you a bit silly. You go and lie down for a spell.'

He literally lay down on the dirty deck and rolled roaring with laughter. Then he got up and looked at his filthy clothes.

'And now no more of these revels,' he said. 'I won't deny I felt a bit hysterical for once. Now let's get about it—our cargo, in ballast—and hey for England, home and beauty!' And not another word could I get out of him.

He worked like a demon, but his fit of silence never left him. When we got away it was just the same: a grunt for yes or no, and not a word of any kind beyond. The voyage was longer than usual, to Yealmpton, in Devonshire, where the *Luck and Charity* was launched; but he made no answer to my remarks on that or any other subject, and 'Kiah and Rance were the only company I had on the voyage.

When we reached port, and almost before we tied up in the Yealm River, Voogdt came on deck in his shore clothes.

'I want a run ashore,' he said. He hadn't spoken as many words in five days.

'Are you going to desert again?' I remembered that a fit of silence had preceded his leaving us at Guernsey.

He shook his head. 'Back tomorrow,' he said shortly. 'Perhaps tonight. For certain by tomorrow night.'

For once I was almost glad to be rid of him, and got about my business ashore, glad to have someone to talk to for a change. Night came, but no Voogdt; he was missing all next day, and I was reading in my bunk late at night before he returned. Then I heard him come aboard, cross the deck and descend the companion, and put down my book to see him enter.

I thought he was drunk. He looked it, exactly: flushed, his eyes wild, his speech incoherent; and the first thing he did was to put a gold-topped magnum on the cabin table and rout out two tumblers from a locker.

'Been painting the town red?' I asked.

He made no answer, but opened the champagne, smothering the report with a handkerchief wrapped round the cork, and handed one tumbler to me. 'To you, partner,' he said, and drained the other at a gulp. 'That's good. That's the first today.'

'Looks like it,' I said dryly.

''Tis, all the same. Things are oft not what they seem. Do I look drunk?'

'You do.'

'So I am.' The only sign of sobriety about him was that he kept his voice low. 'Drunk with joy. A most intoxicating tipple. Oh! I am pleased with myself, James . . . Not that I've any reason to be. These past wasted months . . . The blind mole I've been! To think that Accident should do what mighty Reason could not achieve. Here's to Accident and Reason, Luck and Charity, Voogdt and West.' He poured out and disposed of another tumbler of wine.

'Where've you been?'

'To Plymouth—fool that I am. I ought to have gone miles inland—miles and miles and miles from any seaport town. But how was I to know? And time was short. I've found out where the profits come from, Jem.'

'You haven't!' I said, jumping up so that I hit my head against a deck-beam.

'I have. I've got the company in my vest pocket. Thousands of pounds, Jem. Thousands. And I think we're entitled to a partnership in the show.'

'Has it anything to do with the shooting business and our being nearly run down?'

'The shooting, almost for certain, and perhaps the other thing. 'Tisn't all clear to me yet, and I'm not going to tell you much until it is. But we've got the Axel Trading Company by the short hairs, and there's enough profits hanging to the business for us to have a share without hurting anybody. And that share I mean to have.'

'Is it very fishy?' I asked.

'It isn't too fishy for me,' he said. 'And I think I can guarantee it won't hurt your conscience. In fact, I really can't see that it's dishonest at all. It's smart dealing. That's Ward, of course. Cheyne hasn't the brains. But I can't see that it hurts anybody. Enough of it. I've finished talking for the present. Are we loaded?'

'We shall be by tomorrow evening.'

'If we aren't, we'll sail all the same. There's no further need to keep up this cargo nonsense. It's only a waste of money. That business'll have to be rearranged. We must get back to Terneuzen as hard as we can lick to meet Ward.'

'He isn't there.'

'He will be before we are. I sent him a wire today that'll give him palpitation of the heart. Oh ho! there'll be a sitting in council when we arrive. Now finish the fizz and turn in. Not another word do I say about it till we're out at sea. The very deck-beams might shout it aloud. I was so scared I shouldn't get back to you—that I should be killed in a railway accident or something of that sort—that I posted you a letter before I left Plymouth to put you on the track, in case of my demise, and now I'm nervous about that letter. You'll get it in the morning—and mind you do get it, too. Goodnight, partner.'

A letter card addressed in Voogdt's writing awaited me at the agent's next day, and I took it back to him unopened.

'Since you're not dead,' I said in explanation, as I handed it to him.

'It's your letter, strictly speaking,' he said. 'You're too conscientious. Stick it up in the pipe-rack and open it when we're past the Mewstone tonight. That'll please both parties.'

Seeing he treated it so lightly, I forgot all about it in the course of the day's work, and it was late that evening, and we were well past the Start, before Voogdt, who was at the wheel, recalled it to me.

'Don't you want to read your letter?' he asked slyly.

'I'd forgotten it.' I ran below, took it from the rack and tore off the edges. It seemed at first sight to be a collection of initials.

'DEAR J.,—Ask a chemist what WO2 means.

'A. V.'

I went back on deck with it in my hand.

'What does WO2 mean?' I asked.

'Ask a chemist, I told you. Ask Ward. I wonder whether he'd shoot you or poison you if you did?'

'Don't talk like a fool. Ward's an honest man.'

'I think so, too; but, mind you, it's no good blinking the fact that if we were out of the way it'd mean big money in his pocket. These things make one ponder. That running down business—I'm not saying it had anything to do with our people, because I'm pretty well sure it hadn't—but it would have been a fine thing for them if it had come off. We happen to represent Ward's one mistake. I suppose you were down on your luck when he met you, and he took you for an ordinary coasting skipper. As for me, I'm not at all the sort of man they want poking round their wharf. The average coasting Jack wouldn't have given any trouble; he's too stupid to try smelling into his employer's affairs, as I do. There's the result of your hand. Tear it up in little bits and throw it overboard.'

'I'm as wise as I was before,' I said, doing as he told me.

'You've only to go to a chemist to know as much as I do, and then there'd be two more in their secret. Up to now I fancy it's confined to five people.'

'Who's the fifth?'

'That solicitor clerk of theirs must be in it, I think. Carwithin, he's called. To think how they've been skimming the cream off the market these last eighteen months. This German company means complications, though. Van Noppen's streets ahead of Cheyne. That explosive pretext is noble.'

'I'm still in the dark,' I said. 'Do get it off your chest straight, instead of hinting like this. You muddle me. Where do the profits come in, and what is WO2?'

'WO2, my son, is the chemical formula for wolframite or tungsten dioxide,' he said. 'Its commercial value is about two hundred and forty pounds per ton. And that mud we've been ballasting with is almost pure WO2. Now do you see the game?

'Reckoning in the *Olive Leaf* and the *Kismet*, I calculate they're turning over about fifteen thousand pounds a week. Think of it! Of course all this secrecy means awful waste but they can't be netting much less than three or four thousand a week at the worst. And that's been going on for eighteen months! Get your mind attuned to those figures and you'll begin to understand why the Germans shot at me and why we must watch Ward and Cheyne like sworn enemies until we know them better.'

I breathed hard, fairly staggered for once. I couldn't realise such figures. Four thousand a week—two hundred thousand a year—over a quarter of a million pounds in eighteen months. Our footy little freights, thirty pounds a voyage, or so, shrivelled to nothing in the face of such a sum, and I said as much aloud.

'Four thousand a week! Three small boats and rent to pay out of it—a hundred and twenty at the outside. What a profit!'

'Not so fast,' Voogdt interrupted. 'That four thousand is all profit. I tell you their turnover is nearer fifteen thousand a week. I've allowed two-thirds of that for working expenses.'

'But that's nonsense. How on earth can they possibly spend more than a hundred and fifty a week? They couldn't do it, man.'

'Ah!' said Voogdt. 'But there's one item you don't take into account, and I'll bet it's monstrous—awful.'

'What item?'

'Waste. Ghastly waste. Think a minute of all the precautions they've taken to ensure secrecy. Do you think they dare sell those heaps of stuff just where we dump them on the ballast quays? Not much. That stuff's rubbish—just mud ballast—till they've got it stowed away in their inland warehouses. They daren't even look anxious about it; it lies on those quays for anyone to take away. I expect it often is taken away by barges. Who knows how many small craft round the coast at this minute are carting it about in all good faith as ballast, never dreaming there's a little fortune under their hatches? No, you mark my words: we shall find waste is the biggest item against the firm; and heart-breaking waste, too, for they daren't put out a finger to prevent it.'

'What's the good of the stuff?' I asked.

'It's used for hardening steel—especially engineers' saws. Rum stuff, it is. You know when ordinary steel gets hot it loses its temper and goes soft. Well, tungsten steel don't. Friction only makes it harder, so that saws made of it cut the better for use, and don't wear out half as fast. That's what sends up the price. When wolframite was only used for chemical purposes you could buy it for about twenty-five quid a ton. Then some genius discovered its effect on steel, and its cost jumped almost a thousand per cent. at once. And it's used for electric filaments too. I wonder what effect this supply of ours has had upon the market so far?'

'What are you going to do when we reach Terneuzen?'

'Play with my cards face upwards on the table. Tell them plainly how much we know, and ask for a sixth share between us. That's not greedy: there's enough and to spare, and since we're doing the work and standing the risks, I think we're entitled to our whack.'

'Who d'ye mean by "we"?' I asked.

'You and myself. I did think of letting 'Kiah in, but not Rance. Even 'Kiah—he's a good chap, but I doubt whether sharing profits is likely to do him any good. He might only lose his head and play the fool with the money. What do you think about him? Wouldn't it be wiser to give him a decent rise in screw and put away good bonuses for him from time to time without his knowledge?'

'Seems to me you're busy counting your chickens before they're hatched,' I said. 'Better wait till you've got your share before you start spending it.'

'Maybe; though I think we're safe to get decent terms. But, as you pertinently remark, there's nothing can be settled till we've reached Terneuzen.

I turned in, but of course I couldn't sleep. For a couple of hours I lay awake figuring out the results of the discovery. Ward and Miss Lavington—and the Brand girl, too—came into my mind, and the more I thought of them the less I liked the notion of forcing them to accept us as partners. They'd always treated me well, and it seemed a scurvy way to repay them.

Then Voogdt. I'd always liked the man—liked him from our first meeting, when, dusty and hungry and cheerful, he had thrown his broken boots into Exmouth Dock and philosophised over them. He'd been a good shipmate to me, and I had been glad to know he'd benefited in pocket and health by cruising with me. Now that was all altered—turned upside-down. Here was my friend, a joyous-hearted pauper, proposing to take my employers by the throats, so to speak, and wring money out of them, money that he wanted me to share. It was too much of an inversion of things to please me, and I couldn't pretend I liked it. He'd talked of 'Kiah being spoiled by money: how would money react on him?

At last I pushed open the skylight and called him.

'Wheel ho! Voogdt.'

'Hello, yourself.'

'I don't approve of this business. It's blackmail.'

'Quite right,' he answered. 'So it is. And I'm going to do it.'

'I ain't,' I said. 'I stand out. Where's your philosophy, you who scorn property?'

'Money isn't property,' he said. 'Money's a tool. I never objected to tools—things to do things with. Scythe, spade, plane, ships, machinery—I love 'em all. It's clothes and furniture, houses, farms and land make me tired. They'd weigh me down, man. But money! Money's the grandest tool of all. Property—go to! It's fluid energy—compressible energy. It annihilates space and time, makes war and peace, makes grass to grow, builds ships and houses for fools to live in. With it I can carry the labour of a thousand men bottled in a scrap of paper in my vest pocket. No, money's good enough for me. Call it property, energy, a tool, what you will, I'm out after it this trip. And I'm going to get it.'

I slammed down the skylight, conscious of a crick in my neck, turned in again and managed to catch an hour's uneasy nap before change of watch.

CHAPTER X

OF A PARTNERSHIP IN CRIME

Besides the distaste I had conceived for the whole business, I was naturally inclined to be anxious about the reception we were to get at Terneuzen. If the German company could find it worth their while to try to run us down and shoot at Voogdt, what were we to expect from our own people when we came demanding a share in the concern? I had never liked Voogdt's habit of poking his nose into their business, and now they would be sure to think me a partner in his precious attempt at blackmail. The worst of it was that I couldn't pull out very well. If I refused to stand by Voogdt, that didn't prevent him using his knowledge. If we had a row about it subsequent inquiries might arise, or suspicions be roused on the part of 'Kiah or Rance; and if I went straight to the company and repudiated Voogdt altogether, for aught I know he might be shot at by somebody else, and this time with better aim—and I liked him a lot too well for that. In a word, I didn't know what to do. I couldn't persuade him to lie low and do nothing; I couldn't quarrel with him; I couldn't take the company's side against him, and yet I didn't want to be his partner in the matter. So I did the next best thing: said nothing at all. This I was the more able to do, for Voogdt took the whole conduct of affairs out of my hands from the moment we landed at Terneuzen.

I had no mind to complain of that. His brains were worth double mine; his was the discovery, and his the right to exploit it, but Cheyne bitterly resented his attitude of command, and tricked as he had been by his antagonist from the very start, I admit he had some of my sympathy.

Voogdt, in the highest spirits, met sulks with light chaff, and his manner, a blend of good temper and condescension, would have irritated a saint. It drove Cheyne to the point of ferocity. Even as he tried again and again to address me as the principal member on our side, so Voogdt persisted throughout all their first conversation in treating him with patronising politeness, as though regarding him only as an agent of that more worthy antagonist, Ward.

All this took place early on a rain-swept morning off the wharf. Cheyne, dressed in slovenly fashion, with a coloured kerchief about his neck in place of a collar, and a general air of frowsy sleep under his dripping mackintosh, came off to us in a boat from the shore, and greeted me sullenly.

"Morning,' he said. 'Come below, will you? I want a word with you.'

When Voogdt followed us downstairs Cheyne looked at him savagely.

'What d'you want?' he demanded.

'To hear this word of yours with the skipper. Don't look so sulky, my dear sir. We're partners, you must know. There's our registered trade-mark.'

He pointed to the little looking-glass over the piperack. On it was written, apparently with the corner of a cake of soap, the formula WO2 in letters six inches high. Cheyne went livid.

'You fool!' he said savagely. 'Anybody might have looked in through the skylight,' and he rubbed the letters into indistinguishable blurred streaks with his fingers before he sat down again. 'Now out with it,' he said. 'What's your price?'

'Are you empowered to deal?' Voogdt asked sharply.

'Of course I am.'

'I don't see that there's any "of course" about it,' said Voogdt. 'I understand Mr Ward and Miss Lavington are the largest shareholders, and I prefer to deal with principals. All the same, it may save time to tell you that our price is a sixth share in the concern. You can mention that to Mr Ward, and if he consents he can come and say so.'

'A sixth share! And if we don't consent?'

'Then Messrs. Voogdt & West start in opposition to you within a week.'

'That'd be a terrible blow, wouldn't it?' Cheyne tried to sneer. 'What harm could you do us, with your one twopenny-ha'penny boat?'

Voogdt leaned over and tapped him on the shoulder.

'We should be the worst opponents you ever had,' he said. 'And shall I tell you why? Because we don't want a lot. Three full cargoes, or four at most, dumped the other side of the water, and then sold openly, would make us and finish you. Two hundred and forty tons at two hundred and forty quid and we retire from business with over fifty thousand pounds between us. Half of that's enough for my simple needs, and I think I can say the same for the skipper here.'

'You've got to find a market.' Cheyne objected.

'Advertisement'll do that. "To engineers and steel-founders. Two hundred and forty tons of wolframite for sale in sixty-ton lots. Purchasers can view on quayside at Shoreham, Southampton, Portsmouth and Newhaven." That would suit your book, wouldn't it? That and the consequent inquiries into the source of the stuff. It's no go, Master Cheyne. We've got you in a cleft stick, and you may as well climb down.'

Cheyne cursed us both roundly. 'You haven't thought the thing out yet,' he said. 'You don't know the losses. Besides, a lump like that would cause a drop in price immediately.'

'It wouldn't knock the bottom out of the market,' Voogdt said calmly. 'That'd happen later, when the deposits here became known. That one sale would be enough for us, and we should be able to retire from business. You needn't grumble, you know; you must have all made a decent pile in the last eighteen months. That's our weak point, I won't deny. The only way by which you can hurt us is by realising you've got enough and giving the show away yourselves. That would knock us out, I freely admit. You see I'm open with you. But you won't do it. Better take in two new partners. As to the losses, I'm not over-sanguine. I can guess what those losses mean pretty well; but we'll manage to cut some of them in future.'

'How?'

'That I'll tell you when the new partnership's in existence. Mr Ward's in Terneuzen, I suppose? Yes? Then you'd better go ashore again and arrange a meeting as soon as we land. No sense in wasting time.'

We got alongside the wharf after breakfast, and soon afterwards, looking through the cabin skylight, saw Ward's tall figure, accompanied by two women, hurrying along the embankment through the driving rain.

'He's brought the girls,' I said, in surprise.

'Bother!' said Voogdt. 'But perhaps it's just as well. May as well have all parties present.'

I watched them go into the office together, and shortly afterwards Cheyne called down to us to say they were expecting us.

Voogdt shook his head. 'Not much,' he said. 'We'll meet them on our own ground, here in the cabin. I'm shy of the whole lot of them since that scare the Germans gave me. Come aboard,' he called to Cheyne, 'and bring the others with you.'

That delayed them a little, but in a few minutes they all emerged from the office door in a little group and came hurrying down the wharf. We helped them across the gangway and into the cabin, where they sat down, and then we all sat and stared at each other without a word. I don't know which of the six of us was most embarrassed, but if anyone of them felt worse than myself I'm sorry for him.

I say 'him' advisedly, for neither of the two girls showed a trace of nervousness. When I made some bungling remark about the filthy weather and asked them if I should take their cloaks, Pamily Brand tittered aloud and then tried to look preternaturally solemn. As for Miss Lavington, she slipped off her dripping wraps with a smile and handed them to me as though she were entering the box of a theatre. That was their air; they might have been just onlookers at a play. I could understand it of the Brand girl, she being only a small shareholder, and besides, for all her ease of manner, I thought I saw the light of war in her eyes; but it gave me a good impression of Miss Lavington's nerves that she could be so tranquil and composed. As for me, I felt like a pickpocket caught in the act, and Cheyne looked hangdog enough to be my accomplice.

Ward led off, blinking curiously at Voogdt through his spectacles.

'Mr Voogdt? How do you do? I wish I could honestly say I was pleased to make your acquaintance.'

Voogdt nodded with a smile, not in the least perturbed.

'You may even come to that in time,' he said pleasantly. 'I'm sorry to be in the role of blackmailer on our first meeting, but I hope to prove myself a useful member of the syndicate later on. I'm glad to meet you, in any case. I've read that paper of yours on Emil Fischer and his work, and it interested me very much.'

The Brand girl peeped sideways wickedly at Ward to see how he took this form of attack, but he took no more notice of her than of Voogdt.

'Are we here to say pretty things to each other or to talk business?' he asked dryly. 'Are we to understand you ask a sixth share each?'

'No, no. One-sixth share between us.'

'And how much time do you give us for considering your offer?'

'No time at all. I'm sorry to hold a pistol at your heads in this way, but I needn't point out to you that this business is—well, somewhat precarious, need I?'

'Lord, no!' said Ward, with a half-comic half-rueful grimace. 'We are to understand, then, that your price is one-sixth share in this concern from this date?'

'That's so. We don't want to meddle with your accumulated profits. You've always treated us decently.'

'Thanks. Therefore you repay us by blackmailing us. And do you propose to continue running this boat in return for your sixth share?'

'I hadn't thought of that.' Voogdt hesitated, so I thought it my turn to cut in.

'Yes, we'll do that,' I said. 'We're prepared to go on acting under your instructions.'

Voogdt looked round at me with his chin stuck out.

'Not so fast,' he said. 'I'm making terms, not you. The present methods of trading are too wasteful. You'll all agree there?'

They all four assented.

'Then we must alter them a little. If my suggestions are impracticable—and we'll decide that by the views of the majority—then we go on as before. Now—yes, or no, please?'

'We'd like a few minutes to consider,' said Ward.

I got up, Voogdt following my lead at once.

'All right,' he said. 'You can have ten minutes,' and we went on deck together to await their decision.

After what seemed a long ten minutes Cheyne appeared at the companion, beckoning us, and we went below together.

'We've no choice but to consent,' Ward said, as soon as we were seated. 'D'you want anything in writing?'

'Does any partnership deed exist between you at present?' Voogdt asked. 'No? Then, speaking for myself, your word's good enough for me.'

'Let me say one thing,' I said. 'I'm not responsible for any share in this business, and I feel thoroughly ashamed of putting the screw on you in this way—'

'So you ought,' said Pamily Brand sharply, and Cheyne grunted some sort of chorus to her.

''Tisn't either of you I'm thinking of,' I went on. 'As for you, Cheyne, I'd rob you like a shot, and I don't suppose Miss Brand's loss as a small shareholder is anything to cry out about. But if it's any use apologising to you, Ward, and to Miss

Lavington, I do apologise most sincerely. And I won't touch a penny of this sixth share.'

'Then I shall bag the lot,' Voogdt said coolly. 'Don't you try and be a bigger fool than Nature made you, Jem West. They can afford it well, and we're going to be valuable partners to the firm.'

Ward said nothing, only wrinkling up his eyes and looking at me keenly—to see if I was in earnest, I suppose; but Miss Lavington unexpectedly took Voogdt's side.

'I think that's silly, Mr West,' she said, in her lazy way. 'We've quite made up our minds to paying in any case. In fact your friend might have insisted on a larger share, if he'd liked, and I don't see how we could have refused him. If anyone is entitled to share you are, after the discomfort of this winter's trading for us.' Ward nodded. 'I agree with Miss Lavington,' he said. 'You may take it from me, West, that I shall pay with much greater pleasure if I think you're getting a fair share.'

Both of them were evidently sincere, and I looked at Miss Brand to see if she agreed with them. She sniffed derisively.

'Nobody imagines you're at the bottom of this bother,' she said. 'You're too stupid. But since your partner wishes it'—she glowered at Voogdt—'I think you're entitled to a share in the proceeds.'

'Good enough,' I said. 'That's a majority. I accept the partnership.'

'And now,' Ward said, turning to Voogdt, 'we'd like to hear your suggestions.'

'The first suggestion is that we pay off the other two boats and run only the *Luck and Charity*. And the next is that we sack our two paid hands and ship Mr Cheyne here as first mate.'

That upset things at once. I couldn't see much sense in the suggestions myself but I knew Voogdt must have good reasons for them, so said nothing. Ward was silent too, and Miss Lavington only made a mild protest. But Pamily Brand was up in arms in a moment and Cheyne swore aloud. He'd be hanged if he was going coasting; he had enough to do where he was. When he'd done laying down the law, Ward cut in.

'Reasons?' he asked Voogdt.

'Two good reasons. Economy's the first. You've got three boats, and for a guess you're wasting two cargoes out of every three. Is that about the figure?'

'Very nearly.'

'Good. Then the *Luck and Charity* can save 'em all. Now West and myself know what we're doing, we can help in arranging the removals from the ports. One boat can distribute them better, too, and with less risk of suspicion. You've been planting the stuff too thickly. There must be heaps of it lying in nearly every port from Inverness to the Land's End. And you've got to wait your chance to touch it. All that means risk.'

'As if we didn't know that already,' said Cheyne contemptuously. 'How shall we be any better off if there's less heaps to choose from?'

'You forget there'll be no need hoodwinking your one crew. You and I and West between us can get the stuff shifted. With care, we shouldn't lose one cargo in four—that's better than two in three. And the *Luck and Charity* trading one week to Plymouth and the next to Sunderland won't get noticed as much as if she was going over the same ground month after month, as she is now.'

'That's sense,' said Ward. 'Now why discharge your men?'

'That's the same as the second reason for paying off the other boats. I was coming to that. We've no right to risk any lives but our own.'

Cheyne laughed aloud. 'Risking lives!' he cried. 'In the coasting trade! What a risk to be afraid of!'

Even Ward looked curious, and it was to him Voogdt addressed himself, disregarding Cheyne entirely.

'Don't you know of extra risks?' he asked. 'Would it surprise

you to know we've had a near shave of being intentionally run
down, and that I've had a bullet through my leg in this trade?'

I think Ward, like myself at first, thought Voogdt suffered
from illusions, for he turned to me for corroboration, and I
nodded and said it was quite true.

They made Voogdt tell the whole story, which he did very
well, and then Ward said he thought Voogdt's suggestions would
bear consideration. Again the girls agreed; but Cheyne said
nothing, which was just as well, since we were five to one against
him. Voogdt's tale had sealed the partnership. There was no
longer any feeling of divided interests. I was glad to see how
Ward's opinion of him had altered.

'We shall have to devise ways and means, Mr Voogdt,' he
said. 'I'm afraid you'll find some difficulty in acting as agents
ashore as well as sailors afloat. Besides, who's to look after the
business here?'

'I'll do that,' said Pamily Brand, in an instant.

'That you won't,' I said as quickly. 'This is no place for a
girl with those German sheds handy.'

'They wouldn't hurt me,' she said.

'They won't get the chance. No, if you want to help, take
charge of the Snow Hill office and send Carwithen here.'

Ward laughed. 'I must really congratulate you on your knowledge of the business. How on earth did you know about
Carwithen?'

I indicated Voogdt with a nod of the head.

'He's my general information bureau,' I said. 'I think he
knows your business backwards.'

'There's one thing I don't know,' Voogdt said. 'I don't know
how you discovered this stuff here. That's puzzled me more
than a little. Would you mind satisfying my curiosity?'

'Not at all,' said Ward, and told us the whole story, the others
interrupting every now and then with comments or corrections.

It seemed that Cheyne was the accidental means of the
discovery. He'd been at Ghent in one of Warbeck's vessels

loading for Rio, and whilst his boat was waiting to be let out of Terneuzen Locks he slipped ashore to have a final drink before they sailed. By some means or other—I suppose he'd been saying farewell more than once—he dropped his watch over the embankment, and, flying open as it fell, the inner case got coated with mud. The watch, a good English lever, went on working, so instead of wiping the mud off, he used to show it about as a curiosity—letting people see what a fine watch he had, to work with dried mud all over its vitals. On his return from that voyage he was holidaying in Birmingham and called at Mason College to take his cousin, Pamela Brand, out to lunch. Miss Lavington and Ward joined them, and with two students and one professor present the talk of the table drifted round to chemistry. Cheyne, thinking to puzzle Ward, scraped a little of the mud from inside his watch and defied Ward to tell him what it was. Ward took it away, analysed it and pronounced it to be nearly pure wolframite.

Even then Cheyne only laughed at him. He was too big a fool to appreciate the value of the discovery. But the others soon convinced him of that, and, once persuaded, it was his suggestion that they should try to do a deal in the stuff. His methods were crude: at first he was all for just loading Miss Lavington's steamers with the mud and selling it openly. However, they soon saw that game wouldn't answer, and Ward and Cheyne between them devised the plan of hiring small coasters and shipping the mud as ballast. Miss Lavington sold her steamers to provide the necessary capital, and for eighteen months all had gone well, and would have been going well even now if it hadn't been for Ward's mistaking me for the average coasting skipper, with a taste for liquor to boot.

'Do you mean to tell me that all this embankment is solid wolframite?' Voogdt asked, amazed.

'Far from it. It only occurs in patches, so far as we've been able to discover. Of course we couldn't attempt anything like a survey. That would have attracted attention at once. When I first came out here to look into the matter I pretended to be botanising and got most of my specimens for analysis by pulling up weeds and sampling the earth that clung to their roots. Give me a scrap of paper, will you?'

I tore the fly-leaf out of a book from the little shelf over his head, and on it he drew a rough map of the wharf, embankment, and lock-gates, with part of the pasture fields behind him.

'There,' said he, roughly shading on one or two patches with his pencil. 'You can see the deposits are rather scattered. The bank on this side the lock-gates is nearly pure, but it was impossible to touch that with traffic passing at every hour of the day and night. Besides, we shouldn't have been able to take away canal embankments, of course. Thence it spreads in a fan shape into the fields behind, and then thins out and disappears. There are two other small patches between here and Terneuzen, but where these cut through the embankment we have taken care to repair the path and cover them with road metal. Then comes the deposit we're working—a large patch, almost as rich as that forbidden piece by the locks—and another lot crops out in the fields about a quarter of a mile west of us.'

'Now about the German sheds?' I asked.

Ward shook his head. 'I don't know. The moment we decided working here we stopped taking samples. There was more here than we should ever be able to take away, and if I'd gone on collecting specimens it woud have been certain to attract attention sooner or later. And from what you tell us they certainly don't encourage enquiries down there now. That's the worst of the business,' he burst out, impatiently. 'We daren't ask questions, or show curiosity, and all the time we're working in the dark, not knowing what other people are thinking of us. To think this shooting business could have happened to you here right on our ground, and that we were altogether ignorant of it!'

It may seem like wasted sympathy, for he was prosperous enough now; but I thought how he must have felt, those first few months, before the initial outlay had been recovered, and I felt downright sorry for the man, knowing what he must have gone through. He had thrown up his position; it was on his advice that Miss Lavington had parted with her capital to embark in the most risky enterprise ever heard of; and discovery, which might have taken place at any moment, would have meant financial ruin for both of them. I don't think she was the sort of woman to blame him if it had, but I wouldn't have been in his shoes at the time, for all that.

It must have been a maddening business take it all round, despite the big profits. Remembering Pamily Brand's 'I hate waste,' I began to make apologies for even her temper, for waste had been the keynote from the first. Waste of energy, waste of material and waste of money, under the most tantalising circumstances, often under their very noses. Time and again the mud-heaps had been taken away to sea by other boats as ballast just as Voogdt had guessed. Tons and tons had been removed by farmers' carts as a top dressing for land, and railway companies had dumped hundreds more over their embankments. Sometimes port by-laws had interfered with them—out-of-date rules and regulations prohibiting the removal of ballast from the quays by land. Worst of all, they never dared to show the slightest anxiety about the stuff. Ward described his emotions through one long summer's day at Looe, where he had gone to try and arrange for the removal of one consignment. In the morning he had worried because children, playing on the heap, were taking away the mud on their boots, but the afternoon brought him a sterner lesson of self-control. He had to sit and grin and bear it, whilst a gang of navvies shovelled the lot—five thousand pounds' worth of his property—down behind the piles and planks of a new quay extension.

Cheyne topped that story by instancing the three cargoes we had taken to Dartmouth in the past nine months, not one of which, he assured us, had come to hand.

On the whole, it was with mixed emotions that we contemplated our new partnership. The matter of paying off the other boats and men was left over for later discussion; and, the rain lessening a little, Ward and the girls returned to Terneuzen, whilst Cheyne and we two set about getting off hatches and preparing our hold for the first consignment of wolframite in which we had an interest.

CHAPTER XI

OF A LADYLIKE YOUNG PERSON

IT was queer to see the change of attitude on their part after Voogdt had told his tale about the shooting business. It was as though we were accepted as partners upon a friendly basis forthwith. I thought Pamily Brand held a little aloof from me personally, but she wasn't really unpleasant in any way, and as for Ward and Miss Lavington, they were as nice as they could be.

Cheyne sulked, certainly, but one could find excuses for him. He stood to lose most by the new arrangement, for Ward agreed with Voogdt about paying off the other boats—not at once, but each in turn, with an interval between them, so as not to excite remark—and it was decided that Cheyne should go to sea with us.

Small wonder he kicked at the prospect. Hard and fit though I was, I couldn't call the winter cruising a trifle, and I never remember looking forward to spring as I did that year. And Cheyne was anything but fit: a year and more of shore life, self-indulgence and fuddling had knocked him all to pieces, and he was flabby, soft as a woman. So he sulked, and Miss Brand was cool to me, apparently considering me responsible for this part of the arrangements. It wouldn't have been any good trying to lay the blame on Voogdt. He and she were hand in glove: she'd turned right round since his story was told, and in her eyes he couldn't do wrong now. Naturally, being the clever chap he was, and she a quick-tongued hussy enough, they often squabbled; but they took a delight in it and were only the better friends for every spirited quarrel. I believe she used to come aboard on purpose, and he'd turn her accusations

118

to chaff and her statements to nonsense, and draw her on about the Suffrage and the woman question till she was fit to swear.

I told her so one day when she was down watching us work and arguing with Voogdt. We were putting a patch in the foresail, and, as it was wet weather, were working in the cabin. The place was full of the crumbled heavy canvas and she had to stand by the door. First she started bossing about, of course. Our sewing was all wrong, according to her, but after a weak demonstration of how it ought to be done she took off the heavy leather sailmaker's palm, gave up her needle to Voogdt and started arguing about something else.

I forget what it was all about—something over my head, most likely—but Voogdt posed her with a remark she pretended wasn't worth answering.

'So I'll answer it as men answer their wives when they're worsted in argument,' she said. 'I'll swear. That saves mighty man the trouble of thinking. "Damned nonsense," he'd say, and call it an argument. And your argument is damned nonsense.'

I looked up from my sewing and told her how she reminded me of the kid breaking the teacup. Voogdt laughed aloud, and she turned on him in a flash.

'Who's mother?' she demanded.

'Oh ho! I know,' said he. 'And so do you, Miss B.Sc. She's a big, old lady is mother and her name begins with an N. You wait till she's got time to beckon to you. You'll get it. You'll find trouble waiting for you somewhere.'

That was his way of talking. I could make neither head nor tail of it, but Miss Brand seemed to understand well enough, for her face went crimson. But she stood her ground.

'I defy her,' she cried, laughing too, for all her flushed face. 'I defy her. Others she may discipline, but not me. I'm an educated woman. What's education for, if we can't shake off these chains? How about you, if it comes to that?'

I stared in astonishment, wondering what on earth she meant; but Voogdt took her up quickly enough.

'Time enough,' he said. 'Besides, I'm a looker-on by temperament.' Then he turned serious. 'I'm tainted, too. I've only half-a-lung on one side. Keep to the point: you talk of educated women; haven't there been any desertions from your ranks?'

'Dozens. The weaker vessels. We grow stronger by eliminating them. I shall never desert. I'm armed at all points.'

'Say that to me ten years hence,' said Voogdt, shaking a finger at her. 'I tell you mother's coming for you, teacup-smasher. In the dusk of some warm evening or the cool of some fresh dawn when the birds sing—just when you least expect it—she'll come downstairs and you'll find she's got a slipper handy for her naughty child. Poor slipper,' he said, laughing slyly.

'Dropping into proverbs is the surest sign of a failing intellect,' she retorted impudently. 'Proverbs, scripture, or poetry, you can quote 'em all both ways.'

'Here's a proverb for you Miss Brand,' I said. '"A stitch in time saves nine."' There's a little tear in this sail just by your foot, and if you'll kindly step outside the door or sit down and lift your feet off the canvas for a minute I'll pull it round so that I can mend it.'

She sat on a locker, her feet stuck out straight before her, and by the time the tear was mended the conversation had shifted to some other subject.

The wind hanging in the west, now light, now strong, we had a week ashore, and a very pleasant week it was under the circumstances. There was work to do, of course, but nothing out of the way, and we patched sails and set up shrouds and pottered about generally from morning till dusk. Ward would join us at about midday and the girls in the afternoon; then after tea they went back to Terneuzen together and we put on our shore clothes and joined them at dinner.

Very jolly, those parties were. Sometimes we'd chat and sometimes play cards; but whatever we did we always felt we were welcome. I believe Ward would have admitted he was rather glad of the partnership than otherwise. All the sea part of the business had been in Cheyne's hands hitherto, and whether Ward trusted him or not I could never tell. He couldn't like him much, that was certain; no man could stand the chap for long, especially the quiet student type of man. He was too blatant, too ignorant, for even me to like; and Ward in his heart may have been glad to have Voogdt and myself to share his responsibility.

In pursuance of the new arrangements I sacked Rance, giving him his fare home, and told 'Kiah he must be prepared to leave us at the first English port we touched.

He refused to go, as flatly as a South Devon man can refuse anything, which is as much as to say he argued about it.

'Wha's that for?' he demanded.

I told him our employers were cutting down expenses, and that Mr Cheyne was going to help work the *Luck and Charity*, whereupon he promptly offered to stay for nothing.

'Yu, and 'e, and Mr Vute, there idn' one of 'e can cook,' he said.

'Nonsense. Two of us can as you know.'

'Skipper an' mate cookin'! 'Tis redicklus. Yu let me stay. I don't want no pay f'r a month'r tu. I done middlin' well out o' yu lately—an' there won't be nothin' goin' on 'ome till March, when salmon fishin' starts. Yu let me stop along o' yu an' bear a 'and for my grub an' lodge.'

'Orders are orders, and go you must,' I said. 'And there's an end of it.'

But he only grumbled and maundered on. 'What du 'em want t' sack me for if I don't want no pay? Funny sort o' comp'ny they be, not to let a man bear a' 'and when 'e's ready to du it f'r naught. Yu let me stay before when times was 'ard.'

'Funny sort o' comp'ny,' struck the note I feared—the note of suspicion—and again I began to feel sorry for my partners in crime. They'd been dreading these little suspicions for months, but this was my first experience in that line, and I didn't like it. So I said no more, and at dinner that night reported the whole conversation.

'Do you think he suspects anything?' Ward asked.

'Suspect? Not he!' Voogdt took the words out of my mouth. 'But he'll talk, if he's sacked. Half the South Devon waterside'll hear of it in a fortnight: how West, who allowed 'Kiah to spend a winter with him on no pay and a fish diet, sacked him on the plea of economy and replaced him by Cheyne, who obviously is a more expensive article. We shall have to keep him on.'

'I won't have it,' I said. 'It's all very well to risk our own lives, but—'

'He must take his chance, that's all. All's risk at sea. You daren't raise his pay now, but we'll insure his life behind his back in favour of his relatives, and bank him a good bonus now and then. That's as much as we can do. We daren't sack him.'

'More expense,' Cheyne growled, but Austin spiked his guns at once.

'My dear chap,' he said affably, 'the extra expense is really a small matter. It needn't touch the founders' shares. West and myself'll do all that. Besides, see how much trouble is saved all round. You stay over here managing the part of the business you're accustomed to. There'll be no need to shift anybody here in your place, or to make changes, anyone of which may excite remark. On reflection, I'm sure you'll agree it's the best plan.'

Cheyne agreed at that, you may be sure; but the other three looked thoughtful. I said nothing, meaning to go for Voogdt later, but Miss Brand, as usual, had some remarks to make.

'I quite agree with the bonuses and all that sort of thing' she put in. 'But for one I'm inclined to agree with Capt.—Mr West as well. If there's going to be any risks of shooting, 'Kiah should be warned. I'll do it.'

We all cried out at that, Cheyne loudest of all. 'You'll give the show away,' he said.

'No, I won't. I'll scare the big lump out of his sea-boots, though, if I know my Devonshire.'

'You're not from Devon, are you?' I asked.

'Not I. I'm Lancashire. But I know something of the Celt, and I know sailors. Leave it to me.'

When we got outside the hotel I went for Voogdt.

'You're not playing the game, Austin,' I told him.

'Guilty, I admit,' said he. 'But look at the thing dispassionately, Jem. Isn't the winter trade risk at best?'

'Granted. But—'

'You grant it. Well, this is an extra risk for which 'Kiah'll get extra pay. If you sack him, what happens—to him, I mean? He'll go home, and idle, and grumble and slack about with his cronies, and his family'll live on him till salmon time comes. Then he'll go out in the boats every day, and get drunk with the other men every night till the season's over, and then he'll want another job. By that time he'll be no better off than when you first took him on. Better keep him on board, even with the extra risk, for his own sake.'

'You'd argue black was white, if it suited your purpose,' I said doubtfully.

'Not in this case, for I think as much of the man as you do. But here's my own case, apart from 'Kiah's interests. If he's sacked he'll chatter. You know he will. Then the Topsham boats'll take the tale to Exmouth; Exmouth'll tell it to Budleigh and Dawlish; and they'll talk about us in the drift boats by night and over the crab pots in the morning till in a month 'Kiah's grievance has been discussed in every pub and every port and every boat between Lyme Regis and the Start. Next time we go west, every eye on the coast'll be looking out for us, every tongue wagging about our business; and, I tell you straight, I don't mean to have this plum snatched away just as I'm getting it to my mouth. And there's another point which may appeal even to you—'

'What's that?'

'Cheyne. How long could you stand having him aboard, think you? Here are we—you, 'Kiah and myself—a happy family. But Cheyne—'

'Say no more,' I said. 'I give in. My principles won't stand that strain. But, mind, we must do the square thing by 'Kiah, behind his back. Those bonuses—'

'Of course we will,' said Voogdt, and there the matter ended for the time being.

Next day Miss Brand came down to the *Luck and Charity* in the middle of the morning. Rance was gone, and 'Kiah was busy in the forecastle getting our midday meal. After a few words with us she went forward and sat down on the top of the companion ladder, apparently discussing methods of cooking, by way of setting 'Kiah at his ease. Within half-an-hour she was down in the forecastle, sitting knees to nose before the stove, deep in conversation. Having occasion to go forward I confess I lingered by the hatch to listen, and as far as I could judge she was giving 'Kiah thrills up the back.

I went aft to where Voogdt was reeving a new mainsheet.

'What's she doing down there?' he asked.

'Frightening 'Kiah with ghost stories, as far as I can make out.'

'What a ready-witted hussy it is,' he said admiringly. 'Not one of us would have thought of that. Bet you anything you like she scares him ashore.'

'I'll bet you she doesn't,' I said. I felt bound to stick up for 'Kiah, but I confess I was doubtful, for they're queer cattle, some of the men from the Devon waterside. Besides, I'd heard a quaver in his voice that was a testimony to Miss Brand's story-telling powers.

In the end her plan had results none of us had anticipated. Though I suspected he was badly scared, 'Kiah stayed on without remark, which gave me a better opinion of his intelligence. But the evening we were due to sail, when the warps were cast off, the *Luck and Charity* refused to move. Her bows swung free of the wharf, but her stern was immovable, and try all we could we were unable to shift her. We pushed and strained until we were nearly exhausted, and in the end had to give up the attempt. 'Kiah, questioned, suggested sulkily that we had been 'overlooked,' by which he meant bewitched; but low tide revealed a length of chain made fast round our rudder and lashed firmly to the piles of the wharf. 'Kiah at first denied all knowledge of it, but afterwards broke down and confessed with tears that Miss Brand having dreamed three times that we sailed on an evening tide and were drowned, he had taken this means of ensuring a departure in the morning. Voogdt choked, and bolted below to hide his laughter, and though we had missed a tide I could scarcely keep a straight face whilst I gave 'Kiah the slanging he deserved. He whimpered, wiping his eyes on his sleeve, and then went forward and got on with his work. I am positive that he considered he had saved our lives, and had been rather harshly treated in return for such a service. However, we had no more bother of the same sort, and that was the last attempt to induce him to desert us.

CHAPTER XII

CONCERNING THE ETHICS OF PARTNERSHIP

With Rance gone and Voogdt's insatiable curiosity allayed we put to sea, partners now in the concern, with fairly bright prospects, and I naturally thought everything in future would be peaceable and pleasant. We had made all arrangements as definitely as possible: the superfluous men and ships were to be paid off, and now that we were no longer working in the dark it seemed to me all we had to do was to make quick voyages and our fortunes at one and the same time.

True, the German menace, as Voogdt persisted in calling the competing firm, remained a puzzle, and we were unable to come to any agreement about them. Sitting in council, Cheyne had insisted that they were *bona-fide* traders and pooh-poohed Voogdt's tale of the shooting.

'Can't blame you for being suspicious,' he said. 'This trade makes one suspicious, as I've found. But their explanation holds water as far as I can see. It was just an accident, only you were scared and made more of it.'

'Fifty quid paid by a quay lumper to a fo'castle hand for an accident?' Voogdt sneered.

'Accident or no accident I don't care,' said Cheyne. 'What I go by is my own observations. Five coasters have called down there and left cargoes, and not one of them has ballasted from there. On the other hand they've sent away two small barges loaded deep and flying the B swallow-tail—the red powder flag. Rifles or no, you can't get away from that.'

'But what are we to do?' he asked. 'Are we to take no notice of them at all?—treat 'em as if they were just fools, or be on our guard against them? The syndicate's opinion, please.'

126

Ward shrugged his shoulders.

'I don't profess to know anything about it,' he said. 'You three must settle this affair between yourselves.'

'Miss Lavington?'

Miss Lavington agreed with Mr Ward, but of course Miss Brand had something to say.

'This running-down business—are you sure it was intentional, and can you connect that with the shooting?'

'We can't connect the two attempts,' Voogdt said. 'But intentional? Yes; I'll swear it was that.'

She turned to me. 'And you?' she demanded.

'They certainly cut down the dinghy. I can't positively say more than that. But I think Voogdt's right, all the same.'

'Then if they're not *bona-fide* traders, and if they were behind that attempt, it won't do to regard them as fools, will it?'

'They're not fools, be sure of that, Miss Brand,' Voogdt said. 'I don't think they're traders any more than we are, but even if they were we must pay them the compliment of believing them intelligent. Our pretence of genuine trading must be kept up, if only for their benefit.'

'I think so, too,' she said, and I agreed. The other two declined to interfere, so though Cheyne sneered and talked of waste it was decided that we must go on as before, shipping cargoes at a loss, but exercising all possible care to see the precious ballast consignments didn't go astray. The idea of those sharp-eyed, unscrupulous people at our very door worried me, I confess; but I couldn't see any way of avoiding them, and Voogdt had no suggestions to make, so we had no alternative but to keep a sharp look-out, get on with the work and—unless they molested us—make our fortunes, quick and easy.

There we were mistaken. The German firm didn't bother us again; we had our old happy family aboard; the suspicions and conjectures that used to worry us were all at rest; winter was wearing on to spring; and yet we found more worry as partners than ever we had as employees.

To start with, we made a bad passage, foul weather all the way, and once arrived at Dartmouth my first experience of the syndicate's shore methods nearly worried me sick.

We had all our ballast out, lying on the quay—thirty-five tons of it, worth a good eight thousand pounds—and were moored off in midstream waiting for tide, when I saw a labourer come up with a horse and cart and start loading up with the mud. I'd had two days of fidgeting at every pore every time a child walked over the heap, and this sent me into a cold perspiration.

'See that?' I said to Voogdt.

He nodded. 'We must put up with it,' was all he said.

'I can't,' I said. 'I must go ashore and find out where that's going.'

'Sit tight,' said he. 'You can't do anything. Grin and bear it.'

'Man, he'll take away many hundredweights of the stuff.'

'Half-a-ton, or thereabouts.' He tried to speak calmly. 'Over a hundred quid at a time. Ghastly, isn't it? But we must sit tight and put up with it. I'm beginning to feel sorry for our partners. They've stood this sort of thing for over a year.'

'I can't stand it a single hour,' I said. 'I'm going ashore to find out who he is.'

'I'll go,' Voogdt said. 'You'll make a mess of it, for certain. You're too much the simple sailor. Stay here, and I'll find out all I can.'

He went ashore in our new dinghy, returning half-an-hour later.

'He's working for a Salcombe farmer and has orders to take ten cartloads to Kingsbridge. He doesn't know what it's for, but fancies it's top dressing for land.'

'Oh, Lord!' I groaned. 'Ten loads—five tons! Over a thousand pounds lying and spoiling on fields. I can't stand it, Austin.'

'What are you going to do?' he asked, and posed me. What could I do? Nothing—I could see that. I didn't dare meddle.

'I'll wire Cheyne,' I said, in desperation. It was the only thing I could think of.

'Not from here. If you must wire go to Newton Abbot or Plymouth, and be guarded in your message. You mustn't forget this may be all right. This chap may be working for some agent of ours.'

There was no confidence in his voice, and, speaking for myself, I couldn't believe such a thing possible, so I went to Newton Abbot that afternoon and wired to Cheyne.

'Ten tons of goods being removed to K instruct,' was the message. I didn't dare give the name Kingsbridge in full.

No answer arrived till next morning and then it came from Birmingham: 'K on rail quite correct Carwithen,' it ran, and we both heaved sighs of relief.

Before we sailed again other carts had taken up the good work, and thirty tons had vanished into the interior of the county. But, as Voogdt pointed out, it was a useful lesson in self-control. I thought of Ward's story of the navvies and the quay extension and wondered whether I should ever attain that much command of myself. It's a queer business, having to sit still and see thousands of pounds worth of your own property being taken away from under your very nose in broad daylight, not knowing whether it's going into your pockets or going to waste, and unable to say a word or stretch out a finger to help it in the right direction.

When we got back to Terneuzen we were told the *Olive Leaf* had been paid off and our next voyage was to Kirkcaldy, on the Firth of Forth. That meant new charts and a new voyage, and our first experience of the North Sea winter trade made me regret the departed *Olive Leaf,* who presumably had got accustomed to it, as eels are said to get accustomed to skinning. It was bitterly cold, the weather had gone easterly with the approach of March, and when next we got back to Terneuzen we both reviled Cheyne heartily. Why couldn't he keep us in the Channel till warmer weather? we demanded, and he grinned and said he'd do his best.

Our first two voyages were almost entirely successful.

Deducting 'Kiah's bonuses, which we had placed to his credit without his knowledge, Voogdt and myself reckoned ourselves richer by fifteen hundred pounds apiece; but after those two trips we hit a streak of bad luck. Out of three loads, deposited in Channel ports, only fifteen tons came to hand, which divided into six shares made six hundred pounds a piece. With 'Kiah's bonus deducted—a quarter of our joint share—that left us each two hundred and twenty-five pounds. A hundred and twelve pounds a voyage was very good pay, past denial, but after our first two voyages we were rather inclined to turn up our noses at it.

Our payments were as unbusinesslike as our methods of trading. Sometimes we asked Cheyne for money, and found he would advance up to a hundred pounds without remark. The larger sums were sent us in all sorts of currency—postal money orders, banknotes, sometimes gold packed in strong boxes—delivered by registered post at the ports where we touched. The money orders were sent in different names, and we were advised by Carwithen as to the offices we were to cash them at and what names we were to sign on them. I didn't care for such methods; the false names displeased me, for one thing; but I believe Voogdt positively enjoyed it.

'I wish I was at the head office,' he said once in Southampton Water. 'This game of hiding one's tracks appeals to me.'

'It doesn't to me,' I said shortly. I'd just had no end of a bother trying to cash a money order inland, at Salisbury. Carwithen had instructed me to apply in the name of Collings; I had spelt the name Collins; and it took me a long hour to get the money, the fool behind the counter fencing with me, playfully assuming that I couldn't spell my own name. I couldn't very well tell him it wasn't my own, either.

Voogdt laughed. 'How much was it for?' he asked.

'A hundred and seventy. Rotten, potty, silly methods. I shall ask for mine to be banked for me in Birmingham in future.'

I wrote Ward that night, and from that time left the handling of my money to him—only drawing from Cheyne as occasion required. Voogdt approved when I told him what I had done.

'Ward's all right,' he said. 'But don't trust Cheyne in the same way.'

'I thought you liked him,' I said, rather surprised.

'H'm! Perhaps I do—fairly well. Whether I do or not, he must think so. I like him as well as one wolf likes another in the pack. We hunt together, but he'd eat me—or I him—if other quarry failed. Somebody must keep in with him, you chump. Don't you see that in all this muddle and grab he holds the reins? What's to prevent his doing the lot of us in the eye, if he likes to ship the stuff away when we aren't there? I mean to go on loving him. Then if he tries any little games he may invite me to help.'

'And I thought you had taken to the chap!' I said. 'D'ye think he'll try it on?'

'You never know. No harm in being hand in glove with him for the present, anyhow.'

About the middle of March we had a bad scare. We had learnt from Ward that our continued shipments had not been without some effect on the tungsten market. He told us that he was now getting from ten to fifteen pounds a ton less than when the syndicate began operations, and warned us that a number of cargoes successfully delivered would in all probability cause a further drop in price. Voogdt said that couldn't be helped; our holding was too precarious for us to attempt maintaining a demand. 'Thieves are forced to sell in a bad market,' he said. 'I've always had a sneaking sympathy with burglars, when I've reflected how the fences swindle them. We must just sell as fast as we can for the best price we can get.'

Naturally we looked at the market reports anxiously every time we were ashore, and landing at Southampton, in the second week in March, found tungsten had come down with a rush to a bare two hundred pounds a ton. There was a further announcement that wolframite had been discovered in paying quantities in the refuse of an exhausted tin mine in Cornwall.

'Game's up,' I said.

Voogdt shook his head. 'Don't worry. It'll pay us well at less than two hundred a ton. This is only a flash in the pan. If there'd been any promise of a constant supply it would have gone lower than that.'

A letter he had received from Ward with supplies made a brief veiled reference to 'recent discoveries,' but as far as I could make out neither Ward nor Carwithen appeared to take the matter seriously. Cheyne, however, was in a lather when we got back to Terneuzen.

'Game's up,' he said, using my very words.

'Looks pretty bad, doesn't it?' said Voogdt, teasing him, I thought. Cheyne cursed and grumbled and swore, and ended by asking us both to dinner. We accepted, but when he had gone ashore Voogdt suggested I should stay aboard.

'I'll grub with him by myself, if you don't mind. If he's going to start stealing, this is where he'll begin. If I'm alone he may give me a clue to his intentions. If you're there, he won't. He pays me the compliment of thinking me a rogue, and you've already had the sack once for your transparent honesty, don't you see. So you stay aboard and keep anchor watch, Jem. I'll tell all necessary lies on your behalf.'

He got back after midnight, and before he opened his mouth I could see that something had upset him.

'I knew he would. I knew he would!' he said. 'The sweep! He wants us to split a cargo, leaving the better half at a port not yet decided on, and report to Ward that we've had an accident and had to jettison the stuff. Not a bad scheme, either, I confess I admire his ingenuity.'

'And that sweep is to marry Pamela Brand!' I said.

'Oh ho!' said Voogdt. 'Is that the way the land lies? He wants us to dirty our hands by thieving for him, and little long-tongued Brand is the first thing you think of. Sweet on her?'

'Certainly not,' I said, rather hot about it. 'The girl's nothing to me. In fact, I don't like her—much. But she's straight—straight as a line—and 'tisn't fair to marry her to a swab like that.'

'Never mind about her just now. The question is, what are we going to do?'

'Give him the hammering he deserves and then write and inform Ward.'

'Have a holy row, in fact. Kick Cheyne out; bust the show; and see tungsten quoted at fifteen pounds a ton or thereabouts next time we get ashore. Sorry to disappoint you, but that won't do, Jem. Telling Ward's all right. I'll do that myself. But we can't afford a row royal. Cheyne must be induced to leave the sales to me, and we must just keep another banking account.'

'Can we do that?' I asked.

'We'll manage it that way or some other. We can*not* afford a row at any cost. Remember that, whatever you do. We must keep this beast sweet; help him, even, and just report each move to headquarters. Ward knows you're straight, at all events.'

Cheyne came aboard next morning, Voogdt meeting him at the gangway. They both went down into the cabin at once and then called me through the skylight.

'I've told Cheyne you're all square,' Voogdt explained, when I entered.

I said nothing, but Cheyne seemed not to notice my manner.

'No good paying out six shares when we can make it three, is it?' he asked.

I grunted some sort of an agreement. More I couldn't do, for it was all I could manage to do to keep my hands off him. But it seemed to satisfy him, and he and Voogdt began to explain what he wanted done.

Our next voyage was to Swanage, and we were to put into Newhaven on the way and discharge twenty tons. Thence he wanted us to cable him, but Voogdt had said that meant complications and insisted on wiring the customer himself. Cheyne jibbed a little, but he had no choice, and so gave Voogdt the name of one of Ward's customers that he knew personally and agreed that Voogdt should communicate with him direct. As far as I could make out, the whole thing had been planned beforehand between him and this customer, who must have been another rogue of the same sort, and they had only been waiting their opportunity.

I said nothing: sat like a dummy and grunted yes or no. My fingers were itching to get at the beast, and I didn't try to be civil. At last even he saw it, dense as he was, and soon after took his leave, Voogdt going on deck to see him off.

'Is he all right?' I heard him ask, the skylight being a little open.

'As straight as a line,' Voogdt reassured him. 'He's a bit sulky because he's been trying to persuade me he ought to have a half-share instead of a third, that's all.'

'What's he want that for?'

'He says it's his ship. Of course I told him we couldn't do it, and equally of course he daren't make a fuss any more than the rest of us.'

'Good enough,' said Cheyne. 'If he shows signs of being nasty, promise him a bonus. We can manage that, I daresay.' And off he went.

'You must try and disguise your feelings a bit,' Voogdt said when he came below. 'He's been asking if you were to be relied on.'

'I heard him. Faugh, the swine! He, to ask whether another man is to be relied on! He, that's cheating women, and his own relations at that.'

'That thinks he's going to cheat them, you mean,' said Voogdt, with a grin. 'Come, man; put a more cheerful face on it. Think of him here counting his chickens and Ward, with that wooden face of his, hatching the eggs in Brummagem for all of us. We can work it well. See how: we land the stuff, advise Ward by code wire, and depart. From the next port we advise Cheyne's customer, who swoops down on his prey, to find it gone. Having arranged for cartage and so on, he'll talk to Cheyne like a Dutch uncle. Cheyne can't explain it, nor can we. It's just another cargo gone wrong, that's all. Here's Cheyne at one end, slaving away to get the stuff off, and Ward at the other disposing of it.'

He drew such a funny picture of Cheyne's rage at his disappearing cargoes that even I was bound to laugh, and after that it was no good holding out against the arrangement. But I wrote Ward that night, exposing the whole business, and next day we started loading the stuff Master Cheyne already regarded as his own.

CHAPTER XIII

SHOWING A FOWLER IN HIS SNARE

At her best no one could ever have mistaken the *Luck and Charity* for a yacht. She was too heavily built for that; but for the first two years I had her she looked a cut above the everyday coasting ketch. She was new then; I was able to keep her clean, her decks scrubbed and her brass work polished, and to indulge her with some little vanities, such as take a sailor's eye. Her clumsy tiller was abolished, for instance, and replaced with a neat little mahogany wheel; there were white gratings for the steersman's feet; the compass stood in a binnacle of bright brass and mahogany, and awnings hung from the booms in port.

But now her chipped and clay-stained wheel, with all its brass and wood work scratched and tarnished, was the only trace remaining of her man-millinery. That starvation winter in Exmouth had swallowed everything saleable, and working up and down the Channel ever since had accounted for the rest. The gratings had gone; all that was left of the awnings was a patch or two in the stained canvas of her sails; a ring of screw holes on the dirty deck showed where once the polished binnacle had stood, and we steered now by a clumsy floating compass of antiquated design clamped upon the after end of the skylight. Her once spotless decks were filthy with trampled mud and coal, her brass fittings had given place to galvanised iron, and neatness and lightness in her appliances had been replaced everywhere by clumsy strength.

And yet, soiled and weathered as she was, I think I liked her better now than ever I had done in the days of her prosperity. She was built for rough work; shining brass and white awnings were never her proper wear. Like most men and some women she looked better in her working dress, aproned and bare-armed, than in any ballroom rig. The more I looked at her the more I liked her, and when Voogdt came up to relieve me at midday I spoke my thoughts.

'A dear good old packet she is,' I said. 'Honest as a woman. It's a shame she should be put to dirty work like stealing for Cheyne.'

'How many more times am I to tell you she is not stealing for Cheyne, you pudding-head?' he demanded.

'I don't want to think otherwise of women,' I said. 'I've met 'em all over the world, good and bad, and there's good in the worst of 'em. D'you think any woman would have thought out a dirty, treacherous game like this scheme of Cheyne's?'

'P'raps not. I don't know. Lord forbid that I should shake your faith in woman, lovely woman, even if you do express it like a Surrey-side melodrama. I don't think women'll ever hurt you much, at all events. Give us the wheel. East by nor, half east, is it?'

'East by nor', half east,' I repeated mechanically, And then, not feeling sleepy, sat down on the skylight for a chat.

It was a fine day, not too cold, and the breeze being well behind us, it was pleasant on deck. The cruel winter was nearly over, I was making money, and things generally looked more cheerful but for this Cheyne business. That soured me. I couldn't keep it out of my mind, and before my pipe was well alight we were discussing it all over again.

Voogdt, like myself, had written Ward before we sailed and pitched the letter across the cabin table for me to read before he sealed it. It was a brief, concise report, such as only a skilled penman could write, with nothing to confuse the reader and nothing omitted. Even I, knowing the whole business as I did, felt I had a clearer notion of it all after reading his description. My letter, written in the heat of temper, had been full of abuse of Cheyne, yet somehow Voogdt's simple state-ment, extracting the gist of all he had said, point after point, seemed to show him more clearly as a rogue than all my adjectives had done.

He laid the whole thing before Ward, enclosed a short list of code words he'd drawn up so ingeniously that it seemed to me they provided for every contingency, and also enclosed— what I had forgotten in my haste—the name and address of Cheyne's customer. He said the deal was 'possibly prearranged'—hit off in two words what I had taken half-a-page to say. The concluding paragraph made me chuckle: 'To avoid alarming Cheyne I suggest that consignments misdirected by his order be divided into five shares instead of six. Should he find himself credited with a share in goods he believes lost, he may get confused and be unable to discharge his duties as efficiently as heretofore.'

I chuckled as I remembered it. 'Think Ward'll have a plan ready?' I asked.

'If he's the man I think him he will. He'll have to do that double entry business we spoke of. "Oh! what a tangled web we weave, when first we practise to deceive." Who would have thought we were in for such an interesting business that day you took me aboard at Exmouth?'

'It's a bit too interesting at times.'

'Rot! It's the risk makes the sport. Half the time we're working in the dark. Look at these German people, for instance. We don't know what they're up to; they may shoot us or run us down or blow the company's sheds sky-high any day, for aught we know. Anyone of a hundred chances may wreck our plans: a row with Cheyne, an astute man watching the markets, another tramp like myself suffering from curiosity. The business was only founded on an accident, mind you—a half-drunk sailor dropping his watch. Interesting? I should jolly well think it was. I'm not one of your placid breed: I believe you'd rather be selling things over a counter, or trading regularly from port to port, or drawing a settled income. Not me, Jem. Life's a gamble at best, and though you safe players may leave the table with most of the counters, I swear you don't get most of the fun.'

'I'm certainly not getting much fun out of this so far,' I said. 'Three bad voyages on end. Cheyne a rogue, and our never knowing what these Germans may be up to any minute. I don't like it. I can't be civil to one, and watch another, and keep different accounts going in my head all at the same time. Acting a part before this rascal and that—'

'Pooh! The salt of life,' Voogdt interrupted. 'That's what makes life worth the living. How sweet this old boat steers before a wind. On that one point I agree with you, anyhow: she's a good, homely ship, and I've grown fond of her, too.'

We held the breeze into Newhaven, making a quick voyage of it with no bother at all, but once in harbour our troubles began in earnest. The harbour master, a slow-witted, distrustful South Saxon, led off by asking us, very properly, what was our business.

'Our orders is to get ballast out and be ready to load,' said Voogdt incautiously, and the man went away.

'Now you've done it,' I said. 'D'you think we can leave half our ballast and take away the other half without exciting suspicion after that?'

'We'll see. I'm sorry. Meanwhile, don't hurry about getting the stuff out of her.'

He wrote Ward again that night, taking full responsibility for his hasty answer, and next day we dawdled over our work until the harbour master wanted to know if we'd bought the ballast quay. 'There's others besides you,' he said.

'We're in no 'urry, guv'nor,' Voogdt said placidly. 'We ain't got our orders yet. If anybody wants to ballast they can lay outside so's we can discharge into 'em direct.'

Naturally neither of us thought the offer would be accepted, but it was. There might have been twelve tons out on the quay when another coaster, the *Teresa* of Waterford, warped alongside us in the afternoon. We started emptying our tubs into her hold perforce, but our pace wasn't fast enough for her owner, Irish though he was.

'Talk o' th' Irish bein' lazy,' he said, with supreme contempt, after watching us for an hour. 'Sure, fleas won't bit a South Dev'n man thinkin' th' poor fella's dead. 'Nless he's in a hurry, an' then they schwarm on 'm, perceivin' he's only aslape. Here, Byrne an' Lar'nce, jump aboard that floatin' rest cure an' show them dead slugs how t' shift ballast.'

'You keep your men off my decks,' I said.

'Pho! Sure ye can take up the carpets before they come aboard. You, an' y'r decks! D'ye think my men are dirtier than y'r—plankin'?'

'We don't want your Irish fleas coming aboard to be disappointed,' said Voogdt. 'If you don't like our pace, get out in midstream again, and wait your turn at the quay. We don't get extra pay for loading you.'

'I tho't ye did, the way ye're flyin' at it. Holy saints! I believe I'd get ballasted quicker on the moorin's with the weeds that 'ud grow on our bottom.'

The altercation brought the harbour master round to us once more, and the Irishman appealed to him. Fortunately the ancient hatred of Celt and Saxon served us.

'First come, first served,' said he stolidly. 'They was here first. If you don't like their ways, you must wait your turn.'

'This is a useful way of escaping notice,' I said to Voogdt, when we got a minute alone in the cabin. 'And the ballast is being lost, too. Got any further complications up your sleeve?'

'Don't worry. Smile,' said he. 'Ward'll be here tonight, and I rather fancy I see trouble for Cheyne in this.'

'I see more trouble for us,' I said. 'There's a hundred quid thrown away every time a tub's emptied into that Irishman's hold, work as slowly as we will.'

'Don't worry, I tell you. Wait for Ward. This'll be a coup, or I'm mistaken.'

Ward arrived that night, and sure enough they managed it

between them. Next day he passed the word that we could ballast the *Teresa* as fast as we pleased. She was bound for Neath Abbey to load coal, and Carwithen was already arranging to remove the ballast on her arrival. For ourselves, we were to empty our hold, load with a cargo of deals Ward had bought, and take them to Swanage instead of the ballast as originally arranged. He had chartered another coaster lying in harbour and instructed Carwithen to arrange a coal cargo for her at Jarrow-on-Tyne, where she would take the ballast we had already thrown out on the quay.

'But what about Cheyne? He'll ask questions.'

'Let him,' said Voogdt, and Ward's post-office mouth quivered a little at the corners. 'With half the cargo at Jarrow and half at Neath Abbey, let him ask all the questions he pleases.'

'But what about the sixth share of the lot we were to have landed at Swanage? He'll want to know about that.'

'We'll credit him with that,' said Ward.

'Suppose he hears we went there with deals?'

'He won't hear of it in the ordinary way, and I don't think he'll dare ask questions. If he does, he can only learn that you have discharged half your ballast on the quay, and that another coaster took it. That's happened to us many times before. He won't suspect anything from that.'

'What do you think of Cheyne?' I asked.

'I'm very sorry for the whole business. I thought better of him. It's very fortunate you two are partners with us.'

'You put it mildly. Now, let me get this business straight in my head. When Cheyne asks questions what am I to say?'

'Say you discharged about eighteen tons here, and sailed for Swanage. That's all you need bother about.

'A few more attempts like this and we shall make a slip and give the show away.'

'It's more than possible,' Ward said. 'But obviously I can't interfere. The remedy lies in your own hands. If you persuade Cheyne of the risk and difficulty, perhaps he won't try it again.'

He did, though. He tried it the very next voyage. Complications arose after we left Newhaven, and when we met next he was raving. His customer had sent a haulier to fetch away the mud, and the man, naturally ignorant of the stuff he had to deal with, hauled ten tons of worthless ballast dumped by a dredger and put it on rail. The customer, advised of its departure, sold it, rubbed his hands, and woke a morning or two later to find a bundle of furious letters on his desk ordering him to remove his rubbish. Cheyne was dancing mad, cursing and furious, and accusing us of having mucked the affair. Voogdt tried to pacify him, pointing out that removal from quays was one of our ordinary risks, and then joined me in the cabin. I hadn't seen much fun in it up to then, but now we literally cried with laughter, stuffing our mouths with tablecloth to stifle the noise. It cheered me up considerably, that.

The customer was bullying Cheyne and requesting delivery of the promised consignment, so he pressed us to have another try on the same lines, and this voyage very nearly gave the show away. Our port of destination was Goole, and we were to leave the stolen half-cargo at Yarmouth. Here, being questioned, Voogdt told a story of fussy owners who insisted on over-ballasting us, and said we were lightening the boat against orders. I never heard a more improbable tale, and of course the harbour master's suspicion was excited at once.

'What'll he think when the stuff gets carted away?' I asked, when we were clear of the harbour.

'It won't be carted away. I wired Ward in code: "Amanuensis Syllable," which, being interpreted, means "Suspicions aroused, remove by sea."'

'Think he'll manage it?'

'Bet your life he will. He and Carwithen are two men with big heads. I'm developing a sound respect for the pair of them now I've had some experience of their trade. They'll manage it all right.'

They did and when we got back to Terneuzen from Goole,

Cheyne was past swearing even. His customer had been compelled to buy from Ward to fulfil his first orders; Ward, smiling quietly, had squeezed the price up to its top limit to punish him, and the customer had written Cheyne a letter that nearly turned him grey. He got little comfort from us.

'Tell your customer they're ordinary business losses, under the circumstances,' Voogdt suggested maliciously.

'What's the use of talking that sort of rot? He threatens he'll accidentally give me away unless the goods are delivered.'

'He doesn't write you here, does he?' I asked, startled.

'No fear. Antwerp post office. I go there to fetch his letters.'

'He must know you're thieving, or he wouldn't talk of exposure.'

'Thieving!' He didn't like it put so brutally as that. Choose your words better. And if it is thieving, you're in it too.'

'We know all about that,' Voogdt interrupted, suddenly taking the offensive. 'We're in it, right enough, but where does our pay come in? You make a lot of promises; we do our part of the business, and then all you have to show us is a letter from your customer to say he hasn't had the goods. That's no manner of use to me. You've got to pay us for delivery on shore, and that's all there is about it. If things are bungled after we've done our share of the work, that's no fault of ours.'

'They're only ordinary business losses.' Cheyne, aghast at the sudden attack, found it his turn to plead our disregarded excuse.

'That may be. We haven't learnt the game as well as you have,' said Voogdt truculently. 'All I know is that we've done thieving at your orders and now we aren't to get paid for it. You'll oblige me by brassing up a hundred apiece—fifty quid a voyage—to compensate us for our trouble.'

Cheyne was flabbergasted. 'When you get a cargo through, I will. I promise I will. But surely, my dear chap, you don't expect me to pay you on top of my losses?'

He was livid, and I must confess Voogdt's sudden turning of the tables had taken me aback.

'I do expect it. And, what's more, I mean having the money. So you just get out your cheque-book before we go any further into the matter.'

Cheyne protested, pleaded, cursed and swore, but all to no effect. We had him fast, and in the end he fished out the cheque-book from his desk and wrote us one apiece to the tune of a hundred pounds shaking with rage and funk.

'Good enough,' said Voogdt coolly, pocketing both the slips. 'Now, about this next voyage. Dumping half-a-load of ballast on this quay, and another half-load on that, doesn't appear to work out properly. And it's dangerous, too. The lies I had to tell at Yarmouth this last voyage wouldn't deceive a sucking child, and the next thing'll be that we shall blow the gaff. We'll work one more cargo through for you and then I'm finished. And that cargo won't go ashore at all. You or your pal must charter a barge, bring her alongside in some anchorage in France for preference—Brest. Roads'll do as well as anywhere—and we'll unload into her.'

'That'll never do—'

'It's got to do. It's all very well for you to be careless—you've made your pile. I haven't, and I don't intend this show shall be given away until I have. So make your own arrangements, but remember we don't put another ounce of stuff ashore for you anywhere.'

Cheyne had to give in, of course. We were to make a couple of voyages on the square and by that time he thought he could arrange for the transhipment Voogdt ordered.

Confused by all the mist of lying, I could yet see that Voogdt's was a very good plan and, when Cheyne had gone, taxed him with double dealing.

'Thanks to you, he'll pull that off,' I said. 'Are you playing straight, Austin?'

'Straight!' said he cheerfully. 'Straight, did you say? What is there straight in the whole business? The firm is stealing—from the Dutch Government, I suppose; Cheyne's trying to steal from them; and we're blackmailing him. But what can we do, Jem? We dare not go on playing Cheyne's game; we dare not open his eyes; and we dare not let his customer make trouble. I'm acting as I believe Ward would act in my place. I propose to let them have this one cargo to shut the customer's mouth— reporting it to Birmingham, of course—and after that we must hope Cheyne's too scared to try it again. If we refuse to help him he'll get somebody else, and that means more risk. The two hundred we've got out of him and our two-thirds share of the theft we'll send to Brum to be divided in the usual way. That'll go towards squaring the loss on Cheyne's share of this next stolen cargo. Add the two cargoes we've bagged and he hasn't, and I should think the firm is a bit ahead on the game. Can you suggest a better plan?'

'Not I. Devising roguery isn't my strong point. But you're a bit of a marvel, Austin. It beats me the way the chap's been headed off at every turn. You're a wonder.'

'Rot!' said he, chuckling. 'That's Ward's doing. Look how he tackled the situation at Newhaven. It's been good fun, so far. But, mind you, once a man's off the straight track it's not so easy for him to pull up. Probably Cheyne won't try this dodge again, but we must watch him. He'll be up to something else, or I'm much mistaken.'

Ward met us at our next port, Erith, in London river, and Voogdt made his report. He listened saying nothing until Voogdt proposed the payment of our shares and Cheyne's two hundred pounds into the common fund of the syndicate. Then he raised objections.

'There's no reason for that,' he said. 'Keep it for yourselves.'

Voogdt shook his head. 'No. We don't want more than our fair share as agreed, and, personally, I don't want extra profits out of Cheyne's defection.'

Ward looked pleased, but he still protested.

'We've done well, and are ready to retire. You're not: your pockets aren't full yet. Take it. At this rate the business may collapse any day, and since you've been so fair with us I should like you to make your profits before the end comes.'

'Speaking for myself,' I said, 'I absolutely refuse to touch Cheyne's hundred pounds. It's blackmail, nothing better, and though he's a sweep, and I'm not over-particular, I draw the line somewhere.'

So there we were, at another deadlock. Neither of the others wanted the money, and for the moment it looked as though Cheyne had been bled for nothing.

'Add it to 'Kiah's bonuses,' Voogdt suggested at last. 'As for the profits of the thieving, we both wish them to be sent out and divided in the usual way;' and after we had pressed the point a while, Ward eventually agreed.

CHAPTER XIV

OF A DIRECTORS' MEETING

BUSINESS once concluded, Ward had a personal message to deliver. Miss Brand was at Erith, and please would we join her at dinner that evening? We thanked him, and promised to come, and then, as he had only mentioned one girl's name, I asked if Miss Lavington was with her.

'Not this time,' said he. 'She's on duty at Snow Hill. Carwithen's busy and wants her help.'

'Does she take an active part in the business, then?'

I ought to have known better than ask the question, the two girls having been present at so many sittings in council. But I never really associated either of them with active work—especially such work as shipping business, and a sort of modified piracy at that. What with Pamily Brand being related to Cheyne, and Ward and Miss Lavington almost as good as engaged, I looked upon them as a sort of family party and regarded the girls' talk as something to be listened to, for civility's sake, but not to be considered as anything important after that—so the idea of Miss Lavington actually doing office work at Snow Hill struck me as strange.

'Of course she does,' said Ward. 'We all help. Didn't Miss Brand go through your papers once at Dartmouth?'

'She came aboard and looked them over, certainly. But, to tell the truth, I never imagined she understood them.'

I expect I spoke awkwardly, for I couldn't well tell him I believed she only came aboard with a view to luring me on to try to flirt with her.

'She understands the business very well,' Ward said, interrupting my thoughts. 'I don't know how we should have got along without her—and Miss Lavington. You see we couldn't do with paid employees. The business ashore wanted intelligence, and if we'd hired quick-witted people our secret wouldn't have been our own for very long. Cheyne and myself tried to do all of it at first, but soon found that impossible, so took in Carwithen. As a paid manager he would have been a danger; as a partner he's been worth his weight in gold. When we got into touch with more purchasers and the business again got beyond us, it was at his suggestion that we asked the two girls if they would help us.'

'How could they help?' I asked curiously.

'They did help, I can assure you. They flung themselves into the business whole-heartedly. Miss Lavington learnt to use a typewriter and took over the correspondence and book-keeping. She and Carwithen have charge of the office and most of the work inland—the actual selling to customers. I help them a little in that, the London and south and west of England sales are in my hands, and I also see to removing the consignments from the ports along the English Channel. That's how it is you've seen more of me than of the others.'

'What does Miss Brand do?'

'Hitherto she's had the east coast and Scotch ports in her charge. Now that the *Olive Leaf* and *Kismet* are paid off, she's supposed to be helping at the office, but there's really very little for her to do there with only your cargoes to watch. So she's come down here with me as a sort of holiday trip.'

I said that Erith in March didn't strike me as much of a place for holidaying.

'Ah! But she's the sort of girl that can make a holiday out of a ride on a bus. I fancy one of the attractions here was the chance of another squabble with you.' He looked at Voogdt, with a smile. 'By the way, when you see her don't harp on this business of Cheyne's. She's partial to him. They're related, you know—were playmates as children—so she takes this more seriously than the rest of us.'

His way of speaking was quietly frank, and seemed to put us on the footing of personal friends as well as partners. That was just the difference between him and Cheyne. The one never mentioned Pamela Brand but I wanted to kick him, even when he only meant to be affable. But when I had been an employee Ward's manner had never held offence, and now, without gush or effusiveness, he spoke as though we were two members of the family party and had been so all along.

'Has she said anything about Cheyne?' I asked.

'Not to me. But Miss Lavington tells me she's taking the matter to heart rather. So keep off the subject all you can.'

Erith, being a small but busy port, and near London, had proved a convenient place for the syndicate's operations, and several cargoes of wolframite had crossed its quays during the past twelve months. Miss Brand, in her capacity of agent, had consequently become familiar with the town—had her own regular lodgings in a house out on the London Road—and it was to her rooms that we were invited. Ward was staying at an hotel by the dock entrance, so as to be near us, and we were to call for them on our way up town.

We dressed ourselves for shore in our usual fashion, in clean flannel shirts and collars and our best serge suits, and I was rather amused than otherwise to find when we reached the hotel that Ward had got into evening dress.

'I suppose our clothes'll do?' I said, more in jest than earnest. I couldn't imagine the Brand girl in fine raiment. 'We've a good excuse, anyhow. One doesn't carry dress duds on a coaster.'

'Of course,' said Ward, as though dismissing the question, and we went on our way with minds at ease.

It was dark when we reached the house, and I could only make it out as a fair-sized villa residence standing back from the road with gardens front and rear. A clean, elderly maid took Ward's coat and our peaked caps in the hall, and showed us into a candle-lit room with the table laid and a cheerful wood fire burning. Ward sat down, Voogdt went straight to the fire—

he was always a cold subject—and I was walking round trying
to make out the pictures on the walls, when the door opened
again and our hostess entered. And, speaking for myself, I
wished I could sink through the floor. I don't know when I
ever had such a surprise in my life.

To begin with, I hadn't seen a woman in evening dress close
at hand since my two years of folly in South Devon, and they
weren't—well, the class of women I had known there that went
in for evening dress had always a little tendency towards slovenliness. Only natural, when you come to think of it. The
wasters and their wives, and their wives' sisters and cousins,
had made up all the society I enjoyed then. A waster naturally
marries a barmaid ninety-nine times in a hundred, and of course
her first purchase after marriage would be an evening frock, to
consort with the dignity of her husband's double-barrelled
name. Then the remittances that had been ample for one became
a tight fit for two, and the evening frocks soon got slovenly.
Poor little women—good wives, most of them . . . But, associating with them, and with uneducated sailors ever since, I had
come to link in my mind the idea of a low-necked dress with
some faint suggestion of impropriety. You can't help being
influenced by the notions of the men about you, and the poorer
seamen as a class consider bare shoulders improper in themselves. I suppose they get their ideas from the filthy *cafés
chantants* in the ports.

Then, again, I had lost touch with drawing-rooms. For nearly
a year my home had been a three-cornered box of a cabin, nine
feet long by twelve wide, and I'd shared that with another man.
'Kiah kept it clean enough for our purposes, but his methods
weren't highly polished, at best. We weren't exactly insanitary,
but Keating's powder always made a feature in the grocery list,
and 'Kiah rather plumed himself on it than otherwise, for boats
of our class don't often go to that expense. Our usual cargo
was mud, and the atmosphere of the ports we touched at principally coal dust. We didn't complain, naturally, because

coasting is a rough trade, and cleanliness an unusual luxury for the men engaged in it. I hadn't seen a bathroom for a year: a bucket and sponge in the cabin, or an occasional swim overside had served my needs well enough. And now, fresh from that atmosphere of dirt and slovenliness and sweating hard work, it came a bit queer to be confronted with a girl one had always associated with open air and salt water, and find her dressed to kill, dainty as a flower.

Her dress was plain enough, with no frills or furbelows, and she looked sleek and demure as a kitten, and—what I'd never noticed before—really pretty, too. Remember I'd never seen her before except on board or in some port or another, and there she had always been simply and even poorly dressed. Tweeds were her wear; tweed or serge plainly cut, and often well worn at that, with a straw hat and a plain blouse—that sort of thing. Again and again she had reminded me more of a boy in petticoats than anything else; but now—she wasn't in the least like a boy now, at any rate.

I'm no man-milliner, and to this day I can't tell what she had on, though I can see her plainly enough every time I shut my eyes. I know her dress was a pale dove-grey, very soft and clinging smoothly, so as to show the round curves of her. Her arms were bare, rounded and pinky-white: I couldn't picture them now akimbo on her hips, nor could I recognise in her any trace of the quick little shrew who had squabbled with Voogdt across a cabin full of crumbled foresail. She had taken on an air of costliness; her hair was done elaborately, twisted in coils round the top of her little head, and round her neck she had a collar of pearls. Miss Out-of-doors I'd called her in my mind, but now she looked as though she'd never been outside a drawing-room: it was as though a tough little sea-pink had become an exotic from the hothouse.

I stared so—with my mouth open, as likely as not—that I think she must have felt a little shy—just enough to make her play the dignified hostess for the first few minutes. She blushed, too, and of course that made things worse than ever; and what with that, and what with the strange new daintiness of her, and what with my serge clothes and thick boots, I felt so awkward that I thought I should never get out a civil answer to her greetings. It was all over in a moment: just a 'How d'you do?' and 'I'm glad to see you,' and she had turned to Ward and Voogdt, and left me with my ears burning, wondering at the prettiness of her bare neck and trim waist seen from behind. Whilst she was talking to them I had time to catch my breath, to pull myself together and resolve to try and behave more like a civilised man and less like a 'foremast Jack ashore.

After the first few minutes that came easily, for she hadn't changed her manners with her frock, and her chatter soon set me at ease again. Only when we sat down I couldn't take my eyes off her. Ward sat facing her, Voogdt was on her right and I was opposite him. I think the dinner was simple enough, though I don't know in the least what was served: fish and fowl and sweets, or something like that, with claret to drink and lemonade. The elderly maid waited on us, and until she withdrew with the last of the dishes the talk was necessarily on general subjects. When the door shut behind her Miss Brand took a cigarette, leaned forward and plunged directly into the very subject we had been warned to avoid.

'Business before pleasure,' she said. 'I want the whole of this story about Willis.'

She looked at me, I looked at Voogdt, and we both turned awkwardly to Ward, who answered for the pair of us.

'My last words on leaving the *Luck and Charity* this afternoon were to warn these two to keep off that subject,' he said.

'And why?'

'Well—for your comfort.'

'Comfort!' she cried, with a sudden passion, and slapped a hand upon the table. 'Why will you persist in this attitude of shielding tender woman from the cold wind? Haven't I worked for the syndicate like a man?'

'Better than most men,' Ward answered her.

'Then why can't you treat me like a man?'

'Because you aren't one. Because you approach a business matter with heat, and bang tables and make us all uncomfortable. That's why.'

'I'm sorry.' She was shamefaced on the instant. 'I'm very sorry. But he's my cousin, as you know—and I thought a lot of Willis. I won't be silly again. Now, Mr Voogdt, tell me the whole story plainly. I must know it, you know.'

With her elbows on the table, she listened quietly, never moving except to blink or wave away the cigarette smoke when it got into her eyes, whilst Voogdt went over the whole story again. Now that she was exercising self-control no one would have imagined the matter had any importance for either of them. He spoke without a trace of heat or sneering or emphasis of any sort, and she never once interrupted or showed any trace of emotion whatever. When he had done her manner was as cool and collected as though she had no interest in the affair, and I began to recollect what Ward had said about her business ability.

'You think it wise to let him have this promised cargo?' she asked.

Voogdt gave his reasons, like a man reciting a lesson. 'I don't see any other alternative,' he concluded.

'Nor do I. But—we must do it, I quite see—but it's annoying to be compelled to give them anything at all. And suppose he wants it done again?'

'He shan't do that. We'll make that clear to him, rest assured. And, as I've already pointed out to West, I don't think the firm will be much out of pocket on the deal in the end.'

'Somebody must be there to keep an eye on him,' she said, with decision. 'You'll be away on voyages; there's nothing to prevent him making those voyages long ones; and in your absence he can do as he likes. I must stay at Terneuzen myself after this.'

'If I've anything to say about it, you won't,' I said, finding my tongue at last.

'And why not?' She had never put me on the same footing as Voogdt, but now her manner seemed positively insulting.

'Because it's no place for a woman. We don't know what risks there are, and we do know that Cheyne can't be relied on.'

'Do you think I want Willis Cheyne to look after me?' she said sharply. 'On the contrary. I'm going there to look after him.'

'That's a man's job.'

'I've already told you to consider me as a man. I was doing a man's work before you were a member of the syndicate, and I don't see that your joining it affects my position.' She turned to Ward. 'I'll stay there till the end,' she said.

'The end?' I asked, puzzled, for she spoke as though the end were already in sight.

She still looked at Ward. 'Tell them what we decided when we took them into partnership,' she ordered.

'Oh! that.' Ward spread his hand on the table, examining his finger-nails minutely. 'We—ah—we decided that if we didn't approve of you as partners we would throw up the whole business. We've made enough out of it for our purposes, you see.'

'Why didn't you throw it up at once?' Voogdt asked.

'It didn't matter much, one way or the other. I think West's work throughout the winter decided us as much as anything. Cheyne pointed out that he'd served us loyally through a very trying winter—'

'The deuce he did!' I said. 'Why, he detests me.'

'Whether he detests you or not, he protested strongly against any suggestion of throwing up the business.'

'Has he drawn his profits as they became due?' Voogdt asked, and Ward nodded.

'That explains it. He's broke. I guessed as much, from half-a-dozen little signs.'

'It's impossible,' Pamily Brand said. 'We're—we're all well-to-do. How can he have spent his share in that quiet place?'

'Gambling. The fool I—as if there weren't enough excitement in the business itself. He hasn't been buying securities—such as Japanese loans.' He threw a sly glance sideways at Ward. 'You may as well throw water into a sieve as expect that sort of chap to keep big money. He's just lost his head, and gambled. I'll bet you what you please that he hasn't a thousand pounds in the world, and that he owes more than that. That explains his desire to keep the business going—and explains some other things as well. Thieving, for instance.'

Ward seemed inclined to doubt, but Pamily Brand insisted that Voogdt was right. It was evident that she had tried and condemned Cheyne, and now, like a woman, she wouldn't hear a word in his favour.

'Of course he's a fool,' she said, and then suddenly dragged me in as conclusive evidence. 'Didn't he try to start stealing from his own friends and call you in as an accomplice?' she said, as though that settled the matter once for all.

She took me all aback.

'Me?' I said. 'What do you mean?'

For once she sort of twinkled at me as though I were an old friend, but when I saw that Ward and Voogdt were laughing, I understood she was making a butt of me and it made me furious.

'Look here, Miss Brand,' I said, getting up, 'I'm at your table, and that makes it very difficult for me to say anything. All the same, you should remember I'm your guest and stop your sneering for once. You've never treated me fairly. From the first you've always treated me like a fool—which I am, I daresay. I'm not as clever as you are, and when your cleverness leads to making people uncomfortable, I don't want to be. You sneer at me as Cheyne's accomplice. I never wanted to be. Ask Voogdt, there, whether I didn't want to punch his head at the very start of this thieving.'

'I knew it!' she cried. Her voice shook so that I thought I'd gone too far and frightened her. 'I knew it. I c-could have sworn it.' She turned to Voogdt. '"Punch his damned head and write to Ward and expose the whole business." Weren't those his very words?'

'Those very words, as far as I remember,' Voogdt said. 'If you'd been there you couldn't have reported them better.'

I was standing with my hand on the back of my chair ready to go. Her face I couldn't see whilst she was talking to Voogdt, but when she turned to me again she was smiling quietly, and she spoke as pleasantly as if we were old friends.

'Sit down, Mr West,' she said. 'You take my nonsense too seriously. Now I'll try to speak plainly, so that you can't misunderstand me. When I laugh at you, remember it's a privilege I always claim towards people I consider my friends. Ask Leonard there whether I never tease him. When I said Willis was a fool in choosing you as an accomplice I didn't mean that you were stupid—though you are, to take fire at nothing—but that you were too honest for his purpose. He ought to have known that. I knew it, ever since that night you came to us at Terneuzen, tired out and wet through, poor dear. Another thing: I'm a woman and I mix much with other women, and clever quick-witted men who try to think and talk like women. And that means that they avoid the obvious—put the cart before the horse, so to speak. You don't, you sailors. Willis didn't. He just said what he meant, and it was a blessed change and I liked him for it. And you're the same, and I like you for it. You're honest, and Willis is not, so I like you the better. And you've worked and risked your life in my—in our interests. Do you think I don't appreciate that? Surely you aren't going to deny me my privilege of making fun of you a little sometimes?'

'Sometimes? It's always,' I said. 'And I didn't understand it was just teasing. It seemed sneering to me.'

'Please believe me, it never was,' she said very seriously. 'Come. Shake hands and sit down and be friends. I won't tease again if you don't like it.'

That disarmed me. 'Tease as much as you like,' I said, sitting down, as she told me. 'As long as I know you're only teasing. I thought you were angry with me because I didn't like Cheyne.'

'Well, now you know better, because I don't like him myself,' she said shortly, as though dismissing an unpleasant subject. 'Now, business. Anything further to lay before the meeting?'

Voogdt plunged into the business at once as though to help change the subject.

'Our methods are too primitive,' he said.

'You'll find it difficult to better them,' Ward said briskly, and the two of them began a lively discussion. I said nothing, and Pamily Brand very little for once. She sat listening, putting in a word now and then, and occasionally smiling round at me as though to reassure me of her good will.

Voogdt got out several suggestions, more to make talk than anything else, I fancy, for Ward disposed of them easily enough. Primitive as the ballasting seemed, it was evidently the only practical method of removing the wolframite without arousing suspicion.

'But things are changed now,' Voogdt insisted. 'You haven't any object in deceiving your one crew any more. Surely that should permit of some safer way of doing business.'

'Suggest one,' was all Ward would say.

'What about packing it in bags labelled as fertiliser?'

'It would come to the ears of the farmers at Terneuzen at once. They'd try it, find it worthless, and then begin to make inquiries as to our English market. No good. You dare not betray that it has any value until it's safe in our warehouses.'

'It's losing stuff from English quaysides bothers me,' Voogdt explained.

'We've had to put up with it, and you'll have to do the same.'

'Can't we take the bags aboard empty and fill them from the ballast in the hold when at sea?'

'That's not a bad notion,' Pamily Brand cut in. She must have been listening keenly, for all her air of inattention.

Ward agreed. 'Not a bad notion at all.'

They appealed to me, and I said I thought we could bag some part of each cargo, though not all, as that would mean long delays at sea as well as considerable practical difficulty.

'Then we order the bags here tomorrow and you can get them aboard at once,' Ward said.

'How long will they be making?' I asked.

'A couple of days or so. There's no such violent hurry for you to get away. A day or two of holiday won't hurt you.'

That point settled, we all got up to go. Pamily Brand saw us to the door and shook hands all round, with me last.

'You won't be silly again, will you?' she said. The others were going down the path towards the gate.

'You must forgive me for behaving like a fool,' I said.

'I will,' said she. 'As a token of forgiveness you can call for me here tomorrow morning at eleven, and take me out. I want to do some shopping and you shall carry the parcels. A great privilege. Goodnight.'

CHAPTER XV

CONCERNING MODERN MAIDENHOOD

THE shopping proved to be only an excuse for a walk in the fresh March wind. She called at one or two places to leave orders, but lingered nowhere—as I always thought women were supposed to do, shopping—and there were no parcels at all for me to carry. In half an hour she announced that her marketing was done and proposed a walk before lunch.

Six months earlier I should very likely have been fool enough to think she meant playing with me, as she had at Dartmouth, but last evening's passage of words had disposed of that idea. I confess I didn't understand her altogether, but it had at last been driven into my thick head that she wanted to be friends, in spite of her sharp ways. So I wasn't looking out for causes of offence all the time, and we got on all the better for it. When she snapped at me for slowness or stupidity—as she did often enough, to be sure—I just laughed; and then she laughed too, and we went on as before. It came to me gradually that I'd misjudged her from the start. Of course a man doesn't like being sneered at bitterly and called a fool at first acquaintance; but it was past denying that I had deserved the sneers, and the name too. It was nasty physic to be told so by a girl, but it was physic that had done me good. Remembrance of her anger and contempt had helped as much towards keeping me steady as getting into collar again. More, perhaps: the work had been a sickener during the winter, and I might have gone back to my old ways if I hadn't seen where they led. And being slanged by a nice little quick-tempered girl had opened my eyes to the folly of them more than anything else had done—more even than that winter's short commons at moorings in Exmouth Bight.

Thinking of all this I was pounding along the road full stretch when it struck me I was walking too fast for her and pulled up to say so. She was keeping up well, but with the wind in our faces I expect her skirts bothered her, for she was flushed with exertion. Winter being only just over, she wasn't freckled as much as when I'd first seen her, and again it struck me as it had the night before that she was really pretty sometimes. Her features weren't statuesque, certainly, but her warmed skin was clear, her eyes big and dark, and, if her mouth was impudent, her lips were dainty curves enough. Dark fur was round her neck and with her dark hair framed her face, contrasting with its colour. Her bright eyes and mouth laughed together as I turned to her.

'Penny,' she said.

'For my thoughts, you mean? I thought I was walking too fast for you.'

'What thoughts made you walk so fast?'

'I was thinking how you slapped my face and called me a fool when first we met.'

'You were a fool, you know.' She shook her head in deprecation. 'And you certainly deserved to have your face slapped.'

'For asking you to come for a walk with me? What you are doing at this minute.'

'It's different now, as you know very well. We're friends, aren't we? We weren't then, and I never imagined we should be.'

'Why?'

'Why! Have you any idea how you looked? Filthy, unshaven —a drunken-looking wreck. You were a—a blot on the morning.'

'Why did you trouble to come back and slang me, then?'

'Trouble?' She laughed—a little low chuckle. 'It was a pleasure. I hate dirt and waste and slovenliness. I'll tell you—all the way across in that dirty little leaky boat my fingers were itching to brush the mud off your coat.'

'Why should you take that much interest in me?'

'Oh! the eternal conceit of man! I didn't take any interest in you personally. It was your dirt I was interested in. Grubbiness always wakes me to an active interest in life. It makes me want to scrub and dust, and bang things about, and set windows open. Can't you understand? If you'd been clean—a nice, washed and shaven boatman—I shouldn't have taken any notice of you. See?'

'Don't I interest you now I'm cleaner?'

'Yes, as a friend, you do. I've enjoyed watching that dirty, idle ruffian I found asleep on Exmouth beach turn into a self-respecting man. The wild lust to scrub you has departed, and now I want to see you go on and prosper. You're a friend, see? I've lots of friends and I like to see them do well.'

She spoke the truth, now I came to think of it. She had lots of friends, and a queer, varied set at that. Ward, a clever, well-informed man of science, and Miss Lavington, sleepy and beautiful—both made almost a pet of the little scatterbrain. Voogdt, many-sided man of the world though he was, always had a special smile for her benefit when they met. The old skipper of the *Kismet* had spoken of her in quite a different tone to the rest of his employers. 'Kiah always had a grin underneath his touched cap when she came his way. And though I'd always thought her a wicked-tongued little shrew, I knew no other woman in the world I could talk to as plainly as I could to her, and if I'd been in a mess of any sort and she could have helped me, I would have gone to her readily. I don't think I ever put any credit to her on that account. I should have just taken her good offices as a matter of course. It seemed her proper job, somehow, meddling in other people's concerns. You couldn't know her long without feeling that about her—that she was in her element flapping dusters, and stirring things up, and putting them tidy. It never occurred to me she deserved praise for it.

Her voice cut in on my thoughts.

'Penny,' she said again. 'How you do stride along when you're deep in thought. Don't get thinking on board, or you'll walk overside.'

'I was thinking of what you said—that cleaning and tidying-up is your *métier*. I think you'd look rather pretty with your head tied up in a duster like a little Japanese housewife.'

'Is that intended as a compliment?' she asked, with her eyes narrowing. 'Rather a back-handed one, isn't it—to tell a girl she looks her best when she's partly covered up?'

She laughed freely again. 'I wasn't sure. You mustn't use the word pretty in that tone when you're talking to me, or else you'll find you're steering for another slapped face. I know just exactly how pretty I am. I see my looking-glass every day, and compliments are barred.'

I didn't understand.

'D'you mean—' I began.

'I mean that I know the extent of my personal beauty,' she said tartly. 'I know my nose tips up the wrong way and that I freckle. I hate silly compliments, because I know exactly how much they're worth. I've lived for years with Anne—with Miss Lavington—and nobody dares try flattering her. Whereas—how is it a girl of my type can't talk for an hour to a man without the fool trying to stuff idiotic compliments down her throat? I suppose the magnanimous animal wants to console me because I ain't a beauty, like Anne.'

She talked so simply and so entirely without affectation that I felt as though she were discussing some third person, and I answered her as impersonally, with no thought of compliment—just trying to put the other side of the case, as it were.

'Your eyes are big and dark, and your mouth's very pretty,' I got out and was going on when she stopped and faced me with her eyebrows level—almost scowling.

'You're asking for it,' was all she said, but I dried up, for she looked vicious, and there we stood staring at each other. She seemed to expect some sort of apology, so I begged her pardon and said I was sorry. 'Though what for, goodness knows,' I said. 'I meant no harm.'

'Enough said,' she replied, laying down the law. 'Kindly remember personal comments are forbidden in future. Now we'll go back to the town and you shall give me some lunch. And with the wind behind us you can walk as fast as you please. I'm hungry.'

We had something to eat at a confectioner's, and I enjoyed it immensely, blessing Voogdt's notion of the fertiliser sacks for keeping me ashore this day or two. She was bright and merry as you please, and I didn't feel constrained as I had at her table the night before. I got her on to talk about things that interested her—the Woman's Suffrage business for one—and the more she talked the better I liked it. You can't talk to most women for long without coming back to the only subject that interests them—and that's themselves, nine times on ten. They always seem to be thinking about something else—their own back hair, most likely. But this girl didn't seem to think about herself at all; she gave one the notion that even if her back hair had come down it wouldn't have affected her conversation—unless she stopped to curse it for getting into her eyes. The Sphere of Womanhood was the thing she was most keen on—the Suffrage, and all that, and at first I made her rather wild by laughing at it. When she showed signs of getting really nasty I quieted her by pointing out that sailors couldn't vote either, but that they didn't make half as much fuss about it.

That was a new idea to her. She meditated over it awhile, judicially, with her chin on her hand.

'Why don't they agitate?' she asked.

'Stick hatpins into policemen and horsewhip ministers, do you mean? Because they've got other work to do. If they were ashore agitating what would become of trade, and their wives and kids?'

'Women have work, too.' She was hot about it in a moment.

'D'you think I don't know it? I'm a woman's work myself, and so is every man or woman born. Don't mistake me. I don't say motherhood is a reason against the franchise. I'm all for your having it. But I don't think it's a matter of great importance. I haven't a vote myself, and don't want one—and woman's true work is important—vitally important.'

'Woman's true work, meaning wifehood and the rest of it,' she sneered. 'How about me? I'm not married, and don't want to be.'

'You announced your special job this morning,' I said. 'You've a call for tidying things up.' I chuckled to myself, thinking I had her there, but I hadn't.

'And that's just what I'm doing working for the Suffrage,' said she in an instant, and so scored off me instead.

Apart from the abstract question of the vote, it was amusing to hear her talk of her life and the women she worked with. She hadn't any very lofty ideas of women's ability, whatever she thought of their deserts. To hear their talk made her think of beating to windward in a shallow draught boat, or of making bricks without straw—of any job which meant lots of exertion and precious little to show for it. She had her own word for it. 'Like trying to drive little pigs one way in an open field,' she said, with a twinkle, pleased at the simile. All through she spoke of other women with a sort of affectionate contempt, as though they were a lot of children playing at being grown-ups.

'Poor dears!' she said. 'The poor, muddling dears! Listen to this, now. A woman speaker was sent to me at home, in Edgbaston, to stay the night, speak in Birmingham next day, and then go on again to Rugby. She arrived at ten p.m. in a cab, with a small baby, a nurse, and a trunk about as big as the cab itself. She'd mislaid my address, gone to a post office to get a directory, listed all the Brands in Edgbaston, and driven to each address in turn till she found me. Whilst the baby was being put to bed she argued with me about High Church services versus Low, until the cabman sent in to know if he was to wait. Then she asked me to pay him—to charge it up against head office, of course—and I did so. He said he'd been driving from place to place for over three hours, and the woman said vaguely that she thought that was about right. She seemed to think I was to blame for her losing the address.'

'Poor kid,' I said.

'Are you talking to me?' she demanded indignantly.

'Yes. I was referring to the woman's baby,' I said. I had her that time, and she showed it by getting pink and stammering a little.

'Poor mite. It had slept all the time, the nurse said. She was a capable woman, fortunately.'

'And the mother?'

'Oh, she was past praying for. She went off next day after attending her meeting, and left half her clothes lying about her room. I wasn't going to have that, so I just made a bundle of them and drove down to the station in the hope of catching her.'

'Did you?'

'Did I not! She'd packed her purse in the trunk, and was turning out all its contents on the platform to find it, with the cabman waiting in the background. Her train was gone and she had forty minutes to wait for the next—a slow one.'

'Do you want any more arguments against the movement after that?' I asked.

'Don't be a fool. A thing is either right or wrong, no matter who pleads it. This is right and just, and you know it. Not all the silly women's folly in the world can alter its essential justice. This woman was a dolt, of course, but so are many men. You don't want to disfranchise them.'

'Men don't use hatpins and dog-whips,' I said.

'Disfranchise them wholesale and they'll use rifles and bayonets,' she retorted. 'There, I don't want to spoil our lunch by arguing. Right's right, and wrong's wrong. You know it, and so do I. And what's the use of squabbling about it?'

'Good enough,' I said. 'I've finished. When I'm settled down and have a vote I'll use it for feminine suffrage. That's a promise. And let me tell you this: if you women used more straight talk and less hatpins you'd make more converts.'

'Now you're being nice,' she said, with approval. 'I'm promised a vote, so my day's holiday hasn't been wasted; and I'm pleased with myself and you too.'

The argument and the lunch finishing together, we went out into the street and I asked if I should see her home.

'Not yet,' said she. 'What's the good of spending fine weather indoors? Lets go down to the waterside and say how-de-do to the faithful 'Kiah. I like 'Kiah, and I haven't seen him since I scared him so at Terneuzen.'

'That was a shame,' I said. 'He was really frightened—his life was a misery for days afterwards.'

'I made sure he'd desert,' she said.

'Not he. He's too straight and good a chap for that.' I told her how he'd stuck to me when I was broke. When I'd done:

'He thinks a lot of you,' she said. 'I wonder why?'

'Because I think a lot of him. I trust him and he can trust me. That's why. And it's because you women haven't that sort of trust in you that you can't—'

'Stop,' she said threateningly, her finger in air. 'Stop it. That argument's concluded. I hate flogging a dead horse.'

'Right,' I said, and we walked the rest of the way to the quayside in silence.

A Tyne collier lying next ahead of the *Luck and Charity* was discharging into some trucks alongside, and the din and flying coal dust seemed worse than ever after the walk and cleanly served lunch in a girl's company. We walked round the end of the line of coupled trucks and found our boat wrapped in an atmosphere of idleness, her hatch off, her hold empty, and 'Kiah sitting on the fo'castle companion smoking and admiring his laundry hung out to dry upon the forestay.

That caught her ladyship's eye, of course.

'Look,' she cried. 'Only look! These clothes hung out in a shower of coal dust. Man, the reasoning animal!'

''Kiah would have done better to dry them on the green lawns all round us, I suppose,' I said dryly.

'What do you mean by that?' she demanded.

'I mean that he's got no other place to dry them. Coal dust is clean dirt—better than damp clothes, anyhow.'

'Why couldn't he dry them by the stove downstairs?'

'Why should he trouble? In this wind they'll dry quicker where they are, and a bit of coal dust won't hurt him. It's sanitary enough.'

'I shall tell him,' she said.

'For goodness' sake leave him alone. If you start talking to him about shirts and socks you'll horrify him. Really you will. He'll think you're indelicate.'

'He won't?' she said incredulously.

'He will, I tell you. I know him better than you do. You don't know the queer notions of modesty these men have. Do you realise that he'd think it indecent if you saw him with his feet bare? You'll only make him vilely uncomfortable if you talk laundry. Do have sense enough to disregard his washing altogether.'

Just then 'Kiah saw us and jumped up, touching his cap and grinning a welcome—to Miss Brand more than to me, presumably, since I'd seen him at breakfast-time.

'Where's Mr Voogdt?' I asked.

'Gone ashore,' said 'Kiah, and then turned his attention to helping Miss Brand across the gangway. I stayed where I was, looking at our dirty little home. I suppose it was the 'Mister Voogdt' waked me to thinking what a queer crew we were for a coasting ketch. Me, skipper, with a deep-sea ticket—and extra master's at that—Voogdt, mate, an educated man, with polish and brains, picked up from the roadside, practically starving, and 'Kiah as ordinary a coasting hand as one could meet anywhere. Add that our cargoes were, comparatively speaking, worthless, our ballast really valuable, and that we were practically engaged in piracy, for aught we knew at the risk of our lives, with this jolly little girl as one of our partners, and it struck me anew that we were an unusual trading concern, to say the least of it.

CHAPTER XVI

OF A CONVIVIAL GATHERING

NEXT morning we were up early and away before the turn of tide. The bags had come alongside the evening before, and with the help of the stevedore's men we had the lot aboard before midnight. I had got into the way of hating putting to sea of late, but somehow things looked brighter this morning than they had done for a long time. The day or two of holiday had done me good; there was a touch of spring in the air; once we heard a thrush whistling, halting notes, but sweet and clear, when we tacked close in to the north shore of the river. Voogdt seemed to feel the influence too. He was tending jib-sheets, a job which should have kept him fairly busy beating to windward in a narrow channel, but he found time to come aft and sit on the skylight to fill a pipe.

'Nothing much wrong with this, is there?' he asked, loosening his neckerchief. 'Summer's coming.'

'And a good job too. I don't want another winter at this trade.'

'I don't think you'll get another winter of it. I shall reckon we're lucky if the job lasts us three months longer.'

'Think so?'

'Something in my bones tells me so. How can it last? Our coming in was the beginning of the end. We've broken into a tight little family syndicate, and all of 'em have relaxed precautions a bit. Here in Erith Ward's been aboard constantly, when there were no business reasons for him to be. We've been calling for him at the hotel—dining with the little Brand. I don't say anyone's watching us, but if they were, what would they make of all this friendship between owners and employees? What should we have said, three months ago? Then there's Cheyne. How do we know what surprises he may have to spring on us next?'

'I don't care,' I said. 'If the bottom falls out of the whole business tomorrow, I'm better off than I ever was before. And after this life it'll be a comfort to get back to deep water again. No more slacking about out of collar for me.'

'Same here,' said he. 'I've done right well. I'm sound in health, and I've got real money in the bank. But all the same I can do with some more, and I don't intend Master Cheyne to spoil my game if I can help it. That's what I've been to London for.'

'What have you been doing there?'

'Well—it's as well to be prepared for contingencies In case the business looks like going pop all of a sudden I mean. With help we might at the last moment snatch, a big cargo worth having. I've been seeing about getting that help, at a moment's notice, if required.'

'How? You haven't been talking about the matter to strangers, have you?' I asked, in surprise.

'Have I? Now is it likely? I've whipped up three of the most promising wasters in London, pitched them a yarn about the Secret Service, and they're just hungry to come in. I spun 'em a fairy tale, all about spying on foreign coasts and a Secret Service mission disguised as a trading station. Then I took 'em one by one to my diggings, finger on lip, so to speak, and showed 'em my sea-boots and guernsey and the scar on my leg. That did it. Every one of 'em was keen as mustard after that.'

'You're mad!' I said.

'Not a bit of it. They won't ask questions—the Secret Service wheeze'll prevent that. And they'll be cheap labour, for they don't want pay, being already cursed with sufficient to live on and a bit over. They're just idling about London, bored to death and praying for a change. You don't know the breed.'

'Not know wasters?'

'Not this sort, I fancy. You know the country remittance man who won't work, but these chaps are different. They'd like something to do, only, as I tell you, they're cursed with incomes and so drift into becoming just men about town. They all get sick of that after a year or two, and anything like excitement'll fetch 'em out of it quick enough. Hundreds of the breed went to South Africa—in fact, I met two of my pals out there, one in the Yeomanry and t'other pretending to be a correspondent. There was another there too, in a colonial regiment. He came into money after the war, and then came home and has been at a loose end ever since. Don't look so sour. I've been as prudent as you could wish. We may not want 'em at all, and if we don't we shan't hear any more of 'em. If we do, you'll find they'll come in very useful.'

'Jib-sheets,' I said, and kept him busy for a while, going about every few minutes, so that he hadn't any more time for chatter. I confess I felt very annoyed at his taking such an important step entirely off his own bat, without consulting Ward or myself.

Picking our way down the lower reaches and dodging the incoming traffic was really quite enough of a job to occupy all one's thoughts without wasting time talking. I ought to have kept my mind on my steering and nothing else, but Voogdt's mention of Cheyne had sent my thoughts round to Pamela Brand, and I kept wondering what she was up to now. I suppose that made me a bit absent-minded, and I must have been slack and careless over my wheel. I thought of her walking and chattering beside me, of her pretty neck at dinner the night before, and of the friendly way her eyes twinkled when she was pleased, until a violent shouting almost over my head, and Voogdt's startled face, as he looked back at me, woke me to the fact that we were right in the track of a collier outward bound, and that she was drifting straight down on us with her engines stopped, hooting furiously.

I should have gone out of her way at once if her mate hadn't annoyed me. He was leaning over the fo'castle rail, cursing, and when he saw I was taking notice of him he got personal.

'Are y' in love, bargee?' he roared. The look-out man beside him sniggered, a sort of duty laugh, and Voogdt turned his back, suddenly becoming very engrossed in his work. That made me wild, and I lost my temper, I think. The grinning pair of fools! Being hot and angry and rather at a loss as to what to say, I perpetrated a chestnut I wouldn't have condescended to remember in the ordinary course of things.

'You the mate?' I asked.

'A sure thing I am,' he said.

'Then go and talk to your equals. I'm master of this craft.'

That finished him. To have that hoary-headed old wheeze flung at him—and him in an earnest hurry, too—was more than he could bear. He went aft without a word, and in a minute or two the collier began to drop back a little. Then she got under way again and tried to pass me, but every time she came up I went about and crossed her bows, and she had to stop again. Once or twice it was so near a thing that she had to go astern. Then her skipper actually did come forward to talk to me. I'd had enough of the joke by then and would have let her pass if he'd been civil; but he wasn't, ard so I kept them stopping, and going astern, for a good four miles farther. They brought lumps of coal on the fo'castle head at last and pelted us every tine we passed under her bows, but they never hit either one of us once, and we were well past Tilbury before they had room to get by. I shouldn't have played the fool like that if I hadn't been annoyed with them. As it was, I felt I'd got square with that mate, and the wind taking a slant more northerly just as the river widened, I called Voogdt to the wheel and went below and got breakfast, whistling, very pleased with myself.

We held the slant till the Kentish Knock was abeam and then the wind went round to the west of north, and we had a straight run across, never touching a sheet. Cheyne was very fretful when we met. Terneuzen in winter wasn't a comfortable shop at the best of times, and, being anxious to get the promised consignment of wolframite into his customer's hands, he was more irritable than usual at every delay. Why had we been so long at Erith? What were those rotten fertiliser bags for? He snapped and snarled and grumbled at everything, till I felt ready to kick him. Voogdt took him in hand, smoothed him down, had grub with him, went about with an arm around his neck, so to speak, and soon had him in a more trustful mood again. By the second evening he was quite all right and asked us both to join him at dinner.

'Make a four,' said he, 'and have a four-handed game of billiards afterwards.'

'Who's the fourth?' I asked.

'Van Noppen, the German manager. A decent chap that.'

Here was a shock, if you like. I recalled the last time I had seen Van Noppen, when he was full of explanations about his man's precious gun accident, and now we two—skipper and coasting hand—were to sit at dinner with our betters. I should have started questions at once, but for a warning glance from Voogdt, who accepted the invitation for both of us and then adroitly turned the subject to the proposed theft which Cheyne was arranging at Brest.

When he had gone ashore we looked at each other, aghast. 'What the deuce—' we both began, and then stopped together.

'What is the fool playing at?' I asked.

Voogdt shook his head and got off a Latin tag about the gods first depriving of reason those they meant to destroy. 'What is it little Miss Chattermag says? "Dropping into proverbs is a sign of failing intellect." That's me. This thing beats all. Has that fool taken Van Noppen into partnership already, or only paved the way for it?'

'What are we to do?'

'We must feed with them, that's certain. We can't get out of it without exciting suspicion now. But it'll be a gay party, by the look of it. We don't know how much Van Noppen knows, nor what he thinks of us. That's the hitch, really. What can he think? It would look funny to an outsider if 'twas only Cheyne and yourself dining together. But when I'm included—me, a mere coasting hand . . . How on earth can you smear that over to make it look natural?'

'No good asking me,' said I. 'I can't help you.'

'I'll ask Cheyne,' he said, and off he went ashore at once. When he got back he still looked anxious.

'I can't get any sense out of the fool. All he says is that Van Noppen knows we're his friends and that as he's a guest he'll be civil. I asked him what the man would think of his having coasting hands at table, and he said he wouldn't understand there was anything unusual in that, being a foreigner. A foreigner! Pah! I'm going to turn in and think hard.'

'Thought of anything?' I asked, when he re-appeared at tea-time.

'Nothing. I can't make head or tail of it. What was it I said to you in London river about the beginning of the end. All we can do is to behave as we did before and keep our eyes and ears open. You're still the coasting skipper, and I'm the Cockney hand. That's all. And tread gingerly, Jem, whatever you do. We shall have a critical audience to play to. Try and get him on to drink with you. I hadn't better presume so far myself, I suppose?'

We might have spared ourselves the trouble of such preparations. The dinner was laid in a small back room of the hotel we always used—the hotel by the locks—and Cheyne and Van Noppen were waiting for us together when we entered the stuffy apartment. They greeted us noisily, Cheyne half drunk, and the German not much better. So far from Van Noppen objecting to Voogdt's company, he slapped him on the back and invited him to drink immediately on our arrival.

Voogdt touched his cap, after the manner of the lowly coaster, drank the proffered glass with a 'Best respecks, gen'lemen,' and then stepped outside for a few moments. When he returned he was wiping his mouth, and under his arm was a box of vile cigars which he opened and placed upon the table for common consumption. A certain recklessness in his air that I hadn't noticed before made me anxious even then, at the very start.

When dinner began I thought he'd gone mad. It was no surprise to me that Cheyne should drink spirits, or that Van Noppen, who had elected to take beer, should help it out by a bottle of schnapps at his elbow, which he drank German fashion, neat in a liqueur-glass; but it scared me when Voogdt said that was a fine notion. 'On'y I don't like this 'ere schnapps much, Guv'nor. I'll 'ave whisky, same way.' A bottle was brought in to his order and he set about it like a dipsomaniac. As for me, half dazed by the noise they made, and worrying about his behaviour, I had a bottle of light wine and sat wondering what on earth would happen next, with those three madmen carrying on like that.

By the time dinner was half over they were all flushed and talking one against the other. Voogdt still kept up some pretence of being a coasting hand, but once he contradicted Cheyne flatly, and Cheyne, with his eyes wet and bright, only laughed at the insolence and called him 'old chap' in replying. Van Noppen praised him incoherently for his forbearance.

'It is goodness to be friends all,' was his way of putting it. 'At work—Master. Sir. Yass, all right. But with work done, drink a glass of beer brotherly. Eh?' He was appealing to me.

'A glass of beer,' I said, accentuating 'glass' and 'beer,' for he was drinking spirits in bulk.

'Or two. Three.' He poured out and emptied another glass of neat Schiedam. 'You dring Sauterne, Captain? No good, that. Cold veat'er, drink schnapps.

'Or whisky,' said Voogdt, and suited the action to the word.

'Graves'll do for me,' I said sulkily. I'd never dreamed that Voogdt had this weakness, and I felt sick and sorry. It wasn't so much the danger of exposure—though I saw that was imminent, with those fools drinking as they were—it was Voogdt himself I was sorry for. I'd often wondered whether his weak lung had been the sole reason for his going on tramp. But here was reason enough, if this was his idea of conviviality. The man was a drunkard, and I'd never discovered it till now.

By the time the last plates were cleared—the little Dutch waitress staring at us, half afraid, and keeping on my side of the table all she could—all three of them were half-seas over. Billiards? They couldn't have stood up, leave alone hold a cue. Disgusted, I got up to go. Van Noppen and Voogdt shouted protests, but Cheyne was too far gone even for that. His head was sinking on the table as I moved towards the door, dodging the other two men when they staggered to their feet to try to stop me. By going I should spoil a merry party, they insisted, and therefore I must stay.

I was in the hall, cap in hand, saying goodnight to the landlady, when the door reopened behind me and Voogdt lurched out. He caught me by the arm and in a drunken tangle of Dutch, German and English began trying to persuade me not to go. I snatched my sleeve from him, opened the hotel door and was out in the night without answering him, when he made another lurch and stumbled after me.

'Stop and see it out, you born fool,' he said, in a sober, vicious whisper. 'I'm drinking cold tea'; and before I'd got the sense of the words into my head he had relapsed again.

'I'm aw' right,' he insisted loudly, as if I had tried to get him away. 'Le's go back an' 'ave another. I'm aw' right, I tell yer. Aw' right. Where's my ol' pal, Van Noppen?'

He was just behind us, having followed Voogdt into the hall. He also was evidently very drunk, his fair hair hanging in straight locks over his forehead and his collar unfastened, but he was quiet, and quite ready to go back and resume the fuddling. Voogdt wriggled himself free of my hold and stood swaying, and then, embracing Van Noppen, the pair went back to the sitting-room again, where I followed them with my brain in a whirl.

Cheyne had gone to sleep in his chair, his arms out across the table and his head upon them, snoring heavily. A candlestick, upset by his elbow, was still fuming, its wick spluttering and stinking in a pool of grease upon the tablecloth. Van Noppen extinguished it with the bottom of an empty tumbler—and now that my dull wits were waking I noticed he did it without a slip or lurch—and then shook Cheyne by the arm, shouting in his ear:

'Wake oop,' he cried. 'Wake oop an' 'ave anot'er.'

Cheyne opened his eyes and looked up, utterly unconscious of his surroundings. He emptied the glass Van Noppen held to his lips, and looked around at us, his eyes set and stupid, with no trace of recognition in them, his head lolling from side to side. ''Ave another, you chaps,' he muttered, and collapsed again, snoring and gurgling in his throat.

Van Noppen remained stooping over him, listening to the noises he made, for perhaps half-a-minute. Watching him from behind I could see, now that my suspicions were aroused, that his attitude was intent and alert, not in the least the attitude of a drunken man. Quick as I could I dipped a finger in his glass of schnapps and put it in my mouth, and it was tasteless—only water! Voogdt, watching me, lifted one eyebrow drunkenly, and quicker than it takes to tell I made an H with my hands in deaf-and-dumb language, then held up two fingers, and then made an O, as before. Even as I did it the thought struck me that H_2O something resembled WO_2, and wondered if he'd understand. But he did—trust him—and nodded drunkenly, babbling something to Van Noppen about sitting down and ''aving another.'

Then, at last, I saw how things stood. Underneath all this noise and folly a duel of wits was going on between Voogdt and Noppen. Cheyne and myself had been equally out of it, and Cheyne being now out of action altogether, it was up to me to bear a hand.

I had scarcely made up my mind what to do when Van

Noppen rose erect, having satisfied himself, I suppose, that Cheyne need no longer be taken into account He played his part as before, and I took advantage of it as best I could, getting in his way and letting him knock me sideways with his first lurch. As I staggered I caught at the table as if to support myself—and his bottle of water was smashed on the floor.

'Be more careful,' I said, as though angry at his clumsiness. Voogdt took no more notice than to laugh vacantly, and proffer a drink from his own bottle. He dared that, when acceptance would have meant instant discovery.

But so far we were evidently to windward of Van Noppen. I was strung up to real interest in the game by that time, and it was rich to watch Voogdt pressing him to share the alleged whisky, and his guarded refusals.

'Whisky on schnapps? No goot,' he said, and pretended to hiccup. Oh, he played his game, well, too, past denying. He wanted to fetch another bottle of schnapps, but here I interfered again. I wouldn't let him get it. Both he and Voogdt had had enough, I said, and Voogdt was to come aboard with me. He refused flatly. He didn't care a curse for me or anybody else, and he was going to stay with his old pals and make a night of it. Why wouldn't I stay and be jolly? Van Noppen joined him in drunken persuasions, and eventually I consented with as ill a grace as I could manage. As I'd smashed his bottle I supposed I must pay for another, and before he could offer to fetch it, I'd rung the bell. And when it came in I had the first drink. It was schnapps this time, all right.

I'd drunk with Germans before, and I knew we should whack him when it came to spirits. They're accustomed to light beer, but they're a temperate people, else. He'd had a fair amount of beer already—beer and water alternately—and I'd had the best part of a bottle of Graves, so we started about level; and now I knew I could rely on Voogdt I didn't worry so much about myself. We both kept him at it as hard as we could, and by midnight he was as nearly drunk as ever I've seen a man. My head was humming a bit, and I wanted to talk, but I had the sense to keep off business topics. As for Voogdt, he looked awful—sprawling all over the table, and singing and shouting by turns.

At the last Van Noppen said we could see him part way home—as far as the *Luck and Charity*—but Voogdt refused.

'I aint goin' t' risk my life on them 'mbankmen's t'night,' he announced, with an attempt at sobriety. 'I know when I've 'ad my whack. I sh' sleep 'ere. You better, too, guv'nor.'

'I'm going aboard,' I said.

'No. Sleep 'ere. All sleep 'ere. Don' awn' no Dutch crowner's inquest in th' mornin'. Nasty marks passed about condition, leavin' th' pub night afore. All stay.'

Van Noppen agreed, though he had seemed inclined to come with me when I said I should go, and we ordered four rooms. After a bit of horse-play between Voogdt and Van Noppen, in which more tumblers were smashed, we dragged Cheyne upstairs and put him to bed, after a fashion, and then Voogdt insisted on seeing me in bed too.

'Ol' rascal,' he said, leering. 'Keep an eye on 'im, we must.'

They both stayed in my room till I had turned in, by which time Voogdt was asleep in a chair. Van Noppen stirred him up and got him outside the room, and by an altercation in the passage I judged he was insisting on seeing Van Noppen in bed too. ''Nother ol' rascal,' I heard him say, and finally they went off together.

I was just dozing off to sleep, angry at having wasted an evening, and puzzled to death wondering what on earth Voogdt thought he was playing at, when my door opened very softly, and his voice called me in a whisper. I was out of bed and at the door in a moment.

'What is it?' I asked.

'Dress, and drink a drop of this.'

He pushed a small square bottle into my hands and was gone as silently as he had entered. I pulled out the cork in the dark, smelt a pungent and familiar odour, and took a draught as he had ordered.

I thought I was killed! The stuff caught me in the throat, burning, so that my eyes stuck out and ran with tears, and cold sweat broke out on my temples. Thinking he'd gone mad and poisoned me, I struck a light with shaking hands, and found that the poison was nothing worse than Worcester sauce. Then I saw what he was at. I took a sip or two, more gingerly, and it pulled me together somewhat. Then I shuffled on my still warm clothes again, blew out the light, and sat down in a chair to await events.

CHAPTER XVII

VOOGDT DESERTS AGAIN

THE house sank to stillness and quiet, only broken by a faint growl of voices—Voogdt talking in Van Noppen's room, I supposed—and soon even that monotone ceased altogether. After the silly riot and noise of the evening the silence seemed ominous and depressing instead of restful. I felt rotten: tired, my head beginning to ache, a vile taste in my mouth; and the window being open, I crept to it, stocking-footed, and put my head out to breathe the cold night air, hoping it would freshen me up a bit.

The room was on the first floor, the window facing the sleeping village under the embankment, and the night being clear—though very dark, with heavy clouds hanging low and a slight drizzle falling—streaks and spots of light showed here and there through chinks in cottage window shutters like gold specks on black velvet. It was very still, and the little town was silent as the grave, and but for the sparks of light very near as dark. As I knelt by the sill one o'clock struck from the church spire, and in the stillness the stroke of the bell was like an actual blow upon my aching head.

My head fell forward on my arms, and I was nearly asleep when the door opened again behind me.

'That you, Austin?'

Though I whispered low, he slid a hand over my mouth before leaning out of the window beside me to peer into the darkness below. I looked, too, but could see nothing, strain my eyes as I would. Nor, I believe, could he; but making no more delay, he took my hand in his, made me feel that his boots were tied around his neck, and then pushed a leg over the sill and

181

began to wriggle out after it, holding tightly to my wrists. When his shoulders were level with the sill he stopped as though he had found foothold, felt with his feet for a moment, and then let go my hands and stepped out of sight. In a few seconds his head rose again.

'Roof,' he breathed almost inaudibly in my ear. 'Come.' I only stopped to lock the door and then picked up my boots and slid after him.

Some cookhouse or scullery had been built out from the back of the hotel, and its roof came exactly under my window. To slide from that to the ground was easy enough, and in less than a minute we had crept round the corner of the hotel and were crossing the lock-gates. Through my stockings I could feel their smooth woodwork wet and cold.

My teeth were chattering when we reached the opposite bank and sat down in the muddy roadway to put on our boots.

'What the devil are you up to?' I asked Voogdt angrily.

'Visit of inspection to the German sheds,' he whispered. 'Van Noppen's asleep and snoring. I put in a quarter of an hour lying on the passage floor outside his room to make sure. We shan't get such a chance again. Come along.'

'Which way are you going?'

'Inland and across the fields.'

I followed him, scrambling down inside the embankment, and knee-deep through the ditch beside it, and we set off at a jog-trot across the muddy pastures.

'Run,' said he. 'That'll warm us.' And we ran as best we could, slipping and sliding at almost every other step.

Even at the start I think I must have been too far gone for running to warm me. I only got out of breath, and had to stop and blow again and again, feeling colder than ever. The grass was wet and slippery. the drizzle was increasing to a steady downpour, and to make matters worse the fields were divided by ditches in place of hedges, and as we couldn't jump them in the dark we were constantly having to wade, generally knee-deep, and once as high as the waist. I don't ever remember feeling so washed out, exhausted and wretched.

As far as we could judge we kept a course parallel with the embankment, and at last were rewarded by catching sight of a vaguely outlined hummock that must have been one of our store-sheds by the wharf. Then Voogdt ceased running and advanced more cautiously, whilst I followed stupidly at his heels, too tired even to feel curious about what we should do when we got to the German settlement.

We must have been about half-way from our wharf to theirs when suddenly he stopped dead in his tracks. My eyes were growing more accustomed to the darkness and I could make out that he held up a hand as though to enjoin silence.

'Hear that?' he whispered.

I listened, but at first could hear nothing but the steady hiss of the falling rain. Then I became aware of a sound which obtruded itself on the hearing—a sound quite foreign to soft, muddy pastures. It was a crisp clinking sound, apparently coming from the top of the embankment, and it alternated with a harsh scraping as of stone on iron.

'Hear that?' he whispered again.

'Somebody shovelling stones,' I mumbled.

'I believe you're right. Stay here.'

He disappeared in the darkness and left me standing alone, my head nodding on my breast, half stupefied. The clinking continued, and once I thought I heard men's voices. Before I was sure—indeed, I was past being sure of anything, beyond that I would have given ten years of life to be allowed to fall asleep before a fire—Voogdt was back at my side.

'Come on,' he said, and we set off again in the same direction as before.

Slipping about on the mud behind him, it seemed years—and actually was, I suppose, a quarter of an hour—before we found ourselves scrambling over newly broken ground heaped up into a shallow embankment. Here the mud, bare of grass, was worse than ever, and it was difficult even to stand upright. Once I fell on all-fours, but Voogdt dragged me to my feet; and in another moment we were sliding down the other side of the embankment and sidling our way along a wall that felt as though it were made of plaited rope. By now I was past wondering even at this, only thinking dully that my fingers must be paralysed with cold. When we came to the end of the wall we were standing under the river embankment and looking up at the sheds upon it. They were plainly visible against the sky, owing, I suppose, to some faint reflected light from the water on the other side.

Here Voogdt took me by the shoulders and shook me. 'Pull yourself together,' he whispered angrily.

'I'm nearly gone in,' I said. 'That wall felt just like ropes.'

'It was rope, you fool. Explosive screens. You're all right. I'm going to chance it and see if I can get into those sheds up there. Can—will you come?'

'I'll try,' I said. He dropped on all-fours, and we crawled up the embankment, one behind another, like a pair of otters.

I have only the faintest recollection of what happened after that. Looking back, it all seems like a drunkard's dream, sometimes startlingly vivid and sometimes a blank. I remember seeing Voogdt's head from behind peering round an open doorway against a dim-lit interior, but how he got the door open I have no idea. I must have followed him in, but I have no recollection of it. I remember sitting in a comfortable chair in a clean, neat room with varnished deal walls lit by one lamp, turned very low, and drinking a glass of Schiedam that he handed me, and being very sick after it, and I remember seeing muddy stains from my fingers on the glass. There was a big roll-top desk against one wall, and Voogdt must have broken into it whilst I was being sick, for I watched him stupidly as he pulled open drawer after drawer, stuffing papers into his coat pockets I remember a large brass telescope fixed on a heavy stand and staring blindly at the boarded wall, and wondered why it wasn't at a window, until I noticed that all the windows in the room were above the level of one's head. Then I gave up that problem. There were some coils of insulated wire in a corner of the room, and one or two large accumulators, and after wondering what they were for, I soon gave that up as incomprehensible, too. And the next thing I remember is being back in the *Luck and Charity,* the stove burning almost red hot, and Voogdt plying me with hot tea, and helping me out of my wet and dirty clothes. His face was white and drawn, and he was to the full as filthy as myself. Then comes a longer blank, and I remember nothing more until I woke to find Voogdt shaking me and trying to drag me out of my bunk. It was still dark, and I had a hazy idea that I'd slept the clock round.

'Let me be,' I begged him.

'I daren't, Jem. We've got to be back in our rooms at the hotel before daylight, and it's four now. We must, man. It pretty well means life or death to us.'

'I'm aching all over,' I grumbled.

'I'm no better. You've had an hour's sleep. I've had none. Come out of it. Here are dry underclothes, your next best serge and clean boots. If we get away quickly and wear our overcoats he may not notice we've changed. Perhaps he won't see us, even.'

'Who?'

'Van Noppen, of course. Hurry. Hurry, I tell you.'

I got into the clothes somehow and we staggered ashore and towards Terneuzen. Dawn was almost breaking, but it was still pretty dark, and raining heavier than ever, so no one was about. Even the pilot-house was closed, and only a wisp of smoke from its chimney showed that it wasn't deserted altogether.

That climb on the cookhouse roof about finished me. I dragged off my coat and boots and fell on the bed with all the rest of my clothes on, utterly gone in. As to Voogdt, I don't know what became of him. I must have been asleep before he left the room.

When he woke me again, Van Noppen was with him, and I pulled the clothes up to my chin for fear he should see I was half dressed. Voogdt saw the movement and edged a little closer to the bed in case the German should start any horse-play like pulling off the blankets.

'Halloo, Captain,' Van Noppen greeted me. 'Elefen o'clock . . . How is your het?'

'Awful!' I said. I turned on the pillow as though to avoid the light, and groaned aloud.

'Haf a branty an' soda.' He had a glass of the beastly stuff ready in his hand.

'I'd rather have a cup of tea.'

'Right-o, skipper,' said Voogdt, and rang to order one.

'How's Cheyne?' I asked.

'Mr Cheyne, 'e ain't very well this mornin'. Late howers, they don't agree wiv 'im. 'Es 'ad two brandies an' sodas a'ready— an 'e looked like wantin' 'em.'

'And you?'

'Ow, I'm aw right.' He was pale as death, utterly washed out and wearied, his eyes hollow and dark with exhaustion; but he protested cheerfully: 'I'm aw right, skipper. Not azackly in the pink, per'aps, but you cawn't 'ave sprees wivout payin' for 'em, can yer?'

'I suppose not,' I said, as the tea arrived. 'Now give me that cup of tea and clear out. I'm going to dress.'

Breakfast was the final ordeal. All four of us were wrecks, to all appearance suffering from the same complaint. Either Cheyne or Voogdt would have served a teetotal lecturer as a Terrible Example, and I must have looked every whit as bad as either of them. Van Noppen, with German neatness had made some attempt to brush his hair and tidy himself generally, but his eyes were a beautiful shade of rose-pink and his manner was distinctly depressed. Very likely he was reflecting that his plans for the previous evening had miscarried somewhat. Not one of us had shaved, and taken in the lump we must have made a very pretty picture of a drunkard's quartet. But whilst Cheyne and Van Noppen had no appetites whatever, Voogdt and myself were ravenously hungry, and it was maddening to be compelled to pass one savoury-smelling dish after another, and content ourselves with dry bread and coffee.

But we did it somehow, and got away to the *Luck and Charity* just after midday. Van Noppen came with us, leaving us at our wharf and walking on homewards down the embankment. Before he had gone a hundred yards we were down below, standing at the cabin table eating cold meat and bread with our fingers, and watching his receding figure through the open skylight.

'He's got a surprise waiting for him,' said Voogdt, with his mouth full.

'What did you do down there? I was past taking notice.'

'You were. I never thought you'd collapse like that, Jem. What was the matter with you?'

'Drink, man. I let myself go, sewing up that chap. How was I to know you had this jaunt in view?'

'I couldn't well tell you, could I? I wonder if 'Kiah heard us come aboard? We must find that out amongst other things . . . Oh I I am tired, Jem! And there's tons to do before I can sleep.'

'What's to do?'

'Our clothes to clean; papers to read and burn; our best boots to be burnt or sunk in midstream. We've left tracks in that mud down there, for certain.'

'I'll do all that. You turn in.'

'Dare I? . . . Yes, I will. It'll be an hour or two before Van Noppen decides what to do next. But take care what you're about. We're watched all the time—that telescope—'

'I remember seeing that. But, seems to me it was clamped down facing a dead wall.'

'Pointing dead at us, here, though. The board in front of it was loose, and for certain it's screened from view outside. Where's my glasses?' He put them to the open skylight and stared through them for half a minute. 'Here, look,' he said at last, handing them to me. 'That's the room we were in, the second shed from here.'

I remembered it well—remembered describing it to Cheyne when first the sheds were built. The glasses brought it nearer, and showed a pile of boards heaped carelessly against its hither side.

'I see some deals leaning against the shed,' I told him.

'Yes.' He was getting into his bunk. 'They're there to screen the hole in the wall. Van Noppen can watch us from between them to his heart's content.'

'Sure?' I said doubtfully. Even with my mind full of our crazy night's expedition the idea sounded fantastic.

Voogdt swore at me aloud. Exhausted as he was, I suppose his temper was thin.

'You're the most thick-headed fool I ever met,' he said angrily. 'What are they for else? D'ye ever hear of any sane man storing deals on their ends out of doors in damp winter weather? They'd warp out of true after a single day of such treatment. You know they would. But I'm too done up to argue with you now. Here's Van Noppen's correspondence under my pillow, and I'm going to sleep. You mount guard and don't you let a soul put a foot into this cabin until I give you leave. Wake me if anyone comes this way from the German sheds, and don't forget you're being watched all the time.'

He pulled the blankets over him and I went on deck and had a chat with 'Kiah. He made no mention of anything unusual happening during the night, so it was evident he hadn't heard us come aboard, which was fortunate for once, though it gave me misgivings as to his value as a night-watchman. However, I couldn't remember his having been left alone in the same way before, so that probably his heavy slumbers hadn't harmed us as yet.

Bearing the telescope in mind I didn't pay any attention openly to the German sheds, only glancing down there from time to time out of the corner of my eye to see if anything was doing. A barge was being loaded at their wharf, men going to and fro between the boat and sheds, but there was nothing unusual about that Van Noppen was invisible—watching us, perhaps, though more likely he was sitting indoors scratching his head over the state of his living-room. As for us, we had nearly all our ballast aboard, and when the tide cleared the banks I went below intending to wake Voogdt and ask instructions.

He was out of bed, sitting before the little stove, reading and burning stolen papers one by one.

'Anything interesting?' I asked.

He shook his head. 'Not a thing. Nothing but *bona-fide* business estimates and orders. Looks as if we hadn't done much good by our jaunt.'

'What did you expect?'

'I don't know. But I'll tell you one thing I didn't expect, and that was to find the place deserted and Van Noppen's men all out road-mending at half-past one a.m. of a dirty night.'

'That scraping and clinking, do you mean?'

'Just that. I got as close as I dared, and it looked like road-mending, as far as I could make out. There were three men, and they seemed to be emptying buckets of broken stone or gravel on the embankment, levelling it with shovels and trampling it in. Funny, ain't it? We must have a look at that. But hang me if I know how to manage it, with their telescope on us all day, and the men themselves there after dark.'

'Meanwhile, what are we to do? Go on with the ballasting?'

'Of course. We must stick to our usual routine, now of all times. They mustn't notice anything. But we mustn't sail tonight, unless you can leave me behind . . . Can you and 'Kiah get her across to Erith without me, think?'

'If it's necessary, I daresay we can. Weather seems to promise fair enough.'

'Then that's what we'll do. We'll get away tonight and you shall put me ashore down river, somewhere between here and Flushing. I must be here on the spot for a bit. Cheyne's worse than useless, and I'm getting nervous.'

'What about?'

'Well . . . I'll tell you. Did you notice any electrical apparatus down there last night?'

'Some glass cells and coils of wire? Yes, I did. In the corner, between the telescope and the desk.'

'That's right. That's what I'm nervous about.'

'Why?'

'I can't understand it—and, as you ought to know by now, when I can't understand things they worry me to death. And the road-mending, too . . . No, there's more than buying and selling dynamite going on down there, and I must get at it, or—'

'Or what?'

'Ah! That's what I'd like to know,' said he. 'No good talking any more about it. Come up and get this ballast aboard, and off we go.'

We worked till dusk fell, got the hatches on, and began to wait for tide. Voogdt was so nervous, walking up and down and peering into the growing darkness, that he infected me; but I know questions would only bother him, and went about the usual business of getting ready for sea. He only spoke once, and then it was in a low tone.

'Bet you what you please Van Noppen's here before we cast off,' he said. 'And, what's more, he'll make sure we're all three aboard when we sail.'

'Think so?'

'I shall be disappointed in him if he doesn't,' said he, and, even as he spoke, Van Noppen's voice hailed us from the embankment.

'Sailin' tonight, Captain?' he called.

'In an hour's time,' I shouted back.

'Ah! Shall I come aboard?'

'You're very welcome,' I said. 'Sorry we can't offer you a drink, but this is a dry ship.'

'Dat's all right,' he said cheerfully. But instead of coming aboard he sat down on a bollard at the wharf-side and lit a cigarette. Anybody would have thought he had come after a drink, and stayed ashore because we couldn't give him one.

But as all three of us were on deck, Voogdt's conjecture wasn't impossible, either.

Cheyne came down shortly after, and the two of them were walking up and down the little wharf when we left. Even after they were out of sight in the darkness, their voices came together across the water to wish us fair weather and a good voyage.

Voogdt went below to pack as soon as we were well away, and I went to interview 'Kiah at the wheel. It was impossible to put Voogdt ashore without his knowledge, and for the first time we had to take the risk of letting him see a departure from our usual routine. I gave him no explanations, only telling him he was to land Voogdt in the dinghy at Hoogplaat, a village on the south side of the river about six or seven miles before we came to Flushing, and further, that he was to hold his tongue about it.

He asked questions, of course.

"'Ave 'e been doin' anything?" he inquired curiously.

'What do you mean?'

'Well . . . up there? Up to pub?' He jerked his head over his shoulder. 'I heered there was a bit of a barney when you was up there, night 'fore last.'

Nothing was more natural than that he should think Voogdt had got drunk and come into collision with the police, and he couldn't have got any idea into his thick head that would have served our purpose better.

I winked at him by the light of the binnacle lamp. 'Ask no questions and you'll be told no lies,' I said, very knowingly. 'If you don't know you can't tell, can you? You put him ashore quietly, and if anybody wants to know where he is, you can say you don't know—and that'll be the truth.'

'Kiah, full of delight at being admitted to a part in such high intrigue, winked back at me, gave over the wheel into my charge and got the dinghy alongside with the air of a conspirator. After dropping anchor in midstream, I went below and found Voogdt sitting at the cabin table, writing letters. He was still in his filthy working clothes, but had another suit and some belongings tied up in a parcel of sailcloth.

'All ready?' I asked.

'In half a minute.' He went on writing for a while until he had licked and addressed the last of his envelopes. For a moment he sat looking at them, chin on hand, and then turned to me.

'Sit down, Jem. I want a talk with you. I've been thinking out arrangements . . . If you want to write me, address Post Office, Erith. I'll have my letters fetched from there daily. Date, but don't sign your letters, and don't head them with any address—nothing but the date. Be as non-committal as possible, but never fail to let me know date, place and destination of every sailing from English ports. I shall report myself to you to the same address every other day. If I don't there's something wrong, and you must come and look for me.'

'Where?' I asked, with new misgivings at his earnestness.

'Down at the German sheds. I shall be thereabouts, dead or alive. Don't look so scared, man. I take a bit of killing.'

'I won't have it,' I cried. 'D'you think I'm going to leave you like this?'

'Don't be an ass. You're doing your share of the work and I'm doing mine. I'm giving orders and you must obey them.'

'I won't. Let's chuck the whole job, Austin. We're got enough out of it by now.'

He put his hand on my shoulder, looking very serious.

'Old man,' he said, 'believe me, we can't chuck it. Unless I'm mistaken it's more serious than we've thought' up to now. For a lark I told those fellows in London that if I wanted them it was for a Secret Service job, and I tell you the same thing now in all seriousness. I've nothing more definite to go on now than I had then, but on my honour I believe that that German explosive company is no more a trading company than we are. But they're better men than we. They aren't out for private gain— they're working for national ends, I'll swear; and it's up to us to do the same. So you must sail the *Luck and Charity* across and leave me here. Tell Ward all this if you see him, but don't write letters and don't breathe a word to a single soul else.'

'You're risking your life,' I said.

'And so are you. If these people are what I think, then your life's in danger as much as mine—and has been all along. It may be worth their while at any moment to have you run down or blown out of the water, and if it is they'll do it. Be sure of that. But man, all's risk at sea—or ashore either, for that matter. How would you rather finish—in a sudden and interesting scuffle, or in a wreck, helping to do this job for the benefit of the little island over across there, or in a bed at home? . . . There! Enough said! I've got action and risk, you the same risk with inaction. Mine's the more sporting job of the two, isn't it?'

He laughed straight into my eyes. Going off like that, to risk his life on beastly mud-flats in the dark, he laughed like a schoolboy going out to play. I couldn't say anything to him—couldn't speak, even.

'Now, here's your final orders. The minute you get to Erith stamp and post these letters. They're to my crew. You won't mind their coming now, will you? They'll report themselves within twelve hours of hearing from you. And I think that's all. All correspondence with me *via* Erith Post Office, remember. Goodbye, old man. Good luck.' He shouldered his bundle, ran up the companion, and was gone.

CHAPTER XVIII

OF A NONDESCRIPT CREW

THAT was a trip, that crossing. I don't ever remember a more miserable time in all my life. The weather was fine, and the wind fair, but light and fluky, so that we drifted rather than sailed from Flushing as far as the Girdler light. And all the time I was dancing mad with impatience to get to Ward and set a better brain than my own working on Voogdt's behalf.

There was next to nothing to do aboard, and I spent half the time tramping up and down our tiny deck, thinking, thinking, thinking of Voogdt out alone on those beastly mud-flats till my head ached. If I had left him in a hill country, with some cover about, I don't think I should have felt so bad about it; but, with the feeling of helplessness I'd experienced on that slippery, sliding jaunt still in my mind, it seemed to me there wasn't a dry place for him to hide in, in all west Flanders.

'Kiah made it worse. He was one perpetual covert snigger at the idea of helping to dodge the Dutch police, and went about his work more cheerfully than usual, carrying a face like a summer morning, whilst I was stamping up and down deck, whistling for a wind, mad to get to Erith for news, and making a poor job of trying to conceal my anxiety.

I never for a moment doubted that it was dangerous. Voogdt's word was enough for me. If he'd said Van Noppen was Commander-in-Chief of the German forces I should have believed it, I expect. The way he'd got at the secret of this wolframite business had shown me enough of his quality to ensure me trusting his judgment for ever after. By comparison with Voogdt I was like a blind man—blind and deaf. And the courage of him! To go off single-handed at night, ashore in an unknown district, with clever, sharp-eyed men looking out for him, quite ready to lay him out if they caught him—that was beyond me altogether. And here was I, who had left him to dangers of all sorts, and all unknown, dawdling across Channel in comfort as if I were out on a yachting cruise on a millpond, with that simpering fool 'Kiah for company. I could have drowned myself for the sheer shame of it.

It was a Wednesday night when we left Terneuzen, and we tied up at Erith at midnight of the following Friday. The post office was closed, of course, but I got some stamps at the dock office, posted Voogdt's letters before I turned in, and next morning was at the office again before eight o'clock waiting for it to open.

There was nothing from him as yet, and I went back aboard almost in a fever. Ward had gone away—to Birmingham, I suppose—and I was too worried to go out and see if Pamela Brand was at her lodgings. There was no sign of our last consignment of wolframite at our last berth, so I imagined Ward had managed to remove the cargo all right.

With only two of us aboard it had been impossible to put any of the present cargo in bags; but I took the risk of declaring it as coprolites instead of ballast, and wrote Ward to say I'd done so. Very likely I was running the risk of inquiries, but I'd got past worrying about that. By this time I didn't care if the whole business came out. The partners had all they wanted; they had said so; and as for me, I didn't care for anything beyond getting Voogdt back with a whole skin. Meanwhile the yarn about coprolites would save this one cargo from being taken away, and that was as much as I could do. I wasn't up to working out further ways and means of stealing wolframite just then.

My letter to Ward was curt—almost rude, I suppose, for I felt savage with the whole concern; but, reflecting that I couldn't do without his help, I put an urgent postscript at its foot, saying I was in trouble and that he must come and see me at once.

The first of Voogdt's crew came aboard that afternoon. I

became aware of him standing on the quayside—a sturdily built, clean-shaven man in decent blue serge, with a round sailor's cap and ribbon and the initials of the Southern and Orient Mail in white across the breast of his guernsey. I took him for a quarter-master of that line on a holiday, putting in his time hanging about the waterside, and not even when he hailed me did I guess who he was.

'You Cap'n West? Can I come aboard?'

Busy at the hand-winch, mechanically helping 'Kiah wind up tubs of mud from the hold, and with the back of my mind busy about Voogdt's affairs, I scarcely heard the chap, but absent-mindedly grunted out some sort of permission. He jumped into our rigging like a monkey and slid to the deck beside me.

'Can you give me a job, Cap'n?' he asked.

'What sort of a job do you want?' I demanded, with surprise. A liner's quartermaster asking for a job on a coasting ketch! It was as though a Harley Street specialist had applied for a billet as assistant to a country vet. or a K.C. begged to be allowed to conduct a five-shilling claim in a county court. I looked the man up and down, thinking he was guying me. 'What sort of a job do you want?' I asked again.

''Fore the mast,' he said. He spoke in a brisk, jerky way, but his manner was respectful enough. 'Or maybe mate, if you want a mate. Can I show you my discharges, Cap'n? In your cabin?'

Then I guessed what he was at, and glanced round at 'Kiah out of the corner of my eye. Fortunately he wasn't paying any attention, having his work cut out hanging on to the full weight of the winch. A tub was in mid-air, and for the moment I had taken my weight off the handle at my end.

'Wait a minute,' I said. 'Go aft and wait for me.'

The tub once swung ashore, I beckoned a quay lumper to take my place, and then went back to where the stranger stood by the companion, looking about him, and motioned him below.

When we reached the cabin it was he who asked the first question.

'You really are Captain West?' he said.

I showed him one or two envelopes addressed to me, and then, seeing he still hung in the wind as if doubtful, took down a book from my little shelf and opened it to show the name on the fly-leaf. It was one Austin had given me, and his name and mine together clinched the matter.

'"James Carthew-West from Austin Voogdt,"' he read. 'Good enough. That's all right. You'll know the writing on my testimonial, skipper,' and he handed me a sheet of letter paper. It bore a short note with neither signature, date nor address—just half-a-dozen lines in Voogdt's writing on a half-sheet of paper. 'Report yourself *at once* to James Carthew-West, skipper, ketch *Luck and Charity,* Erith. Ship with him in any capacity he thinks fit until you receive further instructions. Trust him *entirely.*'

'All right?' he asked, when I had done reading and handed back the paper.

'It seems all right. But what the deuce am I to do with you? Quartermasters from liners don't ship on packets like this without exciting remark.'

'Hum,' said he, and then laughed a little. 'My nautical attire was pitched in the wrong key, eh? I'll tell you. The S.O.M. intermediate boats call at Antwerp. I'm going there to join one, and am working my passage with you to save my fare. How's that?'

The idea was good enough, and I nodded in approval.

'But you can't do coaster's work in clean serge.'

'I've brought overalls. Am I to berth in the fo'—castle? What sort of a chap's that hand of yours?'

'A sound man—good as gold.'

'H'm. Has he got fleas, I wonder . . . All right, no offence meant. It's no matter, anyway. Fleas won't kill me: I've had 'em before. Now I'll get my bag aboard and change, and then I'll come and bear a hand with the winch.' And, sure enough, in half-an-hour's time his traps were in the fo'castle and their owner in filthy dungarees, was sweating at the winch in my place, joking with 'Kiah as if he'd known him for months. I began to think Voogdt hadn't been far out when he said there was some difference between his wasters and my remittance men, for no remittance man that ever I knew would have turned to like that. He'd have stuck up his nose in the air at the idea of associating with 'Kiah, and wanted me to go ashore and cement our acquaintance over a whisky bottle.

When we knoked off for dinner I had a word or two with him whilst 'Kiah was dishing up.

'What's your name?' I asked.

'Eh? Oh, I don't know—anything you please. D'ye want my real-name?'

'I don't care,' I said, rather stiffly, for I didn't altogether like his casual manner. 'I only want to know what I'm to call you.'

'Oh—Sellick'll do, won't it? Dick Sellick.'

No such name had been on any of the envelopes I had posted, and I said so at once.

'Never mind. One name's as good as another . . . I say, where's Austin?'

'I wish to heaven I knew,' I said, with sincerity.

'Don't you? Straight? No? When did you see him last?'

'Wednesday night.'

'Where, then? I say, skipper, shut me up if I'm asking too many questions.'

'I don't mind your questions if he's a friend of yours.'

'Friend, eh? Well, you know him, don't you? And he stood by me when I was down with enteric at Bloemfontein. Yes, I guess he's a friend all right.'

'Well, on Wednesday night 'Kiah—our man there—put him ashore at a crib called Hoogplaat on the south side of the Scheldt, and, if you want to know, I'm scared of my life as to what may have happened to him since.'

'He's all right. I've seen Austin Voogdt in tight places before . . . How much does your man know?'

'Nothing. He thinks he was trying to dodge the Dutch police, who wanted him for a drunken row. That's all.'

'How did this letter come to be posted here?'

'I did that at his instructions.'

'Any other letters?'

'Any more questions?' I said. He laughed.

'All right,' said he. 'Enough said. Only I was curious to know whether we should have any more company across.'

'As to that, I don't know any more than you do,' I said; and 'Kiah coming aft with my dinner brought the conversation to an end.

Sellick, as he had chosen to call himself, worked like a Trojan all the afternoon. At tea-time I noticed that his hands were galled and bleeding, and it filled me with amazement to see the way Austin could choose and use such a man. Here was he, fresh from idleness and comfort in London, ready and willing to do monotonous and heavy labour for nothing, just because Voogdt had pitched him the tale that there was danger in it. He seemed to throw himself into his part as thoroughly as Voogdt himself could have done. I heard him say to 'Kiah, as he looked at his bleeding palms, that turning a hand-winch was "'arder graft, matey, than spinnin' the wheel aboard the ol' *Pondicherry*.' 'Kiah said he reckoned that was so. You could see he was very pleased at rubbing shoulders on equal terms with such a marine aristocrat as a liner's quartermaster. That was an exalted social position which he could understand and appreciate.

After tea I went to the post office again, and was rejoiced to find a letter for me had arrived by the midday delivery. By the postmark it had come from Ghent, but it bore no address, only being headed by the date of the day after he had landed.

'All well. Am going to Antwerp and shall be there until I hear from you. Before sailing report who has joined you to V. Austin, George Hotel, Antwerp. If you don't hear from me to the contrary leave Mainwaring and Colley at T. with C. They can desert, if you want an excuse for leaving them behind.'

I heaved a sigh of relief. Surely he couldn't come to much harm in big towns like Ghent or Antwerp. They weren't like the lonely dark marshes I had been picturing in my mind all the time. One name he mentioned—Mainwaring—I had noticed on one of the letters I had posted overnight. The other was altogether strange. For all I knew, one of them might belong to this new hand, and was on my way back to the boat to ask when I met him coming up the street with 'Kiah, both of them apparently bent on spending an evening ashore. 'Kiah had cleaned himself as usual on leaving work, but Sellick still wore his dirty dungarees, and nobody could have distinguished him from anyone of the dozens of other quay lumpers and stevedores' men coming up the street from their day's work at the docks.

I nodded as I passed them and then turned and called him back. 'Hi you—Sellick.'

He came back at once. 'Yes, sir?'

'Your name Mainwaring?'

He shook his head, looking a trifle sulky.

'Colley?'

'No. I say—those two bounders aren't coming. What?' He seemed very disgusted.

'Voogdt advises me so.'

'H'm. Rotters, both!'

'D'you know them?' I asked.

'Sh' think I did—the rotters! What Austin can see in that pair of fools lays over me.'

'Don't you get squabbling aboard my ship,' I said.

He grinned. 'Hardly room, eh? All right, though. No private quarrels. I understand. Anybody else coming?'

'I don't know.'

'Pish!' he said. 'Half the loafers in town, I expect. Nice sort of picnic-party. 'Kiah's my man. I shall stick by him, and cut the rest of 'em.'

'Don't you go making him drunk or any nonsense like that,' I said.

'Not I. Milk—warm milk, in little glass bottles with rubber necks. That's his tipple. I'll nurse him. That all? Right. So long, skipper.' And off he went after 'Kiah leaving me staring after him and wondering whether he meant to be impudent or no. I had half-a-mind to follow them and send 'Kiah back on board, but on consideration decided he was big enough to look after himself. Besides, if the new man's words meant anything beyond mere cheek they implied that 'Kiah didn't want me grandmothering after him. I can't say I took to the chap or his ways either, and if he hadn't been Voogdt's selection I'd have sacked him then and there.

Having an hour at a loose end, I thought I'd go out and call at Miss Brand's lodgings, but I had my walk for nothing. She had gone to Birmingham, the landlady thought, and would I leave any message? I gave her my name, asked her to tell Miss Brand I had called and then went back aboard feeling rather disappointed and more depressed than ever. Of course there was no shadow of reason for expecting to find her there; but remembering our last stay at Erith, this present visit seemed extra dull. What with Ward and Miss Brand gone, and with my worrying about Voogdt, and my dislike of this new member of the crew, I didn't feel over-cheerful.

When I got back to the *Luck and Charity* it was dusk, and though I saw two men standing on the quayside as I went aboard I didn't take any particular notice of them. But no sooner had I lit the lamp in my cabin than I heard feet jump on the deck and there came a light knock on the lid of the companion.

'Who's there?' I called.

'Cap'n West aboard?' somebody called down the stair.

'Yes. Come in,' I answered.

The feet stumbled down the narrow stairway and two men entered the cabin. One was a tall lantern-jawed chap, with a little toothbrush of a moustache, and strong spectacles which magnified his eyes and made them look like an owl's, large and blinking. The other was short and spare, with a pale, clean-shaven face, dark eyes and hair, and a big forehead. He looked a sulky, ill-conditioned beast, and I disliked him at sight. The tall man I rather fancied. His spectacles gave him an air of amiability, as spectacles often do; and he reminded me a little of Ward, which was all in his favour. Even in this first moment of seeing them I thought to myself that it was just as well I liked one of Voogdt's selections, for I naturally guessed at once who they were.

'Cap'n West?' said the tall man, beaming through his glasses.

I took down the book that had convinced Sellick and laid the fly-leaf before them without a word. Spectacles looked it over carefully and deliberately, as though it were some wonderful old manuscript and it was a privilege to read it. The other man just glanced at it, and no more.

'Either of you Mainwaring?' I asked.

The spectacle man beamed and smiled again, as much as to say he was Mainwaring and very pleased about it.

'Colley?' I turned to the other, and got a grunt and a scowl by way of answer.

'You must pardon my friend,' the other cut in, waving a hand towards him like a Master of Ceremonies at a nigger ball. 'He's just gone through a trying time—very trying. He's—'

The other turned towards him savagely.

'Shut your fool head,' he snarled, and again it struck me I'd shipped a pleasant party aboard for once.

'I suppose you've got some sort of credentials or instructions?' I asked.

'I've a letter here from our mutual friend, dear old Voogdt,' the Mainwaring man said, fumbling in an inner pocket. His smooth way began to irritate me, in spite of the liking I had taken to the look of him. Later I found everybody was a dear old chap, according to him, or a dear fellow. He was too affable, by half. After an hour or two of his dear old this and dear old that, one turned to Sellick's jerky talk or Colley's sulks with positive relief. We English are like that, I think. If you take to a man at first sight, it's odds you change your mind about him later on, and very often men you dislike at the start turn out to be right good fellows at bottom.

Voogdt's note to Mainwaring was longer than the other I had seen.

> 'Go and dig up Harry Colley—I've forgotten his address—and the pair of you go to Erith the afternoon after you get this and find out James Carthey-West, skipper of the *Luck and Charity*, coasting ketch, who will give you a passage to Terneuzen, on the south bank of the Scheldt. Don't attract notice, and obey West's instructions to the letter.'

'What are the instructions?' Mainwaring asked, when I handed back the letter.

'I've got to take you to Terneuzen and drop you there. That's all I know. If necessary, you're to desert.'

'And what are we to do now?'

'I don't know,' I said. 'Make yourselves scarce, I should think. I can't ship three extra hands on a boat this size without people noticing it. You'd better clear out until Monday night, and then stow away forward until we sail.'

'Three extra hands? Who's the third?'

'A chap who calls himself Sellick, and who joined this afternoon on Voogdt's recommendation, like yourselves. He's gone ashore now with my man. He knows you—both of you.'

The two men looked at each other for a moment.

'What sort of looking chap is he?' Mainwaring asked curiously.

'Clean-shaven and strongly-built. About five foot ten. Wears blue serge and a Southern and Orient guernsey. Talks in jerks. Says "I say, skipper" at every third word.'

'That fool!' Colley cut in.

'Oh, he's not such a fool,' the amiable Mainwaring protested. 'We know him, Captain. A dear old fellow—a bit of a dilettante, perhaps, but a dear fellow.'

'He said you were a pair of rotters,' I remarked. I thought that would stop his flow of affability, but it didn't.

'The dear old boy. That's only his pungent way of speaking—just a mannerism. And what part is he playing?'

'I don't know,' I said again. 'He's ordered to ship with me, and I've shipped him. That's all I know. I suppose I shall get further instructions at Terneuzen.'

'And what's he been doing since he shipped with you?' asked Mainwaring. For all his affability, there was a tinge of annoyance in his voice.

'Winding up a hand-winch, helping unload clay all the afternoon,' I said.

For some reason or other that didn't please either of them. You could see they were jealous of this Sellick for having got the start of them, and that same jealousy hung about them all the time we were together. As I found out later, Voogdt knew his men and had picked each of them for his own job. I don't suppose anyone else could have got the work out of them he did, and he couldn't have got it any other way than this Secret Service dodge. They were hungry to be helping in it, content to put up with cold and wet and short commons and monotonous waiting, just on the thin chance of being in real danger for once. Keen as boys playing Indians they were, or millionaires stalking big game. Here these two were as jealous as women because Sellick's had put in three hours on a hand-winch hoisting mud out of a coaster.

'Where's Voogdt now?' Colley asked. He had scarcely spoken before.

'I don't know any more than you do,' I said; and then I thought it wise to tell them the whole yarn from the moment 'Kiah had put him ashore. They listened in silence, but when I had done, they both said they agreed with Sellick.

'He's all right. Don't you fear for him. It's a dark night when Austin Voogdt loses his way,' was their verdict.

'I think so too,' I said. 'But I can't help worrying a bit.

However, he'll be safe enough in Antwerp. Now hadn't you two better get ashore and out of sight?'

'Time enough,' Mainwaring said. 'There's nobody about. Let's go for'ard and see our old friend Sellick, his quarters.'

They were standing up to go, and Colley had stretched a hand to the door, when we heard the thump of feet on deck again. I pushed the others aside and put my head up the companion to find it was only Sellick and 'Kiah returning from their expedition. They went below into the fo'castle and I slipped back down the stair to let the others pass. As they reached the deck I heard a tinkling break out forward—string music of sorts—and the two men stopped like pointer dogs.

'He's brought his mandoline,' said Mainwaring. 'No objection to our paying a call on our old pal, is there, Cap'n?'

'I leave it to you,' I said. 'Use your own discretion. My man knows nothing remember.'

'Oh! . . . Well, I don't see why we can't pay a call. We know Mr Sellick, A.B., or bo'sun, or whatever he calls himself. Why shouldn't we come aboard and see him?'

'No reason against it that I know of,' I said.

'Good enough, then. Come along, Colley.' And they went forward on tiptoe, quiet as cats.

Half an hour later, feeling curious about them, I went forward and peeped down through the fo'castle companion. By the dim light of the swinging oil lamp the place looked like an old Dutch picture. Sellick had upholstered the cold stove with a couple of sacks and was sitting on it, cross-legged, picking away at the mandoline, and singing—singing rather well, too. 'Kiah sat on a box near by, smoking and looking at him with open admiration, and the other two were squatting knees to nose in the two empty bunks. The song came to an end just as I arrived, and Mainwaring praised it loudly.

'You can play the mandoline—er—Sellick. I'll say that for you . . . I should like to be shipmates with you for a trip. D'ye think the skipper of this fine commodious vessel would give us a passage across to Belgium?'

'Holland,' Sellick corrected him.

'No. South side the Scheldt is Belgium.'

'It's Holland, I tell you. Ask matey here.'

'Kiah, the deep-sea rover, on being questioned, corborated Sellick.

'Well Holland or Belgium, it's no odds. Would he give us a passage, think?'

'I daresay. He's giving me one. Ask my mate here again.'

'What do you think?' Mainwaring asked 'Kiah.

'Oh, I dunno.' 'Kiah was too busy admiring his talented new shipmate to think of anything else.

'What sort is he?' Mainwaring turned again to Sellick, who was idly picking at the strings of his little instrument.

'All right, by the look of him. Bit of a granny, I should think.'

''E's a better man 'n what you are,' 'Kiah cut in hotly. 'A better man 'n what any of 'ee are, s'there!'

'All right, my dear old chap. Keep cool about it,' said Mainwaring. 'Nobody doubts it.'

'Then what did 'ee say 'e was a granny for? Granny! My—' 'Kiah, excited, used worse language than I had ever discredited him with. 'Granny! Better fit you was 'alf the granny 'e is. 'E'd take you three on with one 'and an' knock 'ee silly, all three of 'ee.'

'He's big enough, and ugly enough,' Sellick said coolly. 'Keep your hair on, matey. Nobody's got anything to say against your skipper. He's a better man than I am, past a doubt.'

'Ah! that 'e is,' said 'Kiah, rather nonplussed by this unexpected agreement; and Sellick striking up another lively tune to end the squabble, I took advantage of the opportunity to retire unheard.

Next morning was fine and clear and, being Sunday, the docks were almost deserted. I went straight to the post office, hoping I might get a letter before it closed at ten o'clock, but nothing further had arrived, and I was on my way back to the boat when I ran right into Ward himself. He was carrying his bag from the railway station and looked tired and done up, having travelled all night, but I was mighty glad to see him, none the less, and he seemed pleased to hear me say so.

'Come to the hotel and have some breakfast with me,' he said. 'Then you can tell me all about it, and we can talk it over at our leisure . . . Voogdt deserted, eh? Well, I expect he had his reasons. A man to trust, that, I fancy.'

After breakfast we lit our pipes and sat in easy chairs by the open window, and I told him the whole story, commencing from the moment when Cheyne had asked us to dinner with Van Noppen. He had let his pipe out before I had finished, but it didn't want that to show he was alive to the importance of it all. He was fairly lost in interest, blinking and staring, filled with curiosity.

'And now you know as much about it as I do,' I said, knocking my pipe out on the window-sill. 'Can you make head or tail of it? Because I can't.'

'Extraordinary!' he said. 'Most extraordinary!' He got up and began to walk about the room, head down and hands behind his back. 'What do you make of it yourself?' He stopped suddenly to stare at me.

'It beats me—all of it. From the moment I put my finger into Van Noppen's glass and tasted that water, to the last thing last night, it's like a crazy dream. I don't doubt Voogdt sincerely believes—'

'You can take it from me—if my opinion is of any value—that when your friend Voogdt sincerely believes anything, he's got reason for it. Take our own case. This wolframite business had been running for eighteen months, and not a soul along the waterside of two maritime countries had suspected anything. Master Voogdt comes along, knowing nothing whatever of the coasting business and nothing of chemistry, and yet he gets to the heart of the whole thing inside six months. A very remarkable man, in my opinion.'

'Then do you think he's right in suspecting these Germans to be in the Secret Service?'

'That I can't say. But I do say that, if he says so, it's an idea worth entertaining. I may be talking utter nonsense in this connection, but of course that bit of coastline from the Scheldt to the Maas is one of the most vital positions in Europe. Half a dozen important rivers—rivers navigable for miles, and tapping the very heart of central Europe—all flow into the sea amongst those forty miles of mud-banks. I know nothing of high politics, but you've only to look at a map of Europe to see that much. Only I don't quite understand what a German post can be doing there at Terneuzen. The place is fortified, I know, but only for the protection of the ship canal.'

'Fortified, is it? I never knew that.'

'Oh, you're not the stuff spies are made of,' said he, smiling. 'I don't mind telling you I'd been there two or three times before I noticed it myself. Those embankments beyond the village—there's a small garrison and some modern guns—but surely one or two men could examine them without exciting notice better than this cumbrous trading station business. I'm still inclined to think they're after the wolframite.'

'Cheyne swears they aren't. He says nothing has left the place except barge loads of explosives.'

'I don't know that I should employ Willis Cheyne to go a-spying, any more than either of us two,' Ward declared. 'No, Voogdt's the man, and we must back him up—at least until we're sure he's mistaken. If it's a national service we must do our best to help. We'll write him here as instructed and ask whether I shall take this information to the War Office, and I'll go back to London and wait his instructions there. And, look here, you'll want money for this business. You must draw on me.'

'I've plenty of money.'

'You won't have, for long. You see, if this business really is a State affair, it will probably be our duty to put a stop to it.

We can do that at any moment, without letting loose the dogs of war or any nonsense like that. But if we do, we put a stop to money-making.'

'How?'

'Simply make public what we know—that Scheldt mud is worth two hundred pounds a ton. In a week, those banks would be covered with Dutch Government analysts, with a regiment or two of infantry and a couple of gunboats patrolling up and down to prevent any more of it being stolen. Under such circumstances I think the explosive factory would be very carefully overhauled, and if there is any spying going on things will be made unpleasant for your friend Van Noppen.'

'Then do I understand you to say that Voogdt's in command of the whole show from now on?'

'That's it exactly. The Axel Trading Company volunteers for Government service. Voogdt is Commander-in-Chief. You're Admiral of the Fleet, ferrying his confidential agents as he directs. Incidentally I should remove as much wolframite as you can before the smash comes. This declaring it as coprolites will serve for half a dozen more voyages, I daresay, and we can't reckon on having time left us for more than that. I'll stay in London as headquarters staff, and remit the sinews of war as required. And that's all. I must admit I was a little sore about the way your friend penetrated the secrets of our wolframite business, but if he circumvents the agents of an efficient, practical nation like Germany I shall feel I have less reason to be ashamed of my useless precautions. So good luck go with him.'

'Amen to that,' said I. 'For the man's my friend and my mate—one after my own heart. And I'll tell you this: if I lose him over this business not all the money in the world'll take his place.'

Ward had letters to write, he said, so, promising to join him at dinner, I went back aboard, meaning to have a sleep; but Sellick was hanging about waiting for me, and at his request I asked him into the cabin.

'Mainwaring and Colley turned up last night,' he began. 'They want to know if you'll give them a trip across?'

'I saw them. They'll stow away for'ard on Monday night before we sail. Who are they?'

'Mainwaring's father was The Mainwaring—the K.C. This fool's been called, but he doesn't like the law. He's a slacker. Messes about poking his fingers into things that don't concern him. He tried to get out to South Africa, but that was no go. He's awfully shortsighted. Then he had a packet of cards printed and bought a hand camera—pretended he was a war correspondent.'

I remembered what Voogdt had said.

'You were there, too, weren't you?'

'Yes. Rotten hole. So was Colley.'

'Who's he, when he's at home?' I asked.

'He? Oh, he's a man—of sorts. I can't stand Mainwaring—smarmy, affable beast. But Colley's a horse of another colour. Father was a steeplejack—factory chimneys, don't you know. Coade and Colley. Big people in the North. Making big money till the Americans knocked out brick and mortar chimneys with iron pipes in sections. They shut down, and Harry Colley looked out for another job. He's got his points—a sound man on machinery. Started a little motor works three years ago, and did well, I believe. Just chucked that, though. He's been learning flying, too. Keen on anything with wheels and works, he is. He's a sulky beast, though. I say, skipper—'

'Well?' I said, for he hesitated.

'What are we playing at, eh?'

'Ask me another,' I said. 'It's all muddle to me. My orders are to ship you, and I've done it. I'm to take your two friends across to Terneuzen without exciting notice, and I've told them to stow away. They're to leave the ship when we get there. And that's all I know, and now dry up and slip it, unless you've any more interesting yarns to tell me.'

He grinned and went on deck. It was all of a piece with the

confused, muddled notions I had of the whole affair that I never learnt the chap's real name. Whilst he was aboard he did his work well and was neat and tidy, yachtsman fashion, and when he left he never as much as shook hands or said goodbye. I hadn't any particular desire that he should, as a matter of fact, for his cynical ways weren't mine. Besides, all the time I knew him he was a rich man playing at poverty, and that's a very difficult role for any man to play without giving offence.

We made a queer ship's company, take us all the way round, and the only point upon which we showed any signs of agreement was a sincere belief and trust in Voogdt, hiding somewhere over there in the Low Countries.

CHAPTER XIX

WHICH TELLS OF A WILD-GOOSE CHASE

MONDAY morning woke us all to activity. Voogdt evidently considered himself what Ward had called him—Commander-in-Chief—for he handed out his orders like an autocrat. Mine came in a letter posted at Bergen-op-Zoom on the previous Saturday and were short and sweet.

> 'All well so far. Ward will join you shortly. Persuade him to act on my instructions posted to him at Erith and Birmingham. Be off Flushing Thursday night, but miss your tide and anchor as close as possible to westward of West Haven light. Stay two tides and keep passengers below decks out of sight. Hope to join you there.'

I went straight to the hotel to tell Ward a letter awaited him at the post office, but found him at the breakfast-table already reading it. Carwithen having opened the duplicate had sent him a code wire telling him to fetch the copy at Erith post office.

'You've heard, too?' he greeted me. 'What are your orders?'

'I'm to persuade you to carry out his instructions, first and foremost.'

'Have you any idea what those instructions are?' he asked, looking at me in a puzzled way through his glasses.

'Not a notion.'

'Read them, then,' said he, and he handed me the letter. It was dated, as mine, on the Saturday before.

> 'DEAR MR WARD,—See Jem West and make him tell you everything he knows about the circumstances of my leaving

212

him. The conjectures which I then imparted to him appear correct. I want to impress the importance of this on you as my reason for asking you to do what may appear at first sight to be a very silly thing. Briefly, I want you to die on Thursday next. Will you therefore please publish an announcement of your death in one or two good Birmingham and London papers on Wednesday morning, and ask one of the young ladies to send Cheyne a marked copy, with a letter of regrets. A rather hysterical and frightened letter, please. Then go away for a spell in the country—or, better to London—and keep out of sight till I tell you to come to life again. This will give considerable pain to your friends and relatives, I fear, but, believe me, it is necessary. And they'll be the more delighted when they discover the report is false. If you think it safe you may take Miss Brand, Miss Lavington and Mr Carwithen into your confidence, and you must give West your future address—but not a word to a single soul else, mind. This will seem mere idiocy to you, but I assure you that it is vitally important, as I hope to convince you after your resurrection, which I trust will take place within a fortnight at latest. Yours in haste,

'AUSTIN VOOGDT.'

'What do you make of that?' said Ward, as I looked up from the letter.

'What's the use of asking me? I've been out of my depth ever since Voogdt left. If 'twas anybody else I should think he'd gone mad. As 'tis—shall you do it?'

'I must, I suppose. We all appear pawns in your friend's game. Doesn't your letter throw any light on the buiness?'

'Not on your dying. There are some definite instructions as to my movements.' I took the letter out of my pocket and handed it to him.

'H'm. This is sane enough,' said he, after reading it over. 'Thursday night's tide. How long will it take you to get across?'

'That all depends on the wind. It's about a hundred and ten miles. With a light breeze, as it is now, say twenty-four hours. If it came on to blow hard easterly we shouldn't get out of the river at all.'

'Then hadn't you better get all your ballast out and sail tonight in case of accidents? You'll be clear of the river, at all events, and, once out in the open sea, you can hang about until Thursday afternoon.'

'That's a good notion. I'll do it. The two stowaways are to come aboard tonight, too, and there'll be no sense in staying here where somebody might see them.'

'Good,' said he. 'Then I'll get back to London at once, and arrange for a cab accident tonight. We may as well put what intelligent co-operation we can into the commandant's instructions. Here's my address.'

He wrote on a sheet of paper—care of some man at Hampstead, an old friend he could trust, he said, and we said goodbye and parted; but I had to go back to join him again, for I hadn't any orders about the *Luck and Charity*. We had nearly all the alleged coprolites on the wharf when it suddenly occurred to me we couldn't sail light, and I ran up to ask Ward what we should ballast with.

'Oh, ballast,' said he carelessly. 'Just ordinary ballast. You've brought a genuine cargo for once and no remarks will be made.'

'How about when we get back to Terneuzen?'

'We've no time now to cross bridges before we come to them. Voogdt'll see you through at the other end. If I go buying deals or coal here now, it'll mean delay.'

So we got twelve or thirteen tons of sand and shingle from the ballast quay, and, by hustling, the hatch covers were on before seven o'clock. 'Kiah and Sellick went up town marketing, and whilst they were gone the stowaways slipped quietly aboard and disappeared into the forecastle. They ought to have gone into the hold, if I'd only thought of it, for there was no hiding-room for two grown men forward; and just before we cast off 'Kiah came to me, much perturbed in mind.

'There's two blooks stowed theirselves away for'ard,' he said.

'No!' said I, trying to look surprised. 'What do the fools think they're after?'

'I d'no,' said 'Kiah. 'They'm friends of 'is.' He jerked his chin over his shoulder to indicate Sellick.

'They was aboard Sat'day night, an' they was talkin' then about 'avin' a trip aboard o' us.'

'I'll trip 'em!' I said. 'Don't you scare 'em out of it, 'Kiah. We'll give 'em a doing. They won't stow away aboard this craft again, I'll bet.'

'Aw right,' said he, impassively as ever, and set about hauling warps aboard, so that we got away without further remark.

The low Essex shore was out of sight and we were nearing the Kentish Knock next morning when the pair discovered themselves. Sellick had just come to the wheel to let me go to breakfast and we'd had a little passage of arms about the course.

'East-nor'-east,' he repeated after me. 'I say, skipper, Flushing lays south of east from the Girdler, or I'm mistaken.'

'Mind your own business,' I said. 'Steer the course I give you.'

'Righto,' said he, the magic of Secret Service evidently working in his mind. 'Beg pardon.'

'Since you've had the manners to beg pardon, I don't mind telling you we ain't due off Flushing till Thursday night,' I told him. 'And then we've got to miss the flood at seven-thirty and anchor close in. But you bear in mind I'm skipper here, and I know my business. I didn't ship you to teach me.'

'Thursday night,' said he. 'That's interesting. Five men aboard for three days, and 'Kiah marketed for three men for one day.'

'Mind your own business,' I said again, angrily, for I hadn't thought of that, and I could see short commons for somebody sticking out a mile.

'East-nor'-east,' he murmured under his breath, staring at the compass like a wooden image, and I had to seek some other object to blow off steam upon. As luck would have it, Mainwaring chose just that moment to make his appearance on deck, and I called him aft, asked him his business aboard, and then let him have it, good. It was no use trying to rile him, though. Like the others, he'd got this Secret Service bee in his bonnet, and if I had him chucked overboard he would have sunk with a finger at his nose, winking at me as much as to say we were all in the know together.

When I'd done slanging him, much to 'Kiah's edification, I asked him if he'd brought any food on board.

'No, sir,' he said affably. 'But I have a friend in that little cabin, and perhaps he—'

'A friend!' I roared. 'How many more of you? What is your little game, anyway? There's another swab stowed away for'ard, 'Kiah. Fetch him up.'

'Kiah produced Colley, and his appearance took a little weight off my mind. He was turning green already, and I saw we needn't worry about his food for the next twenty-four hours. I gave him a dressing down calculated to depress him still further, and then set the pair of them to washing out the fore-castle under 'Kiah's superintendence. After breakfast I felt better and sat down by the wheel to smoke and watch Colley hauling buckets of water aboard and lowering them down the forecastle ladder to his comrade-in-distress. Stealing a look at Sellick, I saw that he appeared very pleased with himself.

'What's the joke?' I asked him.

'Looks to me as if it was coming on fresh out of the nor'-east,' said he.

'Perhaps you won't find it such a joke if it does.'

'Oh, I'm all right,' he said. 'I'm always seasick when I smell salt water, but it's over in ten minutes. I left my supper in London river last night. Now it can blow all it likes for me. It's those two I'm tickled at. I owe them both a turn or two. Harry

Colley took twenty-two quid odd off me at poker coming home from the Cape. Besides, more grub for us, skipper. Two days on one day's tucker won't hurt anybody; but two extra men and two extra days are too much of a good thing. That's cutting it too fine altogether.'

I had one or two tins of meat in the cabin in case of emergencies, but, as he said, five men for three days on the rations of three men for one day was too near a thing altogether, and I saw the emergency stores wouldn't last long. However, he was quite right about its coming on to blow. The north-east horizon was hard and clear against a light sky, and by midday the wind had freshened and was knocking up a lumpy sea. The two passengers declined their dinner and retired to their bunks, where they stayed, only showing themselves on deck once or twice, until Thursday afternoon. So they were no expense or bother to anybody.

Sellick proved handy and useful, and he, 'Kiah and myself took trick and trick about for the next twenty-four hours. The wind being dead against us, we just lay as close to it as we could, quartering the North Sea at our ease, and gaining a few useful miles to windward with each tack.

The *Luck and Charity* being the real good boat she was we stood at the wheel dryshod; but beating to windward isn't the most comfortable business in the world, and once or twice when she bashed her bows into biggish seas, I felt sorry for the two landsmen lying very sick below. We had just jogged across, bang, bang, banging, to and fro, from the Galloper to the Rabs Bank; back to the outer Gabbard; back again to the Schar, only making a mile or two to windward on every forty-mile tack, but not losing anything. It wasn't exciting, but we were obeying instructions, and anyhow there's always a certain amount of satisfaction in knowing somebody else is worse off than you are. So the passengers were good for something, if only to keep our spirits up.

We picked up Lowestoft Light early on Thursday morning

and went about for the last time. Having all day—fifteen hours—in which to do a short hundred miles, we didn't hurry. The wind had eased a bit, and the waves no longer had feathery tops to them, but there was a lump of a sea all the same. We sidled across it, crab fashion, till about four in the afternoon, and then I thought it was about time to think of home. We were then about thirty miles north of the Scheldt-mouth light-ships—the *Wandelaar* and *Weilingen*—so after an early tea we wore ship and ran for it, on a course nearly parallel with the Dutch coast, so as to keep clear of the East Scheldt banks. We timed it nicely, running right under the lee of the Walcheren sand-hills in slack water, and met the first of the strong ebb not a quarter of a mile from Flushing harbour.

The easier motion of running had revived the two passengers a bit, and they wanted to come on deck; but bearing in mind Voogdt's instructions I ordered them to keep below, much to their discontent. It wasn't any pleasure trip for them, from first to last. The ebb drifted us back perhaps five hundred yards before we got the anchor overside, so that we lay a good half-mile from the harbour mouth, for which I wasn't sorry, because a quarter-mile is almost too close to escape notice from the shore, and, besides, our drifting back made the anchoring look a sensible thing to do. Association with Voogdt was beginning to teach me that it's well to have an ostensible sham reason for doing anything besides your own real one.

A big fleet of Scheldt shrimpers came out of harbour on the first of the ebb, and by the time the last of them had passed us it was dusk and 'Kiah was hauling up our riding light on the forestay. He had hardly made it fast when we were hailed by a small boat nearing us, and asked our names and business.

'*Luck and Charity*, English ketch, Erith to Terneuzen, in ballast,' I sang out.

'And God bless her, say I!' Voogdt's voice came cheerfully out of the dusk, and I saw him sitting in the stern of the approaching boat, some Dutch amphibian at the oars. Coming alongside, he slapped the side of our bows as one slaps a favourite horse in a stable.

'Good old wooden packet,' said he, scrambling aboard. 'And good old wooden-headed skipper. Jem West, I'm glad to see you again.'

'You ain't the only one,' I said. 'My aunt! Haven't I been in a sweat about you, just. Where've you been?'

'That'll keep,' said he. 'Have you brought the passengers?'

'Yes. I reported to Antwerp, as you told me.'

'I haven't been there since. Where are they?'

'In the fo'castle.'

'Send 'em aft, will you? They can go ashore here—in that boat alongside. But I want a word with 'em first. How've they been?'

'Seasick,' I told him.

'All three?'

'No. Sellick's been useful.'

'Who's Sellick?'

'The chap who shipped as mate. That's what he chooses to call himself—Dick Sellick. I notice the others call him Frank.'

'What odds? "A rose by any other name . . ." You say he's useful. Let him call himself what he likes. That you, 'Kiah?'

'Ah!' said 'Kiah, very pleased. 'Yu got away from they Dutch coppers, then, Mr Vute?'

'A sure thing I did, my son. I'll do as much for you next time. Just turn out those two seasick coves and send 'em aft to the cabin, will you?'

We went below together, and a moment or two later the others joined us. They were in a bad way, both of them, for seasickness is no joke; but they were evidently glad to see Voogdt again.

'Hello, cockies,' said he, shaking hands. 'You've had a bit of a doing, the skipper tells me. Cheer up! You're going ashore right now. Take the train for Antwerp. When you get there call at the George Hotel—it's near the docks, an English house—and fetch a letter addressed to me in the name of V. Austin. That's right?' he asked me.

'Quite right.'

'Then across the river to the Waesland station, go to Terneuzen, and put up at the hotel by the locks. We shall be there before you, but remember you don't know us, and you never saw this *Luck and Charity* before in your lives. Get that firmly fixed in your heads. And you never saw me, or West, or any of us before. You'd better be English tourists—or artists— or any old thing you like. But you take no interest whatever in shipping. Savvy that? All you do is to loaf about there and wait instructions. And now be off. You've time to get some grub ashore—I expect you're beginning to feel peckish, eh?—and catch the boat train at midnight. Roosendaal's the junction for Antwerp. Don't forget to call for my letter.'

'What are we to do with it?'

'Anything in it beyond the report?' Voogdt asked me.

'No.'

'Then burn it. It's of no importance; but we mustn't leave things lying about, no matter how harmless they are.'

The two were overside with their belongings inside of ten minutes, Voogdt chatting with Sellick in the meanwhile. When the boat had disappeared in the darkness, heading for the pierheads, he came below with me again, and sat himself down, warming his hands. Opening the top of the stove he stared into the glowing fire.

'It's a good thing to be home again, and warm,' said he. 'I've been in some cold shops.'

'Out with it,' said I. 'Tell us all about it. What have you discovered?'

'Precious little, when you come to reckon it all up. And yet—I've got two or three facts. Facts that certainly don't fit in with my theories about Secret Service, though.'

'What are they?'

'Not so fast. I think the best thing to do will be to tell you the whole yarn from the start—from the time 'Kiah put me ashore.'

'At Hoogplaat.'

'Was that the name of the crib? I'd forgotten. I didn't stay there. When he left me—did you know he wanted to lend me a couple of quid when I landed? . . . No? He did, then. Good old 'Kiah! . . . Well, having refused the loan, much to his disgust, I got away from the waterside as fast as I could. There was a road leading southwards, the usual pattern, straight as a line with interminable rows of poplars and dykes on either side, and I followed that. In about two hours I found myself at a village—Iisendyk I think was the name—whence there was a light railway to Eecloo. For a wonder there was a late train, at nine p.m., which I caught, and reached Eecloo just before ten. Stayed the night there and got to Ghent early next morning. What I was after was to trace those German powder barges, if possible. Cheyne said they had all gone up river, but I don't put a lot of reliance on that gentleman, and thought I'd make a few inquiries on my own. However, none had come to Ghent. Three hours' hanging about the dock offices convinced me of that. They understand how to manage shipping over here: 'tisn't the anyhow scramble you find in our ports. With a little palm oil and a few inquiries I was very soon able to trace the record of every boat that had entered the port since the German sheds were opened, and they've sent nothing that way.

'So I took the evening train to Antwerp, and started the same search there. At first it looked like a long job, which is why I told you to write me there; but in the evening I met a chap in the George Hotel, water-clerk to a firm of brokers, who knew the place and business like the back of his hand. I made up to him, pretty mannered as you please, stood him a few drinks, and he introduced me to a man in the Customs. More drinks, more palm oil, and before one a.m. I'd checked every entry of imported explosives that had entered the port in the last twelve months. Not one of them was from Terneuzen.'

I showed my surprise. 'Did they go farther up river, then?'

'That's what I thought till I found cargoes entered for Mechlin. Antwerp's the first port across the Belgian frontier, don't you see, and every load of stuff coming into the country is checked there. The Terneuzen barges would have been entered if they'd only passed the place, no matter where they were going.'

'Where else could they go?'

'That's what puzzled me. I got a map and pondered over it. Get out your North Sea chart and I'll show you . . . Right. Here we are. Axel—Terneuzen. Now then, on up the river. See this little tidal gutter joining the West to the East Scheldt?'

'But that's embanked. The railway runs across it—the main line from Flushing to the Continent.'

'A spidery bridge—not an embankment. It's tidal—pretty hopeless-looking mud-flats, I grant you; but not barred altogether. Once you're through there you're in a maze of mud-flats and islands pierced here and there by the deep channel of a big river, and the islands cut up worse than ever by small canals. In fact, what with mud and what with tides I'm hanged if you can tell where water ends and land begins. Look what a muddle 'tis. Beveland, Duiveland, Tholen, Voorne, Schouwen, Goeree, Beijer Island; just a maze of 'em. A maze. There's no other name for it.'

'Well?'

'Well, I took train to a place called Krabbendyk on Beveland, and on the way looked out of the window and saw this gutter full of water, it being high tide. I walked round the town, admired all there was to admire, which was mostly cows, and then went back to Bergenop-Zoom.'

'I had your letter from there.'

'When I wrote on Saturday I rather thought I should be staying at Bergen, and so told you to anchor here, thinking I could run down to Flushing and join you at the last moment. There didn't seem any other course open. Unless the barges went to sea—which was almost impossible—they must pass into the East Scheldt, and I meant to do sentry-go at Bergen and watch out for the next to pass. However, that very Saturday night, having a taste for low company, I sat in a little waterside pothouse and made the acquaintance of a chap who was engineer of a pleasure launch belonging to some rich coffee merchant at Rotterdam. This coffee man had left the launch at Bergen and gone home by train, and his engineer was on the spree. I joined him, and so charmed him with my affable manners and conversation that he offered to give me a trip back to Rotterdam aboard the launch. I accepted, glad to get out of Bergen for the Sunday, and on our way through this precious maze, what should pass us but a barge flying the powder-flag. That was in this channel—the Keeten—between Duiveland and Tholen, and my engineer pal told me a good many barges from Antwerp took that road to Dordrecht.

'That was enough for me. I left the launch, most ungratefully, at Rotterdam, and skipped for Dort by an afternoon train. Had a look at the docks, but saw no signs of any explosive depot, so went to a cheap hotel, and retired to my bedroom with my map. I fell asleep on the chair, and woke with a bump on the floor. So I chucked myself on the bed and slept for ten solid hours.'

'Did you find any barge at Dort?'

'Never looked to see. When I woke early Monday morning I picked up the map again and—it was an inspiration, no less, Jem—all the tangle of waterways seemed to fall into order before my eyes, just as a child's puzzle maze becomes clear in a moment when a pencil line is drawn through its proper path to the centre. Nearly all the canals leading towards the frontier seemed to converge at Tiel, and to Tiel I went, first train. All as before: low pubs, free drinks, and the information I wanted, before ten a.m. A powder barge had passed through there on Saturday—bound for Arnhem, my informant thought, though he wasn't sure about that. On to Arnhem; to find the barge had left that same morning, bound down the Iissed for Zwolle, on her way to Delfzyl. So off I went in chase, and actually saw her from the train, crawling along behind two stuggy Flemish tow-horses. It was at a lonely part of the canal, and not only was the chap at the wheel smoking, but her cabin stove-pipe was smoking too. And the red swallow-tail flying overhead all the time! How's that?'

'I'm glad I wasn't aboard her.'

'So I thought, at the time. Not that I ever imagined it was powder they were carrying, all the same. Well, this was just before reaching Zutphen. I whipped out my map, left the train at Zutphen, and took another for the frontier. I was going by guesswork, I grant you, but it happened to be right.'

'What had you guessed, then?'

'Shut up. Let me tell my yarn in my own way. This barge was for Zwolle, which is near the mouth of the Vecht. The quickest way from there over the frontier is up that river to Gramsbergen. On the German side the river skirts a God-forsaken morass called the Bourthanger Moor—miles and miles of it, through which is cut a canal, strategic, I suppose—parallel with the frontier. This canal enters the Ems a few miles above Leer, close to the mouth of the river. If anything funny was going to happen that was the place for it—in that watery deserted bog. So I took train to Salzbergen, and stayed there the night, registering at the hotel as a sailor on the way to Emden to join my ship. Next morning I went to Ihrhove, the junction for the West Friesland line, and thence to Weener, where the railway crosses the Ems below its junction with the Bourthanger Canal. This was Tuesday morning, and I hadn't been there six hours before a barge passed under the railway bridge, red swallow-tail and all, bound for—where d'ye think?'

'Delfzyl?'

'Wrong again. Emden.' He looked triumphant. 'She'd changed her mind about her port of destination whilst passing through those morasses. What d'ye think of that?'

'I don't see anything in it.'

'I do, then. This company, with alleged headquarters at Delfzyl in Holland, is sending a steady stream of barges by devious routes into Germany, loaded with wolframite. Think of the tons and tons they're sending. They whack our primitive methods, hands down. Here are we, messing about Channel, with long voyages and short voyages, delayed by all sorts of weather, whilst they're sending a steady procession—forty tons at a time—by safe and certain routes. Explosives be blowed! But isn't it a noble notion? Not a soul dares to tamper with their tarboys, or retorts, or whatever they are. We must do the same business, Jem. I'll put it before Ward next trip, and we must lay in rope-screens and all the rest of the stage properties. A grand idea! Why, we can go on for years. I see myself a millionaire yet.'

'Then you haven't been to Terneuzen at all?'

'What need, man? I've found out the essentials of the business. We know they're on the same lay as we are, and we know where they're shipping their goods. What more do you want?'

'Look here,' I said. 'I grant that your head's worth ten of mine, but I'd like to point out one thing to you. You haven't discovered what you set out to do, and that's the meaning of that road-making at midnight.'

'True,' said he. 'But that can soon be done, now we know what they're at. My conjectures were all wrong—about the German Secret Service business, I mean. They're just the same sort of thieves as we are.'

We got up anchor just after midnight, and had a quick journey up the narrow channels, anchoring again off Terneuzen at three o'clock on Friday morning. There was a light in the office, and in answer to our hail Cheyne came out and called to us to send a boat ashore. 'Kiah and Sellick had just turned in for a few hours' sleep, so I took the dinghy ashore myself, and he came sliding and squattering down over the mud-banks to meet it.

'Have you heard the news?' he asked, when he got down into the cabin, muddied half-way down to his knees.

'What news?'

'Leonard Ward's dead.'

'Never!' we chorused in astonishment. 'What did he die of?'

'Cab accident in Duncannon Street—by Charing Cross. I haven't had any particulars yet, but I've had a newspaper and a letter from Miss Brand. They're scared to death, those girls.'

'And what's to do now?' I asked. 'Who's to take over his work?'

'Ah! Well you may ask. I can't do it and be here too, can I? I don't suppose either of you two can be spared—even if you knew the business—and I don't know what to think, but I don't fancy trusting Carwithen altogether. Eh?'

'What do you suggest?' Voogdt said quietly. 'Haven't you got a proposal ready?'

'Well—look here, you two, what I say goes no farther, does it? Well, then, I don't mind owning that Van Noppen has made me an offer on the quiet to buy us out.'

'What's the figure?'

'I bluffed him, as I thought. Said we wouldn't sell out under a hundred thousand. And if you'll believe me, he rose to it. Thirty-three thousand quid apiece for the three of us. Isn't that very near enough?'

'What about the other partners?' said Voogdt doubtfully.

'Well—what about 'em? They won't make trouble. They're too badly scared over Leonard's death. Besides, what do women know of business? And they've got enough already—more than enough.'

It was Voogdt's promptness saved the beast. Voogdt leant over between us and took him by the button hole.

'This is talking,' he said, in tones of admiration. 'This is straight talk. Now you go on deck, Cheyne, just for ten minutes, and we'll give you your answer.'

The sweep went like a lamb, and Voogdt turned to me.

'Put your hands in your pockets and keep 'em there,' he said. You clumsy ass, you'll muck the show. I'm going to get him down again, and arrange details. You sit tight there, and don't open your mouth, except to say yes or no.'

He called Cheyne down again. 'Look here,' he said. 'As man to man, is that hundred thousand the outside figure?'

'On my honour it is.' Of all things, he chose to swear by his honour!

'How much are you to get as bonus if you bring off the deal?'

'I was to have ten per cent. commission—ten thousand quid.'

'We want half that, just to make even money. Thirty-five thousand apiece for us, and forty thousand for you. Will that do?'

Cheyne was evidently very relieved at our moderation.

'That isn't out of the way,' he said.

'Then tell Van Noppen we'll meet him to discuss the matter in our office this evening at half-past nine. Don't say we accept. We may screw a little more out of him. Agreed? Good enough. We shall be alongside emptying our hold before eight.'

'Is it business to rob women?'

'Taint business to stay on deck cursing early of a cold morning, when you might be down below scheming to get to windward of the swine. Don't you see we're in a fix? If we don't keep in with Cheyne, he busts the show. Our only chance is to get him on our side and stick out for a higher price than Van Noppen'll pay. Come below and I'll persuade you.'

'I won't come below, and I won't be persuaded,' I said. 'I feel as if I'd been rolling in muck and I'll stay up here in fresh air for a bit.'

'All right. Be a fool,' said he shortly, and went below. As for me, I stayed on deck till daylight, disgusted with everything.

CHAPTER XX

OF A DISSOLUTION OF PARTNERSHIP

THE night was over already, really. There was the waking feeling in the air that comes before the dawn. I walked up and down, and the more I walked the more my anger grew. When the clean sky and the first fresh wind of morning told me again what I knew very well before, that Pamela Brand was the only girl in the world for me, I had only to glance ashore to be reminded that Cheyne had once dared to think she was his for the asking. That was the sting of it all; that was what made my anger venomous. Love and hate warred in me: putting the love in the background of my mind, I promised the rising sun that I would square accounts with Cheyne before it set again.

It came up round and clear, turning marshes and river to gold, and then hid again behind a bank of cloud to make its toilet for a fine bright day. Sellick was first on deck, looking about him curiously, and I told him to rouse 'Kiah out whilst I waked Voogdt to help get alongside the wharf. Voogdt and Sellick in the dinghy towed the *Luck and Charity* a couple of hundred yards, and then took the ends of our warps ashore, so that we were tied up within half an hour, and then all hands knocked off to breakfast.

Voogdt gave me a sharp talking-to over the table; but I was tired and sulky, and wouldn't promise anything, until from slanging me he got to asking as a favour that I would give him a fortnight to prepare the business for a shock.

'We've been good pals, Jem,' he said. 'Don't go and spoil my plans now. For heaven's sake keep your hands off Cheyne for the present, and I promise you, as soon as we can possibly manage it, I'll give you the word to go for him?'

'I'm going to give him a hammering,' I repeated.

'He deserves it. No man better. But not now. See here, if we can't get out of it any other way, I'll get Ward's permission to accept this offer. Six into a hundred gives us over sixteen thousand a share—eight thousand each for you and myself. That's none so bad. If Ward consents we'll take that, and you can have a scrap with Cheyne thrown in as bonus on your share. Will that do? Promise you won't touch him, or make trouble before then.'

'Very well. I promise.'

'That's better,' said he, much relieved. 'And now let's get this ballast out and load—load deep for once. No more pretence at ballast. This is coprolites, henceforth. Now come on deck and work some of your bad temper out of you.'

We slung the ballast straight over the skeleton wharf out on the mud, an absence of precaution showing more clearly than anything else could have done that the end of our trading operations was in sight. The hold was almost empty by low water and we were able to get a few tubs of mud aboard before the rising tide stopped our work.

Cheyne didn't come near us all day. He lay abed late, not coming out of the office until midday. Then he only waved a hand, and set out for Terneuzen—for lunch, I suppose. When we knocked off, at about half-past two, Voogdt changed into clean clothes and followed him. He got back about five.

'Mainwaring and Colley are there,' he announced, as we sat down to tea. 'Mainwaring's an English tourist of weak intellect and Colley's his attendant. They're coming down this way for a walk about dusk.'

'Are they coming aboard?' I was feeling much better after a day's steady work, for there's nothing like hard exercise for the temper.

'Coming aboard! No fear. They're going down the embankment towards Van Noppen's show. I'm going for a walk, too. You and Sellick will stay here and keep a sharp look-out.'

He went off about half-past six, after a chat with Sellick, scrambled down the embankment, pipe in mouth, and set off inland, strolling at an easy pace. Sunset was at seven, and just as the great red ball touched the western marshy skyline I saw Mainwaring and Colley coming down the path from the town. Mainwaring was walking jerkily, as though he were on tiptoe, and Colley slouched along a pace in his rear, his hands in his pockets. They were first rate at acting a part, for if Voogdt hadn't told me what they were playing at, I should have put them down as somebody a bit dotty and his keeper. As they passed the wharf, Mainwaring stopped and pointed at us.

'See the little ship, John,' he said, sort of weakly interested.

'Ah!' said Colley sulkily. He spoke exactly as a bored attendant on a madman would speak, and after Mainwaring had twaddled some more about the little ship they went on down the banks as before.

I whipped below and watched them through the glasses until it got too dark to see what they were at, and then I went on deck again. The last I saw of them they had passed the German sheds and were walking farther down the embankment. When I got on deck, I found Sellick going up the gang-plank.

'Here, where are you going?' I asked.

'Ashore. Just a stroll to stretch my legs. No objection, is there? I'm obeying orders.'

'All right,' I said, and he went up the wharf, disappeared behind the office, and I saw no more of him.

I walked up and down for a bit, had a chat with 'Kiah on the fo'castle head, and then, wondering what time it was, peeped down into the cabin. Our clock said half-past eight, and it was getting very dark. I was just beginning to wonder whether Mainwaring and Colley had lost their way when I heard two men walking up the embankment from the direction in which they had gone. Having nothing else to do I went ashore to the end of the wharf to see them pass, but they were only two labourers apparently on their way home to Terneuzen, instead of the two men I had expected. They lingered by our sheds for a moment and then went on, saying goodnight to me in Dutch as they passed. They couldn't have gone five minutes, and I was just sitting down upon a bollard to rest, when Colley came running up the embankment at top speed. He had kept to the grassy edges of the path and was on me almost before I heard him.

'Anything wrong?' I asked, startled.

'No. Got a pair of pliers or stout shears aboard? Anything that'll cut wire. Yes? Run, quick.'

I slipped aboard and brought him a knife I kept in the cabin for odd jobs, which had a pair of wire nippers on it.

'Will this do?' I asked.

He looked at it contemptuously.

'It must, if you've nothing better. Anybody passed here? Two men? That's right. Did they hang about the place at all? Yes? Good. Don't let anybody go near there—near the sheds—till we come back.'

He ran off as silently as he had come, leaving me to wonder what was going on.

As I sat I was facing our sheds, the office immediately oppo-site me, two stores on the left and one larger on the right. Behind, tied alongside the wharf, was the *Luck and Charity*, her bows towards the river and her stern about thirty feet from where I sat. The path along the embankment was wider here, worn by traffic to a good broad road, narrowing off again to left and right in the directions of Terneuzen and the German sheds. The night was fine, but clouds hid the stars and it was very dark, so that it was as much as I could do to make out the shape of the gable-end over the office. From the top of the embankment the marshy horizon all round lay low and dark, blurred a little with the low mists lying on the pastures.

It was a cheerless place by night, low-lying, damp and cold; the only lights visible were one or two twinkles from the houses by Terneuzen dock, and a cheery glow from our fo'castle hatch, shining up through the faint haze that lay over the water. I was just on the point of going down there for warmth and 'Kiah's company when Sellick came from behind the sheds, crossed the road, and sat down beside me on the bollard.

'Where've you been?' I asked.

'Just over there.' He spoke in a whisper, nodding towards the office. 'Squatting on the grass behind that hut. Watching you, for one thing.'

'Colley's just been here. He says we're not to go near the sheds.'

'I heard him. No fear of my going, anyhow.'

'Did you see those two men pass?'

'I did. Shut up, skipper. Listen.'

We listened with all our ears, but could hear nothing except the light breeze sighing in the grass, and 'Kiah whistling some melancholy strain down in the fo'castle behind us.

Suddenly I remembered the appointment with Van Noppen in our office at nine-thirty, and was thinking it was time some of the others put in an appearance when Voogdt came quickly and quietly across the road.

'Time?' he said sharply, in a low voice.

Sellick had a watch and struck a match. 'Ten to nine,' he said.

'Good. We're on time, then. Anything to report, Frank?'

'One of those two chaps stopped by the living shed. Messing about the bottom of the wall, as far as I could see.'

'Whereabouts?'

'Far side. Near the middle of the shed.'

'Right. Clear out, you two. Get aboard. Your work's done. I'm on duty here.'

'Colley says no one is to go near the sheds,' I put in.

'That's all right, Jem. I know. Ah! Here they are. I want you, Harry. Disappear, Mainwaring. Take charge of this, Frankie.'

He handed Sellick what looked to me like a long limp riding-switch, and slipped across the road again, Colley at his heels.

Sellick strolled out along the wharf towards our gang-plank, and I was turning to follow him when something plucked at my trouser-leg. Stooping, startled, to see what it was I found my head close to Mainwaring's upturned face. He was lying prone upon the grass.

'Lie down here, skipper,' he said. 'Frankie'll look after the ship for you. Stay and see the fun. Take cover behind the bollard.'

As I lay down behind him a match was struck behind the office and in less than a minute the other two came across the road, walking slowly and carefully, Voogdt with a bundle clasped in his arms.

'For God's sake don't jolt it, Austin,' Colley's voice sounded very earnest. 'Put it down here on the grass. Gently, now.'

'Not too close to my head,' Mainwaring said plaintively.

Neither of them as much as noticed him. 'Let's have a light again . . . Matches are safe enough,' Colley said. He was kneeling by the bundle, feeling it all over with his hands. Voogdt struck a match and by its flickering light I saw it was of sailcloth, about as big as a man's head, tied carelessly enough with a piece of stout line.

The match went out, but after more fumbling in the dark, Colley seemed to get the bundle open.

'Another match,' he demanded.

The sailcloth now lay flat, and standing on it was a common kitchen saucepan, its handle broken off short, filled with coarse yellow crystals, like brown sugar, only that the crystals were larger.

'My hat!' Colley whispered, in awed tones.

'What is it?' Voogdt asked.

'Picric acid, by the look of it.' He picked out two crystals rather larger than peas and put them by on the bollard. 'Throw away that match and bear a hand, Austin. Take it by handfuls at a time, and spread it on the mud below there. Don't throw it. Walk down and spread it on the mud by hand.'

When the saucepan was empty he took it farther down the embankment and threw it into a pasture field, and just as he rejoined us I heard a step I knew approaching down the embankment.

'There's Cheyne coming,' I said.

At the words our two men disappeared noiselessly into the darkness. I never saw how or where they went. Mainwaring, beside me, gave one wriggle backwards and I suppose slid down over the bank. By the time I was on my feet again Colley had gone too, and Voogdt and myself were alone.

'That you, Cheyne?' Voogdt called.

'That's me. Am I late? Van Noppen turned up yet?'

'Not yet.'

'That's all right, then. I'll open the office. We may as well wait inside as out here.'

His shadowy form approached the office door and I heard his latchkey in the lock.

'Is it all clear for him to go in?' I asked, in a whisper.

'All clear. Got the hang of things yet?'

'An attempt to blow up the shed?'

'That's about it.'

'Are you sure there isn't any explosive stuff left there?'

'No odds if there is. We've cut their wire. Pretty road-making, eh? Now I'll go in to Cheyne. You stay here and keep an eye open for Van Noppen.'

The German turned up punctually to time, and we went into the shed together, passing straight through the narrow outer office into Cheyne's living-room. I'd been there several times before, without taking much notice of the place, but now with my nerves strung and alert every detail leaped to the eye. The frowsy bed in the far corner; the writing-table by the window; the stove bricked into one angle, with a cheap American alarm clock ticking noisily on the narrow mantelshelf; I can see them now as clearly as if in a photograph. In the middle of the room was a table with a green baize cover, and against the partition hung a row of coats and oilskins. Everything was neglected, dusty and uncomfortable. Kept tidy the place would have made decent quarters enough for a single man; but how Cheyne, a sailor, could have ever lived in such a litter beat me. It's queer how little things affect you. Knowing Chyene a rogue and hating him like poison, I yet felt more ashamed at the moment of his untidy house than of his rascality. Remembering the neatness of Van Noppen's room—the room we had burgled—I felt it disgraceful that he should see our headquarters in such a state.

Cheyne was sitting at the table as we entered, the inevitable bottle and siphon before him, and Voogdt sprawled at ease upon his unmade bed. Van Noppen sat down, refusing Cheyne's invitation to drink, and I stood leaning against the office partition behind him. I wouldn't sit in Cheyne's quarters. Behind me, to my right, was the door; opposite, in the far right-hand corner, the fireplace. Opposite to that again, in the far left-hand corner, stood the bed, and immediately on my left was the washstand, set squarely in the corner at its foot, the coats and oilskins hanging on the wall beside it. The window was between the fireplace and the bed, and Cheyne sat with his back to it, facing Van Noppen, the lamp standing on the table between them. I stood behind the German's back, whilst Voogdt, lying on the bed, well back from the light, commanded a view of the whole room, and of all our three faces, Cheyne in profile, Van Noppen three-quarter face, and me full face. Also he had the best view of the door, which was diagonally opposite from the corner in which he lay. As for me, I could see everything in the room except Van Noppen's face, which was turned away from me, and the door, which was behind my right shoulder.

After a bit of palavering round the subject, Cheyne took the conversation in charge, and told Van Noppen he had reported the offer to us, and that we were prepared to come to terms, if possible. Van Noppen looking round over his shoulder at me, as though he wanted me to corroborate Cheyne, I told him at once that I had nothing to say in the matter.

'There's my partner,' I said, nodding to Voogdt. 'He speaks for me. I'm only here to listen, so it's no good asking me questions. What he says I'll stand to.'

As far as I remember, Voogdt, after a lot of haggling, demanded a hundred and fifty thousand pounds. Van Noppen didn't definitely refuse him. He said he wasn't empowered to agree to so much, but that he would consult his principals. That should have ended the matter for the present, but Voogdt started a long roundabout catechism that I couldn't follow at all. At first I thought he was trying to find out the names of Van Noppen's employers, but after a few questions about them he drifted purposely off into a series of questions that didn't seem to me to have any bearing on the matter. How did Van Noppen intend to pay us? What was the present rate of exchange—marks for pounds sterling? Were the Delfzyl Company prepared to make us an additional offer for the *Luck and Charity?* Silly questions like that. And several times he repeated himself, so that even Cheyne at last had to call him to order and tell him he was wasting time. As for Van Noppen, he began to fidget under the cross-questioning, and at ten past ten got up and announced that he must be going, and just as he rose I heard somebody move in the outer office behind me. He would pass on our demands to his employers, he said, and he thought he might get them to spring the extra money. With that he turned to the door and, the conversation being over, Cheyne leaned back in his chair. His movement let the lamplight fall on Voogdt's face behind him, and it startled me. He, the man whose sleepy, silly questions had bored us all, was about as sleepy as a crouching cat. Behind his half-closed eyelids the lamplight shone on the keenest pair of watching eyes I have ever seen. Seeing something was in the wind, I glanced at Van Noppen's face as he stretched a hand to the door. It was deadly pale, and I saw that he was breathing short and quick.

'Half a minute,' Voogdt drawled. 'Half a minute, Mr Van Noppen. I've one or two more questions—'

'Tomorrow,' the man said, and something clicked in his throat as he said it.

'You've left your hat,' Voogdt said, sitting upright on the bed. 'There, on the table. What's your hurry?' Van Noppen glanced at the clock and his face was the colour of ash. Taking no notice of Voogdt or of the hat, he jerked the door open—and fell slap into the arms of Mainwaring and Colley. Entering, they pushed him back into the room.

'Herr Gott!' he said, under his breath. He was struggling to pass them, but Mainwaring, beaming, held him fast, whilst Colley shut the door and leant against it.

'What's the hurry, my dear sir?' Mainwaring asked.

Van Noppen's chin went up as though he were choking. He couldn't answer. Voogdt's drawl came from the corner again.

'The gentleman's pressed for time,' he said cruelly. 'Two questions, Van Noppen, and then you shall go home to by-by. Are your employers a private firm, or the German Government?'

He was choking, frantic with terror, and when he got his answer out it was in German. A private firm, he swore.

'How called?' Voogdt snapped out the question like an order.

'Nobel's,' he said, and with one jerk dragged himself free of Mainwaring's hold and jumped at the door. Colley caught him, Mainwaring was on him in the same moment: there was a short struggle—and they laid him, gently enough, on the floor. He had fainted in their arms.

Voogdt stood over him as he lay.

'Poor devil!' he said. 'I wouldn't go through his last ten minutes for minted gold. Put him on the bed and give him some brandy, Cheyne.'

'What's it all about?' Cheyne asked angrily. 'Who the devil are these chaps?'

'Friends of mine. You see, Mr Van Noppen had arranged an accidental explosion for our benefit. For some time past he has been repairing the ruts in the road down the embankment, and as he filled them in, he laid an insulated wire along one of 'em.

This evening one of his men planted a packet of picric acid under this house, and judging from the time he fainted, I guess it was to have been touched off at ten-fifteen. I expect his men have been waiting this last half an hour to run down and tear up any ends of insulated wire left showing. It would then have been just an unexplained accident. At all events neither you, myself nor West here would have had any explanation to offer, for certain.'

'How did you find it out?' I asked.

'I went down there this evening with these two'—he indicated Mainwaring and Colley—'as skirmishers, scratched up a bit of rut that had been filled in and found the wire. You remember seeing it in Van Noppen's room? So I cut out a four-foot section, replaced the stones I'd dug up, and then came here, and removed the picric acid, as you saw. The two men who brought it passed us on their way here. That's all.'

'The swine!' roared Cheyne. 'What about his offer to buy us out.'

'Ah! I'm afraid that wasn't a *bona-fide* offer. Our business is finished, Cheyne. Full reports of the wolframite deposits will be in all the papers the day after tomorrow.'

'Is that so?' I asked.

'Yes. Nobel's, he said. Didn't you hear him? Subsidised by Government. No more wolframite goes to Germany disguised as explosives.'

'It is an explosive,' Colley cut in.

'Eh?'

'Tungsten acid, of course. Didn't you know that? In its crys-tallised form it's used for making kranzite, the new German army explosive. Is there any wolframite hereabouts?'

'Just a little. The ground you're standing on is mostly tungsten dioxide. Kranzite, eh? And Nobel's in it. I was right, after all.'

We were all silent for a minute, standing round the bed watching Van Noppen, lying so still and quiet. Gradually the sense of what it all meant was soaking into Cheyne's brain, for he turned to Voogdt with a question.

'How will it get into the papers? Can't we hush it up?'

'We could, I daresay, but we aren't going to. I'm going to send a report to the Press Association myself tomorrow—and Reuter's too. I am a real pressman, I assure you, Cheyne dear, not a driver of a waggon.'

Cheyne looked stunned. 'You—you're going to split?'

'I am.'

'Then there's no need for me to wait that fortnight?' I asked. 'Not the slightest.'

Mainwaring took one look at me as I turned on Cheyne slowly. 'What's the next item of the evening's entertainment, Austin?' he asked.

'A boxing contest, by the look of it. Come back to the door, you others. Bring the lamp, one of you.'

'What's the matter with you?' Cheyne said angrily, as I put my hand on his shoulder.

'Nothing. Only your room's dirty and I'm going to dust it out. You're the duster.'

He put up a good scrap, I'll say that for him. But I was in that state of rage I could have pulled him to pieces with my hands, and he never stood a chance from the first.

We had a drink all round, and, speaking for myself, I wanted it. Then the others gave brandy to Cheyne and Van Noppen to bring them to whilst I had a wash.

We all felt very fit and cheerful—hilarious even—all except Cheyne and Van Noppen, that is. The other three put Cheyne to bed, and telling Van Noppen to consider himself a prisoner till the morning, they shut him in the cabin of the *Luck and Charity* and put Sellick on sentry-go at the companion. Van Noppen made no remarks. He was cowed, and went aboard as quietly as a lamb. It was past three o'clock when I went to bed, in the fo'castle, because Van Noppen was imprisoned aft—and then I left the others on deck, sitting and singing choruses to the accompaniment of Sellick's mandoline.

When I awoke the sun was high enough to send a dusty

beam down the fo'castle companion, lighting the grimy place like a lamp. Voogdt was asleep in the adjoining bunk, and Sellick moved about quietly packing up his traps to go. 'Kiah had relieved him on deck, he said, and Mainwaring and Colley were gone back to Terneuzen. When Voogdt turned out he told us we could release Van Noppen, and sent me to the town to hire labourers.

'Get half a dozen stout men,' he said. 'We'll get one last cargo across and I'll keep my startling revelations for the English press. Charity begins at home, don't it?'

Aided by quite a little crowd of men, we got about forty-five tons into our hold before sailing on the evening tide. Cheyne never showed himself all day, and I haven't seen him since. We left him in bed, in a badly battered condition, sole legatee to the sheds, stock, plant and goodwill of that once flourishing concern The Axel Trading Company.

A quick voyage brought us to Erith, where we found Ward waiting for us, ready to greet us like long-lost brothers. A couple of hours' talk sufficed to bring his information up to date, and it was agreed between us that Voogdt should announce the wolframite deposits as soon as he pleased. He told us that Miss Brand and Miss Lavington had come to Erith with him, and that we were to join them at dinner that same evening at his hotel. As to the cargo, which a dozen sturdy dockers were slinging out on the quayside whilst we talked, he would sell that at once by wire, without any attempt at concealment, and so conclude our last deal in wolframite.

When I asked Ward how I stood, he told me the syndicate owed me ten thousand pounds, so we called 'Kiah aft, told him he was a gentleman at large with money in the bank, and I made him a present of the *Luck and Charity*. The fool almost snivelled instead of being grateful, until Ward told him the boat should be done up and turned into a yacht again at his charges, and that he would charter her for three months every year.

'What about you?' he said to me, still sniffing.

'I'm going to sea again. But I'll take a holiday every summer and spend it aboard here with Mr Ward.'

'An' Mr Vute?'

'He'll come, of course.' It was like promising a child presents to keep it from crying.

'An' what be I to do all next weenter?' he complained.

'Lay the boat up at Topsham and work on her yourself, you fool.' I was losing patience with him.

'How be I to get 'er round there single-'anded?'

'Oh, dry up!' I said. 'I'll give you a hand round with her, if that's all. You'll be Cap'n Pym when you get home, man.'

That comforted him a bit, I think, for he said no more and went on deck to survey his new property.

The feeling of ownership soon bore fruit, for in the afternoon 'Kiah informed me that he had arranged with the skipper of an Erith tug to give him a tow down that night as far as the Medway. The tug was taking a string of barges to Sheerness and 'Kiah's frugal Devon soul couldn't resist the temptation of a cheap towage.

'"Tedn' no gude stoppin' about yer, is it?' he asked, rather shamefacedly.

'I'm going out to dinner tonight,' I said. But I shan't be aboard before midnight, mind.'

He agreed, said that would be plenty of time, and went ashore to do the necessary marketing for us both.

When the evening came, and we were all at dinner together, I felt some sympathy with his grumbling. Never was a pleasanter party, but I couldn't hide from myself that it meant saying goodbye to the four people I liked better than any folk I had ever met. Our partnership was over. No doubt we should meet again, often and often: most of the talk at table was about such future meetings; but I knew we should never meet quite in the same spirit as before. There would no longer be the common interests: they would find out that I was a rough-mannered sailor, and perhaps I should feel that they, soft-handed and town-sheltered, weren't my sort either. After dinner came the first farewell, when we all went to see Voogdt off at the station. On the way back I suggested that we should stroll down as far as the *Luck and Charity* and give our regards to Captain Pym. But Miss Lavington said she was tired, and Ward wouldn't come either.

In the end Miss Brand and myself set off together, my knees shaking with funk, for I meant asking her to marry me, and didn't dare set about it. 'Kiah wasn't aboard, and the fo'castle and cabin were locked, so we could only walk up and down the deck and talk and wait for him. I tried to bring the conversation round to herself, but she headed me off every time, and after a long half-hour said she could wait no longer. I said I'd walk home with her. But her manner became chilly at once.

'All right,' she said, not over-graciously, and we went ashore together, she leading the way up the gang-plank.

CHAPTER XXI

OF COLLISIONS AT SEA

Climbing the gangway she slipped, just as Voogdt had slipped some months before, but I caught her from behind and swung her to safety. That one moment did it. When we stood together on the wharf-edge I still kept one arm round her, holding her to me.

Her face, close to mine, looked white and frightened against the night. Her big eyes seemed larger and darker than ever, and the smell of her hair—just the sweet, natural smell of her—seemed to choke me. For the life of me I couldn't speak.

She could, but she spoke low and all her arrogance was gone.

'Let me go,' she said; but she never moved, and for all answer I shook my head.

'You must. Let me go.'

'I won't,' I said huskily, finding my voice. 'I—I love you.'

'That's nonsense.' The words were determined enough, but the voice was something new to me, weak and doubtful. 'Let me go. Please.'

She could have shaken my arm off easily enough, for I held her as gently as a little child; but she never tried, and I plucked up courage a bit.

'I won't. I want you. You've never been out of my mind since that first day—when you slapped my face on Exmouth beach. It was your slap in the face made me knock off drink, and go back to work—and all that. D'you think a man pulls up like that for nothing?'

'You mustn't say it. You mustn't.'

'Why no? I love you, I tell you. I will say it.'

'Not to me. O-oh! not to me.' She almost wailed it: her voice went up in a little shaky whine, and I thought she was going

to cry. Out went my other hand, and she was in my arms. I
suppose she felt like choking, too: her beating heart lifted her,
breast and lips, and in that moment her face was on my shoulder.

'Why—you love me, too,' I said, almost scared with the
sudden surprise of it.

'Do I? I don't know. This love—this awful love!' She began
to cry in real earnest, her face quivering against my cheek.

'Awful, is it?' I laughed, for my heart was singing in me, and
the world only a little ball underfoot that spun to the time of
its beating.

'Of course it's awful. There seems no escape. Haven't I—
haven't I seen the hateful thing everywhere? In the laboratory,
watched through the microscope the rushing together of tiniest
live atoms—shameless little beasts! Haven't I seen how all the
scheme of life was tangled up with it, from the highest to the
lowest, till even I was almost afraid. Afraid, I tell you! Blown
pollen in the moving grasses; bees in the flowers—cell seeking
cell everywhere—all telling the same thing—'

She was crying hysterically now—crying as a trapped animal
cries—her face contorted, her eyes running over and her dear
nose wet and red. Clumsily I tried to kiss it.

'Dear,' I said. 'Dear, what is it? I don't understand—'

'Of c-course you don't. You dear silly, how could you? . . .
But I'm an educated woman, and I looked the thing in the
face—and defied it. In all the crowded world, mad about this
love business, I saw it was thinkers who were wanted—
detached men and women, working for good . . . I'd be one
of them. That was to be my life—to show how a free woman
should live. I wouldn't love: I swore I wouldn't . . . There's
so much to be done for women, and they themselves won't
do it. They'll never do it. They can't. They swear to devote
themselves to the cause, and—and then a man lays hands on
them, and where are their vows? No cause is anything to them
any more. A man holds them and kisses them, and all's over.
To have babies and hang up their washing in the backyard,

that's the outside of their ambitions ever after. But I—I'd be different . . . O-oh, the shame of it! Here am I, crying on a man's shoulder like any housemaid . . . And I wouldn't be anywhere else for worlds!

'It seems a lot of fuss to make about nothing,' I said at length, smoothing her shoulder with my hand. I spoke gently, thinking to comfort her, but she was up again in a moment, struggling in my arms.

'O-oh!' Again she wriggled her face closer against mine. 'Isn't it wonderful? And, oh! I am ashamed of myself—to give in like this. And won't I make you pay for it, just?'

'Make me pay for what?' I was startled at her vicious tone.

'For pulling me aside from the straight path. For giving other women—poor dears, what do they know about it?—the chance to sneer at me as a deserter . . . But it shan't be for long. When this marriage business is over, back I go to the lecture platform.'

'I'm afraid it won't run to that, little girl,' I said. 'You can't keep house for a poor man and run about the country lecturing as well.'

'Poor? What do you call poor?'

'Well, I've nothing but this money we've cleared since you took us into partnership. It'll bring in a few hundred a year—a good useful sum I grant, but not enough to live on, idling. I must get some work as well—'

'A few hundreds!' she burst out, and laughed. 'Why, you dear stupid, I'm rich. I've got thousands of pounds!'

If she'd slapped me in the face again, as at our first meeting, she couldn't have startled me more. 'Good Lord!' I said; and again, 'Good Lord! Where on earth did you get that from?'

'From the same place as you got your few hundreds, of course. I was the biggest shareholder. Nance was only my trustee. And you never knew? We used to wonder whether you did, when you talked as though she and Leonard owned the show.'

'Of course I never knew,' I said. 'I thought you were her paid companion, and she'd given you a share or two out of kindness . . . And you're rich. And after marriage, you want to go lecturing . . . That won't do, Pam'ly dear.'

'What won't do? What d'you mean?'

'I mean I won't marry you on those terms. You rich and independent, and scorning housekeeping! That won't do for me. I love you dearly—love the sight of you and the sound of your voice, but I marry no woman on such terms.'

'What terms do you object to?' Again she struggled to be free. This time I released her and we stood trying to peer at each other in the darkness.

'Your freedom,' I said. 'This semi-detached notion of marriage. A tolerated stupid husband at home, and a clever wife on lecture tours. That's no good to me. My wife must be my woman altogether—my partner—the keeper of my home. To carry half the burden—to love and honour and obey, as the Church service says. Love I think you give. Your honour and respect I'll try to earn. And as for obedience, I'm old-fashioned, Pam'ly dearie, and I'll have that too.'

'Never from me!' she cried.

'Even from you. I needn't tell you again how I love you, but I'll have obedience, or I'll have nothing.'

'Nothing it is, then,' she said, and turned and, stepping lightly and fast, walked away from me along the quay.

For a moment or two I stood still, stupefied; then, thinking she might fall over the quayside, ran along the quay calling her—softly, for fear anybody was about.

I followed her till she reached a better-lighted street and then stopped, watched her out of sight and returned to the boat, wretched. For though she was a little shrew, and though I knew it better than most, I loved her dearly, and I'd hoped for a moment that love would cure her shrewishness. Thoughts of her had been with me always, this long time past, and now I had other memories to add to them—the feel of her breast on mine, of my arms holding her yielding body, and the salt taste of her tears in my mouth. It was a bad hour for me, after I boarded the *Luck and Charity* again that night. I was glad Voogdt had gone, for I couldn't have stood questions even from him just then.

There was no light in the fo'castle, so I judged 'Kiah was still ashore, and I was glad of that, too, for though he wouldn't be likely to come aft and disturb me, it was some small comfort to have the boat to myself. But he had evidently been aboard, for the cabin door awas unlocked, and I went inside, wishing I were dead; and there I sat like a sick beast in a hole, my arms across the table and my head upon them, dull with misery.

Since she wouldn't promise obedience she didn't love—that was all I could make of it, and to marry a rich woman on such terms was more than I could do. So I made up my mind that my hopes were over; that I should probably never see my girl again except from the back of some audience she was addressing, and that my love affair was ended where it began, in those ten minutes of caress and quarrel by a port waterside.

Every corner of the old boat held some reminiscence of her. Dozens of times she had sat where I was sitting now; the little cabin had echoed to her chatter over the teacups, or her laughter at Voogdt's nonsense. It gave me the blues to sit there all alone, and think of her living out her plans ashore.

I heard 'Kiah come aboard and go into the fo'castle, and half an hour later shouting from the barges told me the tug was in sight. When I got on deck the tide was full, the quayside below the level of gunwale, so I called 'Kiah and cast off the stern warp. Muffled in his greatcoat, he came aft to the wheel, stepping quickly and forgetting to cast off forward. I was too miserable to tell him of it, so went and did it myself, and then threw a line to the last barge, already fast to the tug and commencing to swing away from the quay. Somebody in the barge pulled at the line till the tow-rope was aboard, shouted 'All right,' and I went back aft.

'Call me when they cast off the tow,' I said to 'Kiah. He grunted and I went below again.

Head on hands I must have dropped off to sleep, and woke perhaps half an hour later with a start. For the moment I thought it was dawn. The cabin was light as day, the hanging lamp burning a smoky yellow, and there was a terrific row going on outside. Men's voices shouted all round us, and on deck, just overhead, a woman was screeching for help.

I was up there in three jumps, but even if I hadn't been confused and scared out of my wits it was too late to be of any use. When I went below it was pitch dark, so dark that I could scarcely make out 'Kiah's figure at the wheel, but now everything stared ghastly white under the converging rays of three great searchlights centred on us. We were alone in a great circle of glaring light. The tow-rope hung loosely over the side, and the tug and barges had disappeared into the blackness. Not a hundred feet away was an armoured cruiser, her bows crowded with men, coming straight down on us, her propellers thrashing furiously astern. Behind her dim as a street lamp seen from a lighted room, was the Nore light, and I saw we had somehow drifted into the navigable channel of the Medway. In that same glance I saw the cruiser was lowering a boat, men tumbling into it anyhow as it slid from the davits. 'Kiah was nowhere to be seen, and in his place, dressed in his cap and overcoat, clinging to the wheel and screaming with terror, was Pamily Brand!

'Oh, you!' she cried. 'I thought you'd never come. Take this thing, for heaven's sake!'

I measured the distance to the cruiser with my eye, and saw it was a hopeless case. She couldn't miss us, try as she would. That little fool of a girl had steered wide of the barges she should have followed, and either the cruiser must cut them down—and perhaps the tug, too—or sink us. It was no good their going astern; she had too much way on to stop. The thought of the girl under those whirling propellers made me sick, so I semaphored the cruiser frantically with my hands to stop her engines. When she was closer I shouted it, fit to burst my lungs. 'Stop your engines,' I roared; heard them stop, thank God! and then she was on us.

Poor old *Luck and Charity*. Good old ship. She'd been my home through good times and through bad, and it was pitiful to see the end of her like that. Not that I had much time to waste on pity; there was that mischievous devil of a girl to look after. She clung to my arm, quiet now, as the cruel ram of that beastly cruiser slid under my poor old boat, lifted her and canted her over a little, and then sliced off her bows, cutting through hull and spar and rigging easily as a ploughshare cuts through grass roots in a field. It was over in a second; crash and slice; and the steep gray bulk was sliding past us, growing higher and higher as we sank.

There was nothing gallant or picturesque about our rescue. Our navy doesn't wave flags and shout; it just does its job and grumbles about it afterwards. Being all wood the *Luck and Charity* sank slowly, and we sat on the highest part of her stern until the cruiser's boat took us off. We were then about waist-deep, sitting. The boat backed away just as the sinking hull turned; the black water rolled over her, and that was the last of my poor old boat. There was a quiet order, the men gave way at the oars, and we were off in pursuit of the receding cruiser's searchlight.

Drenched and muddled as I was, my wits all woolgathering with the sudden confusion of it all, I never thought of 'Kiah till then—and then with a sudden chill at heart.

'Where's 'Kiah?' I cried to the whimpering, shivering girl. 'You—where's 'Kiah?'

'Ashore.' She was crying quietly, and I ought to have pitied her, but I was past that.

'When did he get ashore?'

'He never c-came on board. I met him and told him your orders were that he must sleep ashore tonight—and then I c-came in his place.'

'What on earth did you do that for?' I asked furiously, but

she wouldn't answer. The men rowing regarded us stolidly, but I could see the midshipman in charge was alive with curiosity, so I asked no more questions.

When he got aboard the cruiser—two men had to help her up the gangway, for her sopped skirt clung about her so that she could scarcely walk—I asked her again what she meant by it. For the moment we were alone, the crew that had picked us up busy hoisting their boat aboard, and nobody was near us but a wooden-faced marine on sentry-go. Still she wouldn't answer, but only stood there sniffing and shivering with her head down, like a naughty child being scolded.

'Tell me,' I said. 'I will know what you meant by it.'

'I wanted to go to sea with you alone.' She looked up at me sideways, and there was a gleam of wickedness in her eye.

'What on earth for?' I demanded, raging.

Her hair was coming down and hung across her face; her clothes dripped, clinging about her, and if ever she looked a child of the gutter she did then. But her tears had stopped and to all seeming she had composed herself, for confident impudence shone in her eyes behind their tangled veil of hair.

'I—I thought I'd show you a woman was as good as a man,' she said.

'You've shown it by sinking 'Kiah's boat.'

'Y-yes. But I can give him a better one. There's something else—'

'What's that?'

'I—I've been away with you alone. You've compromised my reputation. And now you can't in decency refuse to marry me, can you? You will, won't you?' She came close to me, wheedling. 'You will marry me, won't you? And—and we'll decide about that obedience business afterwards. I—I'll promise to say "obey" in the marriage service if you like. It's only a matter of form. Isn't it?'

THE END

THE DETECTIVE STORY CLUB

FOR DETECTIVE CONNOISSEURS

recommends

THE BLACKMAILERS

By THE MASTER OF THE FRENCH CRIME STORY—EMILE GABORIAU

EMILE GABORIAU is France's greatest detective writer. *The Blackmailers* is one of his most thrilling novels, and is full of exciting surprises. The story opens with a sensational bank robbery in Paris, suspicion falling immediately upon Prosper Bertomy, the young cashier whose extravagant living has been the subject of talk among his friends. Further investigation, however, reveals a network of blackmail and villainy which seems as if it would inevitably close round Prosper and the beautiful Madeleine, who is deeply in love with him. Can he prove his innocence in the face of such damning evidence?

THE REAL THING *from* SCOTLAND YARD!

THE CRIME CLUB

By FRANK FRÖEST, Ex-Supt. C.I.D., Scotland Yard, and George Dilnot

YOU will seek in vain in any book of reference for the name of The Crime Club. Its watchword is secrecy. Its members wear the mask of mystery, but they form the most powerful organisation against master criminals ever known. The Crime Club is an international club composed of men who spend their lives studying crime and criminals. In its headquarters are to be found experts from Scotland Yard, many foreign detectives and secret service agents. This book tells of their greatest victories over crime, and is written in association with George Dilnot by a former member of the Criminal Investigation Department of Scotland Yard.

LOOK FOR THE MAN WITH THE GUN

THE DETECTIVE STORY CLUB

FOR DETECTIVE CONNOISSEURS

recommends

"The Man with the Gun."

MR. BALDWIN'S FAVOURITE

THE LEAVENWORTH CASE

By ANNA K. GREEN

THIS exciting detective story, published towards the end of last century, enjoyed an enormous success both in England and America. It seems to have been forgotten for nearly fifty years until Mr. Baldwin, speaking at a dinner of the American Society in London, remarked: " An American woman, a successor of Poe, Anna K. Green, gave us *The Leavenworth Case*, which I still think one of the best detective stories ever written." It is a remarkably clever story, a masterpiece of its kind, and in addition to an exciting murder mystery and the subsequent tracking down of the criminal, the writing and characterisation are excellent. *The Leavenworth Case* will not only grip the attention of the reader from beginning to end but will also be read again and again with increasing pleasure.

CALLED BACK

By HUGH CONWAY

BY the purest of accidents a man who is blind accidentally comes on the scene of a murder. He cannot see what is happening, but he can hear. He is seen by the assassin who, on discovering him to be blind, allows him to go without harming him. Soon afterwards he recovers his sight and falls in love with a mysterious woman who is in some way involved in the crime. . . . The mystery deepens, and only after a series of memorable thrills is the tangled skein unravelled.

LOOK FOR THE MAN WITH THE GUN